T0272402

SANTO DOMINGO STAKEOUT

SANTO DOMINGO STAKEOUT

John Keyse-Walker

SEVERN
HOUSE

First world edition published in Great Britain and USA 2024
by Severn House, an imprint of Canongate Books Ltd,
14 High Street, Edinburgh EH1 1TE.

severnhouse.com

British Library Cataloguing-in-Publication Data
A CIP catalogue record for this title is available from the British Library.

ISBN-13: 978-1-4483-1102-6 (cased)
ISBN-13: 978-1-4483-1107-1 (e-book)

MIX
Paper | Supporting
responsible forestry
FSC
www.fsc.org   FSC® C013056

All Severn House titles are printed on acid-free paper.

Typeset by Palimpsest Book Production Ltd.,
Falkirk, Stirlingshire, Scotland.
Printed and bound in Great Britain by TJ Books,
Padstow, Cornwall.

Praise for John Keyse-Walker

"[An] outstanding, packs-a-punch thriller"
Booklist Starred Review of *Havana Highwire*

"Darkly atmospheric writing, an action-packed plot, plenty of
suspense, and a sometimes-hapless hero caught between saving
his own life and doing the right thing drive this outstanding,
packs-a-punch thriller"
Booklist Starred Review of *Havana Highwire*

"Keyse-Walker captures the feel and power dynamics of pre-
Castro Cuba. Readers will eagerly await the sequel"
Publishers Weekly on *Havana Highwire*

"Twists follow double-crosses as Henry and his street-urchin sidekick, Benny, negotiate the nightmare that is midcentury Cuba"
Kirkus Reviews on *Havana Highwire*

"A likeable, all-too-human hero, vivid characters, a twist-a-minute
plot, and the languid, sun-drenched Caribbean setting make this
an entertaining, engaging read"
Booklist on *Reefs, Royals, Reckonings*

"A tropical treat like no other"
Kirkus Reviews Starred Review of *Palms, Paradise, Poison*

About the author

John Keyse-Walker practiced law for 30 years, representing business and individual clients, educational institutions and government entities. He is an avid salt- and freshwater angler, a tennis player, kayaker and an accomplished cook. He lives in Hawai'i with his wife.

As well as the Cuban Noir novels, John is the author of the award-winning Teddy Creque traditional mystery series and historical cozy mystery *Bert and Mamie Take a Cruise*.

www.johnkeyse-walker.com

To Don Marano – fishing buddy, philosopher, night heron whisperer

In the dark mist of conflict and violence, revolution and confusion, it is not easy to find clear and unclouded truths.

President Lyndon B. Johnson,
Report to the American People on the Situation in the Dominican
Republic,
May 2, 1965

ONE

'I am so tired of listening to this crap song,' Jerry said, draining the last of his drink. He popped up from his barstool with an urgency I had not seen him come close to displaying in our six months of acquaintance and headed off toward the room of La Españolita which harbored the dance floor and the jukebox. His words should have sounded angry or irritated but the tone he used was bland. Just like Jerry was bland. Ordinary. Forgettable.

Pausing at the end of the bar, Jerry asked, 'Will you have Jaime set me up with another, Henry?'

'Sure,' I said. He continued on what had the look of a mission. The last note of the Andrews Sisters singing 'Rum and Coca-Cola' trailed away in the other room, the trio crooning about working for the Yankee dollar. Jerry must have stepped in before the tourist who had played the song three times consecutively could jam more money into the jukebox, because the next song out of the machine was The Kinks' 'All Day and All of the Night'. Ah, back to 1965.

'Another Mamajuana for Señor Pleasants, Jaime, and another Presidente for me, *por favor*,' I ordered.

'Right away, Señor Gore.' Jaime was one of the two reasons I frequented La Españolita. He was the quintessential bartender – generous with the pour, always ready with a light and willing to listen without volunteering advice. The other reason was the jukebox, so American it wouldn't even take the local pesos. Somehow it was always filled with the latest hits. In a place where you couldn't get an American newspaper less than a week out of date, this was nothing short of a miracle.

I had come to La Españolita for Jaime but grew to love the jukebox, especially with all the British invasion music that was topping the charts. Jerry had the opposite experience. He had come for the jukebox, being drawn in the door by the music when he was barhopping one night.

Jerry was the kind of American you could find in almost any port town in the Caribbean. They were a type. Unattached. At loose ends. Mid-thirties to mid-forties in age, working on a paunch from drinking too many Red Stripes or margaritas or rum punches or painkillers. Balding. Sunburned but not tanned. Between jobs but willing to tell you they were living the good life. Misfits at home in the States, they were tolerated in Gustavia or Oranjestad or The Valley because of the trickle of cash they supplied to the second- and third-rate tourist bars and fleabag guest houses that they frequented. They thought they were friends with the locals. They weren't. They thought they were friends with the tourists they met. They weren't. They were men without a country, a family or a future, yet they deluded themselves into believing that they had a life others could only envy.

I was worried about becoming one of them.

Until I met Jerry. Then I realized that I would never become one of them. I guess it was seeing the delusion up close that convinced me.

The ominously dark Mamajuana and the icy Presidente were placed on the bar just as Jerry returned, a fresh Camel dancing on his lips. 'Got a light?'

Before I could respond, Jaime flipped opened his Ronson and applied the flame to Jerry's coffin nail. Jerry blew a blue cloud at the ceiling, which joined the rest of the blue cloud circulating there.

'Hey, is that Camila still your housekeeper?' Jerry's tone was of disinterest but his hungry eyes said otherwise.

'Yeah.'

'Man, she could keep house for me anytime.' Jerry had gotten a glimpse of my housekeeper, Camila Polanco, when he stopped by my place a few weeks before to deliver a copy of John D. MacDonald's *A Purple Place for Dying*. I wasn't home. He had asked Camila for a date, then and there, using all of his gringo charm, such charm consisting of the concrete promise of a square meal and the more amorphous pledge of a good time. Jerry had the expectation that the square meal would be enough to entice the victims he selected and that the good time would be icing on the cake. He hadn't mentioned to me that he had asked Camila out. Maybe he thought I had something going with my housekeeper. I didn't. But she didn't waste any time informing on Señor Unpleasants, as she called him. She did want to have something going with me. She made no attempt to conceal it and put considerable effort into making it happen. Maybe she thought if she told me about Jerry's half-hearted pass, I would be spurred into action. I wasn't.

Jerry sipped his Mamajuana. I sipped my Presidente. The murmur of tourist conversation could be heard from the other room, largely stepped on and made unintelligible by The Kinks' outspoken desire to be with the Girl All of the Time.

Jerry finally broke the silence. 'I'm thinking about blowing this pop stand.' This was a common topic with him. The grass was always greener and the sandy beach always whiter on the next island as far as he was concerned. 'I hear Reynolds is going to open a bauxite mine in Jamaica. They need a manager, one with experience. One who's an American. It could be the ticket for me.'

I hesitated to point out to Jerry that in the six months since I'd met him, he hadn't mentioned any experience in bauxite mining or management in general. It seemed his only qualification for the position was that he was American. And he was barely that. If you believed him, he'd spent the last fifteen years bouncing around the islands.

'Yeah,' I said, to acknowledge that he'd spoken and keep the conversation – if it could be called that – alive. Conversation, any conversation, was what Jerry and I used to convince ourselves that we were not just day-drinking but socializing.

'Hey, why don't you come with me? I'm gonna need an assistant manager.'

I resisted pointing out to Jerry how crazy it was to be making such offers when he didn't even know if there would be a job available and said, 'I'm still on the payroll here.'

'What? You mean for Bosch? He's out and is never coming back. Wessin y Wessin's in for good now.'

'Bosch is still depositing pesos in my account. So I'm staying.'

'Well, suit yourself. Personally, I think it's a waste of your time. You'll be missing a big opportunity.' He pushed up the dirty sleeve of his sport jacket to glance at his watch. 'I gotta take a piss,' he said and headed to the *servicio*.

Little did I know that it would be the last time I saw him before the explosion.

TWO

'Another for me, Jaime.' The words crossed my lips easily – no, effortlessly – as they had in Veracruz and Puerto Cabezas, in Fort-de-France and Saint George's, in Carúpano and Plymouth, in all the ports and backwaters on the slow circuit of the Caribbean Sea I had been making since Castro cut me loose back in 1960. A years-long, far-flung pub crawl that was the culmination of my foolish dreams to move to Cuba, become a private investigator and live the good and easy life in paradise. A fantasy that twisted into me working for the Cuban dictator Fulgencio Batista and mob interests in Havana and ended with me fighting for Castro. And when I was no longer of use to Fidel, he gave me the boot. My time with El Comandante made me *persona non grata* to the US State Department, so I bummed from island to island until I finally landed in Santo Domingo. And found my way to the bar at La Españolita.

In all those bars, in all those towns, on all those paradisiacal islands and coasts, the service was occasionally instant, more often indolent, but always, always that next drink had appeared. Until now.

Now, Jaime had vanished from his post. I stepped a ways into La Españolita's dim interior, figuring him to be busing a table or taking an order. But the bar room's only inhabitants other than me were a local couple secreted at a table in the corner and three middle-aged businessmen with loosened neckties and rolled shirt-sleeves, dispatching a bottle of Bermudez with grim alacrity. It seemed that whatever business the three had engaged in had been a failure and the only way to deal with the fallout was rum. Been there, done that.

Only when I turned back to the bar did I see the note, partly soaked in spilled Presidente. 'LEAVE NOW!', it said. Unsigned. I puzzled over it for a beat or two before I felt the crawl of gooseflesh on my neck and arms. It was the exclamation point on the writing that did it, imbuing the simple message conveyed by the two words with an unequivocal urgency. Jaime's absence added to the imperative; given the note's location, he was the likely author and he had 'left now' himself.

I rose from the stool, tossed a crumpled handful of pesos on the bar and made for the exit. I was out, pushing the heavy mahogany door closed when I hesitated. Was this some kind of a prank, cooked up by Jerry, with Jaime enlisted reluctantly by Jerry's promise of an enticing tip? Was I going to walk back into the bar to guffaws from Jerry and an embarrassed half smile from Jaime?

My hesitation had not resolved when, in a flashing instant, a heavy concussion pushed me to the ground. I was conscious long enough to see the mass of wood, plaster, glass and dust that had been La Españolita headed toward me and then the world went black.

Even through the mouthful of dust and plaster, I could recognize a smell – or was it a taste? – from my Air Force Office of Special Investigations days. We had trained then with a new explosive called C-4, which gave off the scent of tar or burned oil after exploding. The training had only allowed for a single explosion of one block of C-4, but my brain, though fuzzed up from the concussion, managed to search back almost a decade to identify that odor even before I had wiped enough dirt from my eyes to allow me to open them. When I was finally able to see, the sun was still obliterated by a cloud of smoke and my own personal space was darkened by a large flat piece of debris on me. I pushed against it with my hands. It moved an inch. I engaged the larger muscles of my legs. That did the trick. Through the murk I saw that I had kicked away the door of La Españolita. The heavy door had been forced off its hinges by the blast and landed in the street with me beneath it. While the hinges had splintered away, the heavy mahogany planks that made up the door had remained intact and protected me from much of the force of the explosion.

My chest hurt. My legs hurt. I had a splitting headache. My body, every last loving inch of Mrs Gore's favorite and only son, felt like it had been beaten with a Louisville Slugger wielded by Willie Mays. Blood ran into one of my eyes, blurring the vision I had just managed to clear. Despite all this, I was able to stand. A woman came at me through the gloom, her clothing in shreds and covered with blood. Her mouth was open. She had to be screaming but I couldn't hear her. I realized I couldn't hear anything.

Jerry. He was still in the bar when the explosion occurred. I had to find him, get him some help. I took a step and staggered. My vision narrowed to a pinpoint. And then I was out.

THREE

Yellow light came in through my eyelids. I tried to open them but seemed unable to control the muscles. They fluttered like those of a flirtatious ingénue.

'Well, Mr Gore, so good to have you back to consciousness.' The voice was soothing, a bit husky but in a pleasant way. A nurse, my fuddled brain told me.

'What . . . where?' My throat still was scratchy with dust. I croaked the words.

'Don't try to talk yet. You are in the hospital in Santo Domingo. You have been hurt in an explosion.' At that point my brain realized that the soothing voice addressing me was speaking English and for that reason probably wasn't a nurse.

I finally got control of my eyelids and snapped them open. The voice was coming from a woman seated beside me. She had a round face framed by ash-blonde hair. She reminded me of Doris Day. Beautiful but in a wholesome way. She was smiling at me, like she was pleased that I had finally come to. She wore a linen business suit and I couldn't for the life of me figure out why she was there but she certainly wasn't a nurse. She called for a nurse in perfectly-accented Spanish and, from what I could piece together from their rapid-fire conversation, asked that I be brought some water and that a Dr Gutierrez be notified I was awake.

'There now, take a few sips of this,' she said, holding the glass of water to my lips.

I did, and managed to blurt out, 'Who?' before she pressed a finger to my lips to silence me, smiling.

'You must rest. Who? Who am I?' she said. 'I'm Valerie Spicer. I'm from the US Embassy. I'm the cultural attaché there. The ambassador sent me to check on you when we learned that an American citizen had been injured in the bombing at La Españolita.'

I sat upright in the bed. 'Bombing? There was a bombing?'

Miss – or was it Mrs? – Spicer put her hands on my shoulders and gently settled me back into my pillow. Only then did I realize I was wearing a very short hospital gown that exposed parts of me that shouldn't be exposed. I reached for the sheet to cover myself and was rewarded with a shooting pain from the pinky finger of my left hand. I looked down, saw the hand was swaddled in bandages and held it up before my face. The painful pinky finger, even bandaged, was decidedly shorter than it had been the last time I'd paid it any attention.

'I lost part of my finger?' The question was stated to the world. Valerie Spicer answered it.

'You lost about half of your pinky finger, Mr Gore.' She patted my shoulder with a reassuring, motherly pat. 'The good news is that Dr Gutierrez thinks that is your only permanent injury. You have a concussion but he believes there will be no lasting damage from that.'

She seemed so cheerful conveying this news that I couldn't help but respond in my most sarcastic tone. 'That is certainly good news for me and my remaining nine fingers, Mrs Spicer.'

'It's Miss Spicer, Mr Gore.' She ladled out another of her reassuring smiles. 'You should consider yourself fortunate. People were killed.'

Jerry! 'There was another American,' I said. 'Jerry Pleasants. Was he OK?'

'The embassy has no record of another American being injured in the bombing.' She brightened her smile. 'Or killed for that matter.'

'He had just left the bar area to use the *baño*. Maybe he was in there when it happened. Was that part of the building damaged?'

'I'm afraid the entire building was demolished, down to the footers. You and a lady walking on the street outside were the only survivors. A British couple, a Haitian man, a woman from Martinique and three local businessmen were killed. But no other Americans.'

'But there was another American in there. Jerry Pleasants. About forty years old, receding hairline, seersucker jacket, five feet, nine inches tall, one hundred and seventy pounds. Fair skin. Sunburned.'

'There was no casualty reported to the embassy by the local police who fits that description. Relax, Mr Gore. Your friend probably walked out before the bomb went off and doesn't have a scratch.' The motherly pat again, to go with the reassuring smile.

'What about the bartender, Jaime?'

'There was no word from the police about a bartender or anybody by that name.'

'He was a local. I'm sure the embassy doesn't particularly concern itself about the locals but he was there too.'

'Was he now?' Miss Spicer's voice took that tone we've all used when dealing with intransigent children, hysterical adults or mental patients who are convinced the walls are crawling with spiders only they can see.

'Yes, he was,' I said, irritated by the kid-gloves treatment and Miss Spicer's obvious conclusion that I was off the deep end. Then, another concern hit. 'What day is this?'

'Monday.'

'What? Do you mean I have been out for over a day?'

'Yes. And I have been here by your side for the entire time,' she said, pleased with herself.

'Where are my clothes?'

'What clothes?'

'The ones I was wearing before someone stuck me in this bare-assed hospital gown.'

If Miss Spicer was troubled by my coarse language, she certainly didn't allow it to show. 'Your clothes are gone.'

'Gone?'

'Yes. They were basically shredded in the explosion. The doctors cut off what was left when you were brought in.'

'And I suppose they won't let me leave in one of the hospital's gowns.'

'Well, it's not the hospital's gown. The embassy keeps a small supply for Americans who end up in the hospital. Sheets, too. In the Dominican Republic, you bring your own clothing and sheets to the hospital. Americans aren't used to that. Here, your family feeds you, clothes you and washes you when you're in the hospital. And right now, Henry Gore, I am the closest thing you have to family in Santo Domingo.'

The implication of that hit home, and all I could get out was: 'So . . .?'

'So while the doctors finished amputating half of your pinky and took a couple stitches in your scalp, nurses assisting, I was the one who washed the grime off your bare ass.' She smiled beneficently. 'And a fine one it is.'

I felt myself color. Miss Spicer decided to rescue me. 'So, if you want some clothes to get out of here . . .'

'I do.'

'Then give me an hour, and I'll be back with some.'

She went out the door still smiling.

FOUR

Miss Spicer was true to her word. She was back at my bedside in forty-five minutes with underwear, socks, khaki slacks, a white short-sleeved shirt and boat shoes. 'Courtesy of Uncle Sam,' she said, plopping the bag of clothing at the foot of my bed and waiting expectantly.

'Would you mind while I change?' I said, motioning for her to turn and leave the room.

She apparently missed the full import of my gesture, turning her back but staying in the room. 'You know you shouldn't leave until Dr Gutierrez has a chance to look at you.'

'He was in while you were gone. Proud of his nice, clean amputation of my fifth digit just above the second knuckle. I told him I was out of here and asked for the bill. He said the embassy had picked up the tab.'

'You're welcome.'

'Yeah, thanks.'

'Don't feel special. We do that for all Americans who get blown up in Santo Domingo.' Miss Spicer turned back around without first asking about the progress I'd made on getting dressed. I'd only just managed pants and socks at that point. 'Nice tan,' she said.

'Has anyone told you, Miss Spicer, that you are very . . . direct?' I said, pulling on the shirt.

'I am thirty-two years old, Mr Gore. I am a single woman working for the US foreign service in a posting that warrants danger pay. Since I graduated from Bryn Mawr, I've had postings in Africa, Southeast Asia and Eastern Europe. In that time, I've learned that obtuseness begets confusion and directness gets results. But I still smile because being nice counts for much in this world. And I still like your tan. And you can call me Val, Mr Gore.'

'Henry,' I said, a bit disarmed.

'I have a question for you, Henry, now that you're dressed and ready to depart.'

'Yes.'

'Shouldn't you be staying here for a few more days, with the concussion, the finger and all?'

'Dr Gutierrez examined my head wound. Checked my small cuts too. Held up a pen and had me follow it with my eyes as he moved it back and forth. I've lived here for a while. I know that's a rigorous examination by Dominican standards. He even gave me a shot of lidocaine in the pinky.' I wiggled the stub in its bandage. 'See, pain free. I'm off. Thanks for your and Uncle Sam's help. It's the first thing he's done for me in a long while.'

'Well, Henry, if you're not going to follow my suggestion, at least let me give you a lift home. I have an embassy car. Maybe it will further your opinion of your Uncle's generosity.'

'Not of Uncle Sam but definitely your generosity. I'll take the offer of a ride but I'm not going home.'

'Where to, then?'

'La Españolita. Or what's left of it.'

Life was rapidly returning to normal on the block that had once held La Españolita. The explosion which destroyed the bar had had remarkably little effect on the rest of the neighborhood. Some of the adjoining buildings had windows blown out, which had been temporarily covered with plywood. The glass would be replaced in a matter of days. I had seen the same neighborhood struck by a moderate hurricane in my first month here. That rebuild had been completed in short order.

The same could not be said for La Españolita. It had been a freestanding building of wooden construction – the ramshackle type – and now it was a freestanding pile of sticks. A semblance of cleanup was underway. A dump truck was parked where the front door that had saved me had been. A couple of *hombres* tossed sticks and other pieces of debris into the truck one or two at a time. The day was humid and their efforts desultory; I expected the whole job would take several weeks at their current pace.

'Where are the police?' Valerie Spicer asked as we slowed to a stop.

'At the police station, I suspect,' I said.

'Surely they haven't finished combing the rubble as part of their investigation.'

'How long have you been in Santo Domingo, Val?'

'About six months.'

'I take it you haven't had much contact with the police during your stay here.'

'I'm the cultural attaché, Henry.'

'Right. Well, these days, a police investigation never lasts more than an hour or two. If they think they know who did it, the cops round them up and stick them in prison. If they don't know who did it, they pick someone they would like to see in prison and put them there, case closed. Or they declare the crime unsolvable.'

'You said "these days".'

'Yes. Since Wessin y Wessin's coup. Before then, under Juan Bosch, there had been reforms undertaken. Crooked or lazy cops were fired. The police were beginning to be like the police in the States, really trying to solve crimes and not spending so much time trying to extract bribes. But when Bosch went out and Wessin y Wessin and the military junta came in, they brought most of the old cops back. Not just the hierarchy, even the beat cops. Now that they're back, they're very loyal to the junta. And they have quickly reverted to their old way of doing things. There are the handful of good ones around, like there are on any police force. But there are no cops here because this investigation is concluded. Thanks for the ride.'

I got out of the car and walked toward the two workmen. Then I heard the driver's side door open and close behind me. I turned. Val was a couple steps back, moving at a half jog to catch up. 'What are you doing?' I said.

'I'm coming to have a look. You said your friend – Jerry, wasn't it – was here.'

'Yeah.'

'He is an American.'

'I never got a look at his passport but he said he was.'

'Then the US Embassy has an interest in his safety and in learning what happened to him.'

'The cultural attaché has an interest?'

'I am a foreign service officer, Henry, and my duties are many and varied. Sometimes I even hand-hold expat vagabonds who get themselves blown up in dive bars.'

'All right, come on.'

We approached the workmen and, after a bunch of '*no sé*', '*no vi*' and '*no escuché*' answers from them, Val wandered – business suit, sensible shoes and all – into the rubble. I followed after getting a *loco yanqui* look and shoulder-shrug permission from the workmen.

'What are you expecting to find in this mess?' I asked when I caught up.

'Just poking around. Weren't you going to search when you decided to come here?'

'No. I was just going to ask questions of whoever might be here.'

'That got us nowhere. Your passport information said you were a veteran. Air Force Office of Special Investigations. From that I thought you would be enough of an investigator to want to get a little dirty.'

'You checked my background?'

'You were unconscious for a day, remember? I sent a telex to Washington to see if I could get next-of-kin information. The boys in DC did some extra looking.'

We wandered the rubble silently after that, side by side, about six feet apart, lifting boards and kicking away pieces of roofing. It was hot and the wreckage was getting ripe, smelling of spilled beer, rotting food and the tarry odor of C-4. Val was focused, a trooper, never complaining or stopping for a break. After a half hour, I was beginning to think we were engaged in a useless exercise.

'Val, I'm not seeing the point of this. If Jerry had been in here, the cops would have found something of him. He must have gotten out before the place went up.'

Val stopped and wiped the sweat off her brow and a stray strand of hair out of her eyes. 'So you want to give up, Henry? Give up on your friend, Jerry, just like that?'

Her words irked me. 'Not give up, just move on to something more likely to produce . . .'

'Ah!' Val said and bent to pluck something from the debris. Her exclamation and action reminded me of when my mother would spot a four-leafed clover in our lawn. Only what Val came up with wasn't a lucky piece of greenery. It was dirty and blackened by smoke but there was no mistaking it.

It was a severed human ear.

FIVE

The cops arrived right then. I thought it was quite a coincidence that the two uniforms happened to roll up just when Val found the ear. I thought, like Desi's Lucy, that we were going to have some 'splaining' to do. As it turned out, the cops didn't just happen by. They were on a mission. Though Val handled most of the talking, I got the gist of the conversation. They were looking for me, as were all the cops in Santo Domingo. I was wanted for questioning in connection with the bombing of La Españolita. My rapid departure from the hospital had raised some eyebrows at police headquarters.

I thought it might not be prudent to tell the officers who loaded me into the back of their 1960 Ford about the ear. At least not until I knew more about the lay of the land.

Val must have felt the same way. She didn't mention the ear, either, and she seemed to have disappeared it. She piled into the back of the police car with me, after some bickering with the officers and waving around her US Embassy identification card. There were no handcuffs or any other actions indicating I was under arrest. Apparently my trip to headquarters was more in the nature of a firm invitation.

The headquarters of the Policía Nacional Dominicana was not alien territory to me. I had visited the imposing building just off Avenida Mexico many times after I became a consultant to the government of President Juan Bosch. I'd only been in Santo Domingo a few weeks when Bosch, a reformer and proponent of democracy, was elected. One of the Bosch reform efforts was to professionalize the national police force. For that, the government hired a consultant. Me. The limited expertise I had was more than they had. The next months would see me at PND headquarters often, trying to clean out the corruption and infuse some professionalism. I tried to be evenhanded. I may have made some enemies but I thought I made a few friends, too.

My efforts were turned on their head when the military, led by General Wessin y Wessin, carried out their coup. President Bosch fled to Puerto Rico. In the soft manner of most coups in Latin America and the Caribbean, Bosch's followers were not executed or imprisoned but rather just removed from office and allowed to continue living their lives.

Those allowed to continue living their lives included me. I had money saved and life in Santo Domingo was inexpensive and pleasant. And President-in-exile Bosch decided to keep me on the payroll. Since the military coup, a consultant fee check arrived every month from an outfit rather amorphously named Import-Export Corp., LTD. In exchange, I sent the company a report every week or ten days, describing my observations on literally anything that struck my fancy – politics, news and conditions in Santo Domingo and the surrounding countryside. I wasn't exactly undercover. The police and military intelligence had to know I was there. I wasn't exactly a spy. I didn't recruit agents or attempt to infiltrate any organizations. I just made observations and kept a low enough profile that the reconstituted PND and SIM, the Dominican Republic's military intelligence, didn't consider it worth bothering with me.

At least not until the two beat cops picked me up in the ruins of La Españolita. Relax, I told myself. I was just a witness and, indeed, a victim. I was comforted by the fact that a US Embassy officer accompanied me. I was also comforted that no handcuffs were used and that the attitude of the cops bringing me in was, while gruffly cop-like, not hostile. The final comfort came when Val Spicer and I were taken directly to the office of Captain Cosme Salazar.

SIX

'Henry, my friend, first we thought you would die and then we thought you didn't want to speak to us.' Captain Cosme Salazar rose, hand extended, from behind his gray metal desk. The policeman had a wry smile on his face, making it difficult to read whether his words and gestures of friendship and welcome were an actuality or an act. Usually you can look into a man's eyes to get a true understanding in such a situation. Not with Captain Salazar. He had a wall-eye that made him seem as if he was always looking at an object in the distance over your left shoulder. The strabismus pulled one's attention away from his good eye. Looking in his eye to get a true idea of his thoughts, emotions and intentions – normally a reliable test for me – had never worked with Cosme. Perhaps that was why I had never been able to figure out if he was one of the good cops or one of the corrupt ones when I was doing my consulting work for President Bosch or how he managed to keep his job when the regime change took place.

'Always a pleasure to see you, Cosme.' I shook his hand.

He paused a moment, considering a retort and opted instead to turn his attentions to Val. 'And who is this lovely creature accompanying you, Henry?'

'Valerie Spicer, Captain. I am with the US Embassy.' And then Val blushed. After he had called her a creature. I have never understood how he could get away with it. If I called a woman a creature I'd expect, rightfully, to have my head handed to me. Cosme, though, could get away with anything with women. Even with his wall-eye. True, he was a snappy dresser; he had his police uniforms tailormade, with a non-regulation Sam Browne belt. But it was something more than that. He had a mistress and a child by her; a girlfriend who tolerated the mistress; and ongoing side conquests of lengths from one night to several months. He was insatiable when it came to the opposite sex. He was always on the prowl.

'Not this one, Cosme,' I said, feeling protective of the woman who had spent the last two days feeling protective of me. 'She's out of your league.'

'Oh? Oh, I see, Henry.' Cosme's tone was just-between-us-men smooth. 'My congratulations.'

'Whenever you boys are done dividing up my carcass, I assume some actual police business will follow,' Val said. She had stopped blushing and was somehow managing to look Cosme in the eyes, even the wall-eye, in a most businesslike manner. 'I am here with Mr Gore, on behalf of the United States government, to assist in whatever way I can to help you find the persons responsible for the La Españolita bombing. And to protect Mr Gore's rights in any police interrogation.'

Redirected to police business, Captain Salazar smiled sweetly at Val because that is how he conducted police business. 'I appreciate your, and the United States', help in locating the bomber, Miss Spicer. And as for protecting rights during my conversation – not interrogation – with Mr Gore, I can assure you that if anyone needs protection, it is I. Mr Gore has experience which makes mine pale by comparison.' He gestured for us to sit in two straight-backed chairs opposite his desk. Some might think the straight chairs were to make us uncomfortable. Prior experience told me they were the best PND headquarters had to offer. 'By way of formal background for you, Miss Spicer, I lead the Investigation and Identification Unit of the PND. That is our quaint term for the homicide squad, homicide being such a distasteful word. The unit's authority extends to other major crimes, like the terrorist attack on La Españolita, so it is doubly within my purview, as both a terrorist crime and a murder. Seven murders, to be precise.'

I thought about correcting Cosme on his body count but I only had one ear, not a full body, to back my assertion and decided to bide my time. Instead, I asked, 'Do you have any suspects, Cosme?'

'No names, Henry, but criminal elements of the recently-deposed regime are responsible.' He favored Val with another smile. Only then, after all the time I had known him, did I realize how brilliantly white and perfect his teeth were. Perhaps all those women had a thing for perfect teeth. 'That information, of course, comes down from above.'

'You think the Boschists did it? Killed all those people? Why?' I said. The 'why' did double duty – why do you think that and why would the Boschists do it?

'Perhaps you can tell me, Henry. With your close ties to the former regime, I was hoping you might have some insight. And, of

course, I would also like your statement of what occurred, as well
as an explanation of why you signed yourself out of the hospital
and returned to the scene of the crime as soon as possible. I could
ask you a series of questions and we could spend a tedious afternoon
on your answers and follow ups. On the other hand – *como se dice*
– you know the drill and all the questions. Why don't we just have
you move right to your answers and save Miss Spicer the tedium
of watching us spar back and forth?'

'Fair enough,' I said. 'My ties to the former regime – the one
that used to provide your paycheck, Cosme – don't include any
information on any terrorist activities. I can address one thing,
though. It's not their style. You know that. The whole leadership,
from Juan Bosch on down, was about democracy and reform. They
worked for years to gain power politically. If they were just terrorists, there would have been bombings and assassinations before the
elections in 1963. There was none of that because it's not their
modus operandi. They wouldn't do it. They didn't do it.'

'If not them, then who, Henry?'

'I don't know. Another revolutionary group maybe. Someone who
just wants to make trouble for the current regime. Maybe the current
regime itself.'

'Your last five words, said to an officer less open-minded than
me, could get you in serious trouble, Henry. Fortunately, I realize
that you were just throwing out broad hypotheticals. And why would
the current regime do such a thing, speaking hypothetically, of
course?'

'Of course,' I said. 'To set up an enemy. To create fear and allow
them to keep control.'

'Did you see such things happening during your time in Cuba,
Henry?'

I had never revealed to Cosme that I had even been to Cuba but
I suppose it wouldn't be difficult to learn that I had been there,
when, and what I had done. I shot a quick glance in Val's direction.
She had her eyes down, taking notes in a small notebook she had
pulled from her purse. She was unfazed by the mention of America's
most urgent concern in the hemisphere. I guessed that she would
be quite a poker player.

'No, Cosme.' I let my answer stand at that.

Salazar shifted gears. 'Then what can you tell me about the day
of the bombing?'

What could I tell him about that day? That I was day-drinking with someone I didn't know that well, except he liked day-drinking, too, and was an American. That I had picked the place because of the bartender. Jesus, that sounded seedy. I sugarcoated the story. 'I was at La Españolita to meet a friend.'

Cosme's good eye shot quickly from me to Val and back again. He must have thought I had been there to meet a woman and didn't want Val to know. That's why he would have been there.

I preempted whatever dodge Cosme was about to lead me into. 'And the friend's name is Jerry Pleasants. An American. We were there to discuss a business matter.'

'Your friend's address?'

'I don't know. I have never been to his place.' In six months. Why didn't that strike me as strange before then?

'What type of business matter, if I may ask?'

'Jerry was offering me a job. As an assistant manager of a bauxite mining operation that is going to be opening in Jamaica.' There was no lie in what I said, just a bit of omission.

'You are truly a renaissance man, Henry,' Cosme said. 'I had no idea you were experienced in bauxite mining.'

'My experience is more on the general management side,' I said. Val duly noted that, not glancing from the page. At least she seemed to be buying my cover for my day-drinking acquaintance with Jerry Pleasants.

'So you and this Jerry Pleasants met at La Españolita?' Salazar prompted.

'Yes. A while back. We had a mutual interest in music and we became friends. On the day of the bombing, we listened to music on La Españolita's jukebox because it has the latest hits from the States. And then we talked about the job. The management position.'

'Did Mr Pleasants have any other business associates with him?'

'No, just him.'

'Were there others in the bar?'

'There was a tourist couple. Not in the bar room; back in the room where the jukebox was. English or Canadian by their accent. In the bar room proper, there was another man and woman, together. They looked like locals. And there were three other locals, business types, at a table together.'

'You have described those who died, I think,' Salazar said. 'Any others?'

'The bartender, of course. He was the only employee in the place.'

'No waitress or cook?'

'La Españolita didn't serve cooked food.' I saw that register, ever so slightly, with Val. Maybe she wasn't buying the business meeting story after all.

'And this fellow Jerry was there,' Salazar said. 'Anyone else?'

'No.'

'Did you know the bartender?'

'Yes.'

'Well?'

'Yes.' I guess Val knew La Españolita was my second home in the Dominican Republic by now.

'How?'

'From the bar. His name was Jaime.'

'Last name?'

'I don't know.'

'Tell me what happened next.'

'Jerry and I were seated at the bar. We had our business discussion and then he went in the back, to visit the *servicio*.' I hesitated, unsure how I wanted to tell the story for some reason.

'And . . .?'

'Jerry had been talking to me when he left the bar and I had turned in his direction.'

'Talking? What was he saying?'

'"I gotta take a piss."' Not a flinch from note-taking Val. A lot of women these days would find the language slightly vulgar.

'Then what?'

'I turned back to the bar and Jaime was gone.'

'Gone where? Left the building? Gone elsewhere in the bar?'

'Just gone. Disappeared.'

'That would be unusual with a customer at the bar, wouldn't you say, Henry?'

'It was not like Jaime to do that. And there was a note left on the bar.'

'A note?'

'It said, "Leave now". With an exclamation point.'

'What did you do?'

'I looked at the note. I looked around for Jaime. And for Jerry. And then I got up and opened the door to leave the bar. I hesitated at the door, took one last glance inside for Jerry and didn't see him. That was when the bomb went off. I got blown into the street, with the door on top of me. It protected me for the most part but the blast took off part of my little finger.' I held up my bandaged hand. 'The rest, Cosme, you already know, probably better than me.'

'You were lucky, Henry. You and a lady passing by in the street outside were the only injured. Everyone inside La Españolita at the time of the blast died.'

'I thought you said seven died.'

'Yes.'

'Not Jaime?'

'No bartender was found.'

'And Jerry. What about him?' I asked.

'We were unaware of him even being in the bar until you told me just now. He must have left the bar after visiting the *servicio* and you did not notice. There was no additional body found. I am certain that your friend is fine.'

At Captain Salazar's mention that no other body had been found, Val stopped writing, putting her pen and notebook on the corner of his desk. 'That may not be entirely correct, Captain Salazar.' She undid the clasp on her handbag, reached inside and drew out a lacy lady's hanky. 'We found this in the rubble of La Españolita.'

She unwrapped the charred ear and placed it on Salazar's desk.

SEVEN

Cosme Salazar handled Val's delivery of the ear to his desktop with aplomb. 'This is an ear,' he stated calmly, as if women tossing scorched human ears on his blotter was a daily occurrence. He spun his chair to a green metal filing cabinet behind him and pulled out a file. After reviewing it quickly, he placed it open on the desk and fanned the seven eight by ten glossy photos inside like a deck of cards. 'Autopsy photographs of the victims from the La Españolita bombing,' he said.

I picked up the photos one by one and examined them. Val looked at them over my shoulder. They weren't the clearest pictures I had ever seen but they were clear enough to tell that each of the seven corpses retained both ears.

'None of these is Jerry,' I said. 'Or Jaime. But all of them have both their ears. This ear must belong to Jerry or Jaime.'

'How do you conclude this, Henry?' Neither Cosme's good eye nor his wall-eye met mine.

'Process of elimination,' I said, thinking his question was a poor attempt at some kind of sick joke.

'Can you positively identify the ear as that of Señor Pleasants or the bartender Jaime?'

'What? Come on, Cosme. It's a burned ear that's been out in the sun for a couple of days. I'm lucky I can tell it's an ear.'

'So you cannot positively attribute it to either man?'

'Well . . . no.'

'Then it is just a random ear.'

'A random ear? That's a new concept for me, Cosme. Would you care to explain?'

Salazar was unruffled. 'It is an ear to which we can attribute no particular origin. It could have come from anywhere. Someone could have accidentally dropped it in the debris. Someone could have planted it there, to cause confusion in the investigation.'

'Who would do that?'

'A troublemaker. Someone wishing to call into question the clear results of a completed investigation.'

'Clear results? Completed investigation?' I said. 'What clear results? What completed investigation?'

Captain Salazar allowed himself a sad smile, and said, 'Since the National Reconstruction government led by General Wessin y Wessin assumed . . . control, the Investigation and Identification Unit of the PND has become more efficient. As we were ordered to become. In the forty-eight hours since the vicious attack on La Españolita, we have fully examined and released the crime scene, identified all of the dead and wounded, conducted and completed a thorough investigation, identified a number of individuals – all Boschist terrorists – as conspirators in the bombing, and tonight, in coordinated raids in Santo Domingo and the surrounding countryside, they will be arrested, tried and appropriately punished.'

'I see. What about Jerry Pleasants?'

'We found no body that was identified as Jerry Pleasants. No next of kin has reported an American known as Jerry Pleasants as missing. And the fact that only one American – you, Henry – was injured in the bombing is a relief to General Wessin y Wessin, who seeks to maintain good relations with the United States and wishes to show that its citizens are safe here. So, Henry, the Investigation and Identification Unit has no cause to inquire into such an individual. Indeed, we are not sure that such an individual even exists.'

'Jesus, Cosme, have things gone that far downhill here in less than two years?'

You could see it then. Just for a moment and then Cosme Salazar's mien returned to its world-weary old self. But it was there briefly. Embarrassment at what had become of the unit he commanded and the career he had built and maybe, too, a touch of anger at me for having called him out. He said, 'Thank you, Mr Gore, for coming in today and giving your statement. And our thanks to you, too, Miss Spicer, for being present on behalf of your government. It was my genuine pleasure to meet you. You may exit the way you came in.'

'That went well,' Val said brightly, standing in the afternoon sun beside the rubble that had been La Españolita. Cosme had ordered the two officers who had brought us in to return us to where Val's embassy car was parked.

'You think so?' How could this woman find only the good side in everything?

'Absolutely, Henry. You weren't arrested. That means I fulfilled the primary job of any embassy officer who assists a US citizen in an encounter with the police authorities of a foreign nation.'

'That's a pretty low bar, Val.'

'Oh, you'd be surprised how often the embassy staff don't clear that bar. Now that we have gotten your desire to poke around La Españolita out of the way and fended off the local *gendarmes*, I'm taking you home.'

'But . . .'

'No argument, Henry. You have been blown up, concussed, lost part of an appendage, been investigated by the police and haven't had a shave or a shower in two days.'

'I thought you said you had taken care of bathing me in the hospital.'

'Sponge baths don't count. They're no match for a good hot shower. Besides, do you really think you should be jumping into things feet first with no recovery time? Aren't you tired? I know I am and I haven't even been blown up. I only sat up overnight in a chair.'

Now that Val mentioned it, I did feel tired. Hell, now that Val reminded me of it, my body felt like I'd had an encounter with a freight train and come out on the losing, but at least still living, end of it. 'All right, Val. Take me home.'

'And that is where?'

'One hundred and six Calle Luperón.'

'Old school, eh? Funny, I had you pegged for one of the newer places on the other side of the river, in Santo Domingo Este.'

'My place suits my needs.'

'Show me.' And just like that, she had invited herself. We drove through the city streets to the colonial area near the banks of the Rio Ozama. My place wasn't on the river or fronting the Caribbean but it was mine, plenty nicer than my apartment-office had been in Havana, much nicer than sleeping in the jungle with Fidel and his rebels. As accommodating and homey as any place I'd lived in the islands. It was in an old building which looked like Chris Columbus himself had been the architect and builder. It had a brick and stone façade on the street, with wood-framed windows of handmade glass on the first floor and a Romeo and Juliet balcony on the second where my bedroom was. The entry wasn't from the street. You came into a courtyard with an ancient well at the center. Entry doors to eight habitations opened to the courtyard, including mine. A step inside brought you into a low-ceilinged sitting-dining room with white plastered walls and hand-hewn beams. The kitchen was at the back, together with a bath. The upstairs was my bedroom, complete with a made-in-Spain four-poster bed that looked as if the building had been built around it. A bathroom had been added upstairs sometime after the colonial period.

The apartment, which I rented from a Boschist businessman who was a great admirer of John Kennedy, came furnished. And it came with Camila Polanco, who now greeted me at the door by enveloping me in a breath-strangling hug.

'*Dios mío,* Señor Gore. *Ah, Dios mío. Dios mío.*' Camila was stuck like a broken record on the phrase and stuck in our embrace for a period which lasted much longer than proper in the conventional employer–employee relationship. This was probably my fault. Camila was not, you see, the standard housekeeper type. No red hands cracked by scrubbing floors and washing dishes; hers were dark, long-fingered and elegant. They moved as if she were playing an invisible harp. No tired eyes, dulled by years of drudgery, maintaining her employer's household by day and that of a husband and children by night; Camila was unattached. No gray strands escaping from a kerchief as she toiled; Camila's hair, which she wore tied back with a vibrantly-colored ribbon, was glossy blue-black and reached well below her enticing hips. Her demeanor matched her appearance, radiant to the point of effervescence, intelligent, competent and warm-hearted. She was, in short, the kind of *señorita* I had dreamed of finding when I first traveled to Havana eight years ago. When I moved into the apartment on Calle Luperón, I had succumbed to her considerable charms. It had been mutual but brief. The old four-poster bed got quite a workout for a week or two. Then one day I awoke to find Camila watching me in the early-morning light with a look in her eyes that said I was not just a fling, I was husband material. That look told me I had to find a place for her in my heart or else not trifle with her affections. And there was no place available in my heart. That place had been taken, and, even now, eight years later, held by a Midwest farm girl with a pure heart and a difficult life. I brought the romantic side of my relationship with Camila to an end but she insisted on staying on as my housekeeper. She plainly had not given up her hopes for us, being the cheerful and optimistic type that she was. I decided I couldn't be a snake and put her out of a job, so we both pretended what had happened had not happened. Sort of.

'I was frantic, Señor Henry,' Camila said, finally loosening her grip a bit to lean back and look at me. 'I had no idea where you were. And your hand. You are injured?' A new wave of concern washed over Camila's lovely face. A tear crept to the edge of a lower eyelid and glided along her smooth cheek.

'It's nothing, Camila. It's nothing that I won't live through.'

'Well, I . . .' Val Spicer spoke over my shoulder.

'Who is this?' Camila shifted from concerned servant to jealous lover in a flash.

'Valerie Spicer.' Val extended a hand and a dazzling smile. 'I am with the US Embassy. I've just been involved in helping Mr Gore these last few days while he was in the hospital, Señorita . . .?'

'Polanco.' The smile and the official connection with the embassy seemed to disarm Camila somewhat, although she grasped Val's offered hand like it was a fish that had just spent the last ten days fermenting on the sand at Playa Punta Torrecillas.

'A pleasure, señorita.' Val smiled with her eyes as well as with her teeth. Camila parried with the stink eye, which Val ignored. 'So, Henry, get some rest. Eat some food. I will see you in the morning.'

'In the morning?'

'Just a check-in to make sure that you are doing well. You being alone and all. Courtesy of Uncle Sam, just like that sponge bath in the hospital.'

'Sponge bath?' Camila was now incandescent.

'Well, I couldn't return him to you all dirty, dear.' Val gave a little wave of her fingers in my direction and slipped out the door.

'I am bushed,' I said to Camila. 'I'm going to bed for a while.' It's difficult when you have to hide in your own house.

Camila huffed a very Latin huff, conveying a good deal of hurt and a touch of threat, an art that women in the Spanish islands of the Caribbean have mastered. Then she said, 'I will make you food.'

I went to bed, bone-tired and realizing how battered I was from head to foot. I thought I would sleep for hours but I didn't. Camila was taking out her anger on the pots and pans in the kitchen downstairs. It sounded like a marching band made up exclusively of cymbals. I tossed until Camila called up the stairs that dinner was on the table and she was leaving. With the house finally quiet, I dropped off to sleep. I would like to tell you that I settled into a sweet dream of Val – or was it Camila? – giving me a sponge bath, but in truth, I passed the night in one long nightmare of Jerry Pleasants wandering through the smoking ruins of La Españolita, his clothes tattered and his hair singed away, looking for his lost ear.

EIGHT

'Señor Gore is still asleep.' Camila, downstairs, hissed this statement like a provoked feline. She was trying to be quiet but her exasperation bled through into her voice, elevating its volume. Morning sunlight streamed in the windows. I had slept through the night.

'That's all right, dear. I'll take some coffee and wait.' Val's cheery voice in the kitchen seemed amplified too.

The voices traveling up to me from the kitchen didn't quite sound like they were squabbling but they didn't quite sound like they weren't, either. Much as the soft bed and invitingly cool sheets called to me, I decided to get up and make my way downstairs before there was an international incident. I shrugged into a robe and went to the bath. I still hadn't taken that hot shower and my five o'clock shadow had moved all the way around the clock to almost eleven. I turned on the shower and was about to enter when a raised voice, its words garbled but its owner clearly Camila, sounded from below. Shower off, robe back on and down to the kitchen.

On the way, I placed my ignored-until-now left hand on the stair banister. Pain shot through the injured pinky, up the arm and managed to take my breath away. The lidocaine administered at the hospital had worn off. I stopped for a moment on the stairs, trying to regain my composure.

'Nice legs.' Val stood at the bottom of the stairs, looking – or, rather, leering – up.

My robe, in deference to the tropical climate of the Dominican Republic, was – no other way to put it – short. Val, looking upstairs, probably had a view which enhanced the exposure of the abbreviated garment. I hurried down the steps to cut off the viewing angle. Val met me at the bottom, looking pleased with . . . herself, the view, who knows?

'You certainly are the early bird, Miss Spicer.' I thought it best to move back on a more formal footing after the free show my robe and I had just provided.

'Miss Spicer? Why the formality, Mr Gore? Why just yesterday, when we were ear-hunting, we were good old Val and Henry. And weren't we happy then?' Val coupled her remark with her best Doris Day bright, sunny morning face.

I chose to ignore the comment. 'You *are* here early.'

'I just wanted to check on the embassy's favorite blown-up expat resident of the Dominican Republic.'

'I heard a noise in the kitchen.'

'That? Oh, just some girl talk between Señorita Polanco and me.'

I leaned to glance into the kitchen. 'Where is she?'

'I gave her the day off.' Val's cheery voice had no catty edge. 'She was very upset yesterday when you finally came home and she clearly hadn't gotten over it yet this morning. But, look, she made breakfast.'

'You sent her home?'

'Yes. Poor girl. Come, sit down. Your food is getting cold.'

I was going to protest Val's takeover of my domestic situation but my stomach had other ideas. I had not eaten since leaving the hospital, opting to sleep instead of eating the meal Camila had left for me last night. A Dominican breakfast of *mangú tres gloves* waited on the table. The savory smell of the mashed green plantains, pickled onions, fried *salchichón*, fried *queso de freir* and sunny side eggs drew me in. The next thing I knew, I was tucking into the meal. Val did *hausfrau* duty, pouring me mugs of rich Barahona coffee. It was a quaint domestic scene, one to which I was unused. I ate in silence and Val did not speak beyond offering second helpings.

Done eating, sitting in the sunlit kitchen, I relaxed back into my seat. But not for long.

'You positively stink, Henry Gore. Did you not take that shower I recommended?' Val asked.

'I was about to when I heard the cat fight going on and came down to investigate.'

'I don't know what you are talking about, Henry. Go. Go take your shower. I'll clear the dishes.'

The steaming water running over me carried away the gamey scent of my hospital stay. I stood under the shower and tried to let it wash away the last image I had of Jerry Pleasants in my mind – slouchy, slightly drunk Jerry, mumbling, 'I gotta take a piss' and heading to the *servicio*. Walking into eternity. Or maybe not. Maybe he walked out the back door of La Españolita and went on his merry way when the place exploded a few minutes later, not a care in the world. Not a care for his drinking buddy, either. If Jerry walked out of La Españolita, he could not have gone far. Why hadn't he come back to help? To check for survivors? To help me, maybe the closest thing he had to a friend in Santo Domingo, maybe the closest thing he had to a friend anywhere? But he hadn't come back. He got out and left me. For all he knew I was injured – and I was – and he didn't even have enough concern to return. To hell with you then, Jerry Pleasants. To hell with your shabby clothing, your pudgy, florid face, your bad jokes and worse plans. To hell with your good taste in the one thing that joined us together, other than a love for midday imbibing, that being pop music. To hell with you. You left me to die.

But what if he hadn't? What if he had tried to warn me, being somehow warned himself, and had been blown up for his trouble. What if that *was* his ear? Where was the rest of him? Gone, obliterated, removed from the face of the Earth in the single clap and flash of the bomb? No, that could not be. All the other victims, dead and injured, had come out mostly intact. I was whole but for part of a finger. The dazed woman I saw walking in the street after the blast was recognizable as a human. The dead, the seven unlucky ones in the wrong place at the wrong time, were still whole, still bodies, parts missing, mutilated and burned but still entire. But was all that was left of Jerry just an ear? No, he was out there somewhere, injured, maybe alone, maybe not remembering who he was. He was out there. He deserved to be found. I could not write him off, as Cosme Salazar and the PND were prepared to do. Maybe I was the only one who cared what had happened to Jerry Pleasants but I did care.

And what about Jaime? He had managed a note of warning to me but what had happened to him after? Did he escape the blast? Or was the ear his? If he escaped and warned me, was he the bomber? Or did he know the bomber? If the answer to either of those last two questions was affirmative, why had he bombed La Españolita? Being a bartender was a great job in Santo Domingo. If he wanted to blow up things, why would he foul his own nest?

'Henry, are you OK in there?' Val's voice was close, no longer calling from downstairs.

'Yes. Fine.'

'Do you need a towel?'

What was she doing volunteering to provide one? 'No, I have one. Thanks.'

I'm not sure I would consider myself a man of the world when it comes to the opposite sex. I suppose a disinterested observer could look back on my dalliances with the farm girls of Maine while I was in the Air Force; my liaisons, compensated and uncompensated, with the numerous beauties of Cuba; and the pairings with various island girls and accommodating female tourists in my post-Cuba travels around the Caribbean, and conclude that I was. And I had been in love, the truest of true loves, once. I should know about women. I should be comfortable with women. But there was something disquieting in the knowledge that Valerie Spicer had found it perfectly all right to come upstairs, stand in my bedroom outside the bathroom door and casually call in to offer me a towel. I guess a man of the world I am not.

I took my time toweling dry, ran a sink of hot water and shaved the multi-day stubble from my face and finally had to confront whatever waited on the other side of the bathroom door. Robe wrapped defensively around me like an inexperienced bride on her wedding night, I cracked open the door and stepped into my bedroom.

Val leaned on the low dresser across the room, relaxed, winsome, hardly the man-eater my too-vivid imagination had conjured in the shower. 'Feel better, Henry?'

'Yes.'

'See, Nurse Val is always right. I knew you'd perk up after a little rest, some food and a shower. Now let's have a look at that finger. Have a seat on the bed.'

I wanted to tell her that I ought to dress first, that this examination of my hand could take place, effectively enough, downstairs at the kitchen table but she was already at the elbow of my good arm, steering me to a seat on the big four-poster. She knelt beside the bed and gently unwound the bandage that I had so diligently avoided getting wet in the shower.

'Mmmm. You not only feel better, you smell better, Henry.'

Silently cursing the habitual splash of English Leather cologne I had applied after shaving, I said, 'Is it embassy policy to give follow up medical care to citizens injured overseas?'

'Some citizens, if . . .' Val stopped.

'If?'

'If maybe they would not take good care of themselves, otherwise.' Then, brisk and businesslike, she added, 'This looks like it's healing pretty well, considering.'

I hazarded a look at the finger, hoping it wouldn't be too gruesome. It wasn't but it wasn't something I'd recommend showing to young children, either. The most unsettling part was not what was there but what was missing. I touched the top of the stub. It hurt. I winced.

'Bet you won't do that again,' Val said, unhelpfully. 'Where is your first aid kit?'

'Bathroom linen closet, second shelf.'

Val returned in a minute with the small olive drab bag with a red cross on it. 'Rather complete,' she said. 'But rather old. The paper wrapping on the bandages is all yellowed.'

'It's done some traveling,' I said. The first aid kit was Korean War surplus, issued to me as one of Fidel's fighters in the last days before we entered Havana. Bought from America with dollars donated by Americans. I had marveled back then at how much of *La Revolucion*'s equipment was paid for with money from the United States. Not government money but that of individual donors who wanted to see Batista and his American mob friends gone from the Pearl of the Antilles. I never had to use the kit for a combat injury, though I saw a lot of action with Fidel. Day-drinking in Santo Domingo had proved much more perilous than making revolution in Cuba.

Val painted the stub with Mercurochrome and re-bandaged it, winding paper tape over the bandage while gently holding my hand.

'There, Henry, good as new,' she said, looking up from where she knelt beside the bed. Continuing to hold my injured hand in her right hand, she reached her left to the back of my neck and, grinning, pulled me forward and kissed me. Kissed me softly, almost chastely, at first, and then vigorously, with an animal hunger.

I pulled back. I was not ready for this after being bombed and hospitalized and barely knowing her, I guess. I'm not really sure why.

'Oh, Henry, why so shy?' Her words betrayed some small hurt but her aspect was blithe as ever. 'I'm a big girl. I have no virtue to protect. I'm not adverse to a little fun. And you're a big boy, with no entanglements of the heart to keep us apart as far as I can tell. Unless Señorita Polanco has her hooks in you deeper than it would appear. Does she? No, I thought not. So why not have some fun? Come on, it's 1965.'

'Sorry, Val. Things have been moving pretty fast these last few days. I just . . .'

'Too fast? OK, I can see that. You're pretty banged up. People tell me that sometimes I can be what my dear old mom used to call "forward". So I'll back off, Henry. I'll give you your space and let you heal up. Because, trust me, when we get going, you are going to need your strength.'

How does one respond to a statement like that? With a promise of a studly man-performance in the future? With a blush and down-cast eyes? Neither alternative seemed right to me, so I settled for: 'Thanks.'

'You're welcome,' she said. 'Now aren't we polite? Well, I told the chief of staff I wouldn't be back today. Now that I can't get you into the sack, do you have any other amusement in mind?'

'I want to find out what happened to Jerry Pleasants.' When the words came out of my mouth, even I was surprised.

NINE

U ncle Sam, in all of his bureaucratic wisdom, had labeled me an investigator in my Air Force days. Heck, I worked for the Office of Special *Investigations*. But the truth was that my time in the military conducting background checks and my short career as a private dick, doing matrimonials – essentially peeping-tom work – had ill-prepared me to do any truly serious investigations. And locating an American with no known friends other than me, no family and no known place of abode in a Third World country would be serious investigative work. I wasn't sure I was up to the task.

And there was the matter of my investigative partner. Valerie Spicer, Cultural Attaché, certainly didn't have a title that suggested any investigative training or experience. I knew from my time in the world of counterintelligence what her title did suggest – that she was a spy. The job of embassy cultural attaché is so often the cover job for spooks that they might as well just call the position Cultural Attaché and Spy with Diplomatic Immunity. What I couldn't figure out was why Val, as a spy, was wasting her time on me. My history was an open book. My time on the wrong side in Cuba was well known to the State Department, so there was nothing to uncover about me. And because of my expulsion by Fidel, it was not likely that I could be turned into a source or double agent. The blatant pass she had just made at me could be genuine – even spies need to get laid now and then – but more likely it was the first effort at some kind of honey trap to ensnare me. To what end I could not fathom.

These thoughts drifted through my mind as we traveled along the Malecon, the white-gloved Val at the wheel of the embassy Ford. My concussion headache was gone and I believed I was thinking clearly. I decided that, even if she was a spy, I had nothing of value to give her, so why not play along? Besides, she had a car and a set of credentials that she didn't hesitate to flash. I had neither. I needed the car to get around if I was going to find out what happened to Jerry Pleasants. I needed the credentials because they would open doors and I figured that might help in the search for Jerry, too.

'And where are we going, Henry?' Val said. 'Or are we just out for a drive along the Malecon on this fine day? I mean, I'll follow driving directions turn by turn if you insist but I might be of more help if I know our plan. Maybe you could even go all modern man and allow me some input into our little finding-Jerry exercise.'

'I have a plan.'

'And it is?'

'Talk to some people who know Jerry. Visit his residence. Talk to his neighbors.'

'So where is Jerry's pad?'

'I don't know.'

'Guess you can't do the talk-to-the-neighbors part of your plan just yet.'

'No. I'm going to start with the talking to his friends part.'

'Who are his friends?'

'That's another problem. Jerry didn't have a lot of friends, at least that I know of. In fact, I only know of two – me and Jaime, the bartender at La Españolita. And I'll save you the trouble of asking. I don't know Jaime's last name. And I don't know where he lives. What I do know is that it's possible that he had something to do with the bombing.'

'This isn't sounding like a very productive plan, Henry.' Val said this with a spritely tilt of her blonde locks toward me, like we were having a teasing discussion of movies or music and she disagreed with my tastes.

'I do know of someone else who might qualify as a friend. At least enough of a friend to know where Jerry lives. It's a long shot, though.'

'It sounds like long shots are all the shots we've got.'

'Yeah. This would have been easier if you hadn't sent her away earlier. I'm not even sure she'll talk to me now.'

'Camila?'

'Bingo. Turn right here.'

Camila lived in a compact bungalow in a warren of streets in the elbow formed by Avenida Abraham Lincoln and Avenida George Washington. I knew the place because I visited on several occasions in that blissful time before I woke to her looking at me and seeing a husband. I hadn't been back since. No telling the reception I would get today.

'This is the place,' I said.

'Nice, for a housekeeper.' Maybe it was. Maybe I paid Camila a little too much. Guilt money.

'You had better stay in the car, Val.'

'Are you kidding? I'm coming in.'

'After what I heard going on downstairs this morning?'

'That's done. Camila and I have an understanding.'

'Suit yourself.'

The front of the house was shrouded by a pink bougainvillea. The place was old but the stucco walls were freshly painted since the last time I'd been there. I knocked and was warmly greeted.

'Señor Henry, how nice! Oh.' Camila's face fell when Val stepped from behind me. 'Come in.'

Camila's place was the twin of mine. The heavy Spanish colonial furnishings. The quaint kitchen and sitting room. She eyed Val and said to me, 'I thought you came to ask me back to work today.'

'No need,' Val said.

'But return tomorrow,' I said. Camila brightened. 'For today, I have a question.'

'*Si?*'

'You remember Jerry. Señor Pleasants.'

'*Si.*' Camila's eyes darkened.

'He's missing. I'm – we – are looking for him. But we don't know where he lives.'

'*Si.*' The affirmative was drawn out.

'We thought you might know where he lives.'

'Why would you think that, Señor Henry?'

'I know he asked you out, Camila. He told me after you refused him. But I thought he might have mentioned where he lived.'

'He took me there.'

'He took you to where he lives?'

'Yes.' Camila looked hard at Val and then turned her eyes to me. 'After you refused me. One time. I . . . it was a mistake.'

I felt for Camila. I was a dirt ball, a heel.

'I can take you there,' she said.

TEN

Val drove. Camila rode shotgun. I sat in back and worried what might erupt between the two front-seaters. I shouldn't have flattered myself. Apparently, the ladies did have an understanding between themselves. I just wasn't privy to what the understanding was.

Camila gave concise directions, which Val obeyed. No small talk, chitchat, byplay or any other unnecessary communication passed between them. Camila took us across town, across the Duarte Bridge over the Rio Ozama and into the newer neighborhood of Santo Domingo Este. On a quiet side street, Calle Bonaire, Camila pointed to a walk-up apartment building. 'There, on the second floor.'

'Which number?' I asked.

'The entire second floor.'

The building was new by Dominican standards, built in this decade and not showing any of the wear that centuries of hurricanes, wars and blazing Caribbean sun had inflicted on places like mine in the old city. It was nice here. Shaded streets. Quiet. Clean.

'I'll be right back,' I said, sliding out the rear door. I'd gone a half dozen steps before I heard the two front doors of the Ford slam behind me.

'I'm not missing this,' Val said, catching up to me.

'Neither am I,' Camila said, a pace behind.

We climbed the stairs to the second floor and knocked. No answer. A porch with a wrought iron railing extended the full length of the second level. I walked along it, peering into the windows. Curtains blocked my view.

'Shall we go in?' Val asked.

'Break in? I want to find the guy, Val, but I don't want to go to jail doing it.'

'I will get us in,' Camila volunteered, and disappeared down the steps. In five minutes, she returned with the building's caretaker, a white-haired old hand with a ring of keys on his belt.

'What did you tell him, Camila?' I said.

'That you are Jerry's brother from the United States and cannot contact him, so you came to investigate.'

'Have you seen Jerry – Señor Pleasants – recently?' I asked the caretaker in English.

'*No hablo inglés,*' the old man replied. '*Policía?*'

'He wants to know if we are the police,' Camila said.

More conversation in Spanish between the caretaker and Camila ended with the old man shaking his head. 'He said he won't open it if we aren't the police.'

'Tell him we are.' Val stepped up, pulled her embassy ID from her purse, flashed it at the old man and said, '*Policía. Abre la puerta.*'

The trick worked, probably because the old man couldn't read Spanish or English and the ID looked official. He had the door open in a second.

I stepped inside. 'Anybody home? Jerry?'

Val called, '*Policía,*' keeping up the ruse.

There was no answer. The place was spartan, just a table and two chairs in the kitchen and a small sofa in the living room. No books, magazines, pictures on the wall or any of the other trappings of normal occupancy. There were no dishes in the kitchen sink. A few staple food items lined the cupboards – coffee, sugar, canned goods. The bedroom was equally spare, just a double bed, precisely made, with no indication of when it last had an occupant. The medicine cabinet in the bath held a razor, toothbrush, shaving cream and a bottle of aspirin. The way the place looked, Jerry might not have been in it for months or could have walked out just a few minutes before. There were clothes in the bedroom closet, a bare minimum of shirts and pants, a single pair of shoes. There was a hat that I had seen Jerry wear once.

'Neat freak,' Val said. 'Or he doesn't really live here.'

I turned to Camila. 'Was it like this when you were here before?'

Embarrassed, she said, 'I guess. It was dark.'

'Did the caretaker tell you when he last saw Jerry?' I asked Camila.

'He said he tries to respect the privacy of the tenants and does not monitor when they come and go.'

Val stepped to where the caretaker waited at the door. She said, '*Cuándo vis por* última *vez al Senōr Pleasants?*' in a passable imitation of a cop voice, stern in place of her signature smile.

The old boy dropped the tenant privacy dodge. '*Una samana, señora.*'

'A week since he's last seen Jerry,' Val said. 'Before the bombing. Henry, looks like you might be the last one to see your friend alive. If he hasn't shown at his old apartment since the bombing, maybe he was killed. I'm no expert but just because there is no body doesn't mean it wasn't blown to smithereens and there is simply nothing to find of the poor man. Other than, possibly, his ear.'

'I suppose that could be,' I said.

'Why else would he just be gone?'

'No reason that I know, Val.'

Camila couldn't resist working on the caretaker some more, now that he was talking. She posed a swift series of questions to him and he answered with equal speed. I was at a loss in this Spanish language equivalent of machine-gun fire but Camila summarized at the end.

'The caretaker said that Jerry does not mix with the other tenants in the building. He is very quiet, pays his rent on time and makes no trouble. He has no girlfriend who visits or any other guests, for that matter.'

'*Gracias,*' I said to the old man. To Val and Camila: 'It looks like we're wasting our time here.'

The room swam and pitched like a ship in a heavy sea. Then it all went dark.

ELEVEN

I woke in my own bed. The sun was slanted low in the sky through the closed curtains. The humidity of the early evening made the air thick and wet.

'Welcome back to the world, Henry,' Val said. Then, calling down the stairs, 'Camila, our boy is awake.'

Camila appeared in the doorway and rushed to my side. 'Señor Henry, you gave us a fright.'

'You also nearly gave us a hernia. It was everything the two of us could do to carry you up the stairs. It was much easier getting you down the stairs at Jerry's apartment with the help of the old caretaker,' Val said.

'I thought you might be dying.' Camila caressed my cheek, her eyes brimming with tears.

'I didn't, but I called in an embassy favor and had your treating doctor from the hospital come and check on you,' Val said.

'So, am I dying?' I said, more than a little curious but trying to maintain an appropriately masculine detachment on the subject.

'No, Henry,' Val said. 'But Dr Gutierrez did say you need to take it easy for a couple days. As in bedrest easy. Apparently getting blown up has more than a seventy-two-hour recovery time. You will recover completely if you allow yourself to. Oh, while he was here the good doctor also checked your finger. Healing nicely, he said. I told him it was the quality nursing care you were receiving.'

I scooted up in the bed. The room didn't swim. I had a headache but not a bad one.

'Slow down, cowboy,' Val said. 'Didn't you hear what I just said? The doc said to take it easy.'

'Unless you have a bedpan handy, Val, I'm getting up and making the epic trip to the *baño*.' I swung my legs out of the sheets and realized I was naked underneath. 'What happened to my clothes?'

'Señorita Spicer said your clothing would be too restrictive to be comfortable,' Camila said. 'I agreed. We undressed you. Do not worry. We averted our eyes.'

I'll bet. 'Well, better avert them again. Nature calls.'

'I have a better idea,' Val said. 'Here's your robe. We'll turn our backs until you give the OK.'

They did and then escorted me, Val on one side and Camila on the other, the ten steps to the bathroom. Thankfully, they stopped at the door and allowed me some privacy, although they were both waiting like sentries when I emerged. They slow-marched me back to the bed. Five minutes later, Camila brought up a hearty meal of *bandera*. The rice, red beans, chicken and avocado restored me. But all the fussing had to end. I was not cut out to be the sole patient with a nursing staff of two.

'That really hit the spot, Camila. You ladies both have been so kind, rescuing me and taking such good care of me. But now I think it's time I got some of that rest that Dr Gutierrez talked about.'

'Good, Henry,' Val said. 'Camila and I will be right downstairs if you need anything.'

'Actually, Val, there is no need for you to stay. Camila is more than capable of looking after me. And I'm sure you have other work to do at the embassy.'

'Not really,' Val said, brightly. 'But if you and Camila think that three's a crowd, I can take a hint.' She gave me a quick kiss on the forehead and was gone.

I sent Camila out to pick up a copy of *Listín Diario*, Santo Domingo's newspaper of record. I read about the round up of the La Españolita bombers Cosme Salazar had promised. A couple of Bosch followers, it seems, had confessed to the crime under careful interrogation by the PND. I wondered if Jaime was one of them or if he had even been considered as a suspect by Cosme. I dozed.

Five o'clock came and, over her protests, I sent Camila home. Then I put in a call to Cosme Salazar.

'You caught me just before I left for the day, Henry,' the police captain said when the switchboard operator put me through. 'To what do I owe the honor?'

'I called to invite you out for a drink, Cosme.'

'For the first time in a year and a half? Well, the magic hour of five o'clock has arrived. The usual place?'

'Sounds good. See you in fifteen minutes.'

When Generalissimo Rafael Trujillo, dictator of the Dominican Republic from 1930 to 1961, wanted to show the world his enlightenment and sophistication, he did it by supporting the design and construction of an ultra modern hotel in his capital, Cuidad Trujillo. Now Trujillo is gone, assassinated in 1961, but the fine hotel remains, run by the Intercontinental Hotel Corporation, a subsidiary of Pan-American World Airways. This hotel, El Jaragua, is sited on the shore of the Caribbean Sea, along the Malecon. Its grand frontage is lined with palms. It is low-rise, only a few stories into the blue Dominican sky. The curve is its primary architectural feature – a curved façade on the ends of the building, curved walkways, a circular pavilion for shade at the end of the curved pool, round tables with round umbrellas in the outdoor areas. The modernist character and clean lines of the building are a sharp contrast to the colonial architecture of the oldest city in the western hemisphere. It was Trujillo's way to show how modern and progressive his regime was. Unfortunately, he and his lackeys were killing too many people to carry off the illusion. When he was assassinated, Cuidad Trujillo reverted to its old name, Santo Domingo, and its old roots. El Jaragua stands alone as the remaining monument to the Trujillo era.

I was already sipping a cocktail at the luxe El Jaragua bar when Cosme sauntered in. He was a different man out of the office, I had learned in my prior after-work happy hours with him – relaxed, candid, a touch cynical and a good conversationalist. As he approached, I caught myself wondering why we had given up meeting for cocktails once or twice a week at the end of the workday. I guess it was because I was viewed as a Boschist and on the outs after the coup, and he wanted to keep his job, and maybe, as Wessin y Wessin's junta consolidated its hold, his head.

'Henry, so good to see you again.' The bartender immediately appeared, flicking a lighter on the tip of Cosme's Costanza. After taking a long, slow drag on the smoke, he said to the barman, 'The usual.'

'Cosme, you've been drinking without me,' I said. 'The old bartender from two years ago is gone but the new man knows your smoking habits and your favorite drink.'

Cosme smiled. 'Luis, the old barman, left after the coup. Someone decided the barman position at El Jaragua was too good to allow to a follower of Bosch. A shame. Luis was a good man. Ramon, here, started out a little rough around the edges but he's a fast learner and, more importantly, his politics are correct.'

'You may not want to say that too loud,' I said.

'You did notice that I waited until Ramon was serving a customer at the other end of the bar to speak.' Cosme grinned. 'They say the walls in Santo Domingo have ears, my friend, but the bars, they have eyes and ears. Let's take a table.'

We found our way to a corner table. A few seconds later, Ramon arrived with Cosme's 'usual' – a Bermudez rum and coconut water. Ramon also brought me, unbidden, another Brugal and lime. Ramon had learned well, despite his nepotistic affiliation with the Loyalist junta.

Cosme lifted his glass. '*Pa'rriba! Pa'abajo! Pa'centro! Pa'dentro!*' The classic Dominican toast is always slurred, even when sober, and Cosme adhered to the tradition. His wandering eye, when coupled with the lazy speech, would have made the casual observer think that he was already three sheets to the wind, but he wasn't. 'So, Henry, you are now running in diplomatic circles, I see. And with very lovely diplomats indeed.'

'You're thinking that Val is above my pay grade, Cosme?'

'Not at all, Henry. She just doesn't seem to be your type.'

'Oh, but she's yours, you old hound?'

'Well, if she were unattached. But I would never tread on a friend's territory.'

'She's not attached to me, if that's what you're driving at, Cosme. And I'm not running in diplomatic circles, as you say. Val was just sent by the embassy to look after an American who had the misfortune to be in the wrong place at the wrong time. We don't have a thing going. We're barely acquainted.'

'If I may say so modestly, I know a thing or two about women, and what I see when Miss Spicer looks at you is not a woman who wishes to remain "barely acquainted" with you.'

'Trust me, Cosme, it's not a mutual attraction. She's nice and she's smart but she's not for me.'

'I appreciate your candor, Henry. And since you have retired from the field . . .'

'Whoa, there, partner. Just because I'm not in the hunt doesn't mean she's fair game for the Cosme Salazar love-'em-and-leave-'em treatment. She's been good to me. She is a friend, or becoming a friend, and I don't much like seeing my friends romanced, bedded and then tossed aside.'

'Henry, that really is a bit harsh. True, but harsh.' Cosme's pawky smile confirmed that both his designs on Val and the dénouement he planned were as I thought. 'Nonetheless, I will keep my romantic distance from Miss Spicer. In deference to our friendship.'

'Are we still friends, Cosme?'

'Of course, Henry. Of course.' The wandering eye made it difficult for me to discern if Cosme was being truthful. 'How could you think otherwise?'

'This is the first drink we've had together in almost two years,' I said.

'You never called.'

'Neither did you.'

'Touché, Henry. But I had good reason.'

'That being?'

'Shall we say that General Wessin y Wessin and his friends keep close tabs on who is fraternizing with whom. And palling around with a known Boschist like you is, well, frowned upon.'

'So why did you accept my invitation this evening? Wouldn't that be frowned upon? If I was a Boschist, which I am not.'

'There are those who would say otherwise, Henry. But let's not quibble over your status. Your status is that you are my friend. And also a suspect. Which allows me to begin drinking with you again, as now it is also investigating.'

'Suspect? In what?'

'In the bombing of the La Españolita. And, by the way, I don't consider you a suspect. But some in the regime do. Ah, now, I see you look offended, Henry. Don't be. This will allow us our cocktail hours again.'

'I thought the crime was solved and the perpetrators were arrested,' I said.

'There is solved and then there is solved,' Cosme said. 'The case is solved and closed as far as the public proclamations of the junta are concerned. But there remains an interest in determining who really was behind the bombing. So the investigation continues. Quietly.'

'I should be miffed, Cosme, but I know how slippery you are, so it won't do any good. So I'll just come right out and say it. I don't have an interest in finding out who is behind the La Españolita bombing. It might actually be one of those who you've already arrested. It might be Jaime the bartender, who had some advance knowledge and ducked out. I've learned the hard way that it's best to avoid poking my nose into places where it might get broken, or worse. What I am interested in is what happened to Jerry Pleasants. I guess you could call him my pal. Or maybe not. But he just can't be swept away, ignored. That's my interest.'

'And what do you want from me, Henry? My blessing of your search for Mr Pleasants? You have that. It is harmless and if you want to spend your time that way' – Cosme made a 'who cares' shrug with his shoulders and hands – 'but more I cannot do.'

'Can you give me information?'

'What kind of information?'

'On your quiet investigation. We can trade. Your information for mine.'

'You have information, Henry?'

'No. Do you?'

'No.'

'Then it looks to me to be a fair bargain.' Cosme laughed and puffed on his cigarette. 'That is what I always liked about you, Henry, your dry sense of humor. Fair enough. Information will be traded, in both directions. Who knows, we may find your Jerry Pleasants and solve the bombing, too. A win for us both.'

'Worse things have happened.'

'Will you be working alone or will your little sidekick be assisting?'

'Sidekick?'

'Miss Spicer, Henry.'

'Oh, no. I'll be working alone.'

'Too bad. Such a handsome woman and so feisty. Another drink?'

'Yes, now that you mention it.'

TWELVE

'How is my cheery boy this morning?' Val Spicer said from my bedroom doorway. I rolled over and grabbed my Orvin from the nightstand: 7:30 a.m.

'I might be more cheery after another hour of sack time,' I said. The truth was that I had a splitting headache again, although this time I thought it had more to do with the half dozen firewaters I had consumed with Cosme Salazar the night before than the concussive detonation my body had suffered four days ago. Not that the effect was much different between one and the other.

'Oh, don't be such a sourpuss,' Val said. 'It's a beautiful day. I thought we might go to Boca Chica for a swim.'

'I thought I was supposed to be resting.'

'What is more restful than a swim in the clear, warm Caribbean? And after, there's the cutest little inn nearby, where we could get a bite and take a room to . . . unwind.' Val added the hesitation before the last word the way a stripper slowly draws off the first glove when she starts her routine.

'If I wanted to unwind that way, why not right here?' My turn to be the tease, though I had no idea why I should be.

Val opened her mouth to answer but the sound came from behind her at the top of the stairs. 'Señor Henry, you are awake. And you look so well!' Camila effused. 'I have your breakfast here. *Café* – the pearl peaberry you like. And *mi abuela*, she makes these *buñelos* this morning.' She held out a tray. The rich aroma from the steaming cup and the cloying scent of the vanilla cinnamon syrup on the fried yuca balls filled the room.

'That,' Val said, 'is why we need to go to Boca Chica to unwind.' As always, Val said it with a smile but maybe, just maybe, there was a trace of irritation over Camila's omnipresence in her bright blue eyes. And maybe, just maybe, there was a trace of good old Latin anger in Camila's dark doe eyes at this blonde usurper who had the audacity to keep entering her domestic domain, even when she showed up a half hour early and with her *abuela's buñelos* to boot. But each again put on their best face as they silently watched me down the coffee and breakfast.

Fortified, I said, 'Time to be off.'

Camila played her best card up front. 'The doctor said for you to rest, Señor Henry. In bed. Here.'

'Oh, he looks pretty chipper to me, Camila. He will be just fine with a good chaperone. I'll bring him back in one piece.'

Camila sulked. Val preened, thinking the upper hand was hers.

'It's Wednesday morning,' I began.

'Here and over a quarter of the globe,' Val chimed in.

'It's a workday. Don't you have work to do? You are the cultural attaché at the United States Embassy. Don't you have something cultural to do?'

Camila nodded vigorously. If she couldn't keep me for the day, keeping Val away was the next best thing.

'Not really, Henry. One nice thing about culture – it usually doesn't get up before noon. Sometimes even later. That leaves the mornings free. Don't worry, Camila. I'll get him back here right away if he gets tired.' I could see Camila's understanding of Val's last sentence was that she would bring me home tired, after who knows what kind of taxing activity.

Not one to linger over her triumphs, Val had me dressed, filled a tote with beach gear and loaded me into the embassy Ford before Camila could regroup.

As we pulled away from the curb, I said, 'If you plan to go to Boca Chica for a swim and a roll in the hay, you can let me off now.'

With a sigh and a benign smile, she said, 'I plan to go where ever Henry Gore is going.'

'Fine. Go north then, on Duarte Avenue.'

'Yet another woman up there, Henry? Three's a crowd, which we already have with Señorita Polanco. Four's an orgy, which you're not up to.'

'Sorry to disappoint, Val, but there is no additional woman, no orgy and, indeed, we don't even have a crowd of three, despite your and Camila's efforts to create one. Since we couldn't find Jerry yesterday, I thought I'd try the next best thing, finding someone who might know Jerry's whereabouts.'

'And who would that be?'

'Jaime.'

'The bartender again?'

'You've been paying attention.'

'Does he have a last name today?'

'He must.'

'But you don't know yet.'

'Not right now.' I tried to project confidence, despite this admission.

'You remembered where he lives, then?'

'Sort of. North of town and east of Duarte Street. North of the named streets.' Like many of the cities and bigger towns in the Caribbean and Central America, Santo Domingo had a fringe of slums clinging to the edge of its more established neighborhoods. That was where we were headed.

'Gualey? The City of God?' Val asked.

'I'm surprised you're familiar with it. Not too much high culture up there.'

'A lot of things about me might surprise you, Henry. If you just give it a try. So, no addresses there. Do you have a landmark? Or someone with an actual last name?'

'A landmark. Jaime talked about it one night when things at La Españolita were slow. He grew up there, living with his *abuela*. No mother in the picture. He said he used to play and swim at something called "La Poza del Chino". It's a kind of natural pool or pond in the middle of the barrio, a gathering place to relax and take a swim. I'm hoping we can go there, ask around and maybe find Jaime or, failing that, his *abuela*.'

Val raised a skeptical eyebrow. 'I'll bet you play the long shots at the track, too, don't you?'

'Sometimes it's the only bet available. Turn here.'

We made a right on Calle 17. The path of travel took us from an orderly grid of streets to a maze of dirt tracks with corrugated tin, wood and cardboard structures crowding in on both sides. Naked babies played in mud puddles beside the narrow lane. Gray-bearded men in rags sat smoking in the sun. Groups of young men, some with faces scarred from fighting with knives and machetes, lingered menacingly at the intersections. I had been in the slums before, when I was consulting for President Bosch, and these young thugs, known as *Tigres*, were some of his biggest boosters. Bosch's willingness to speak with and for these elements had caused alarm among the military and ultimately led to the coup and the installation of the junta. The *Tigres* and the rest of the people of Gualey had been returned to the hopelessness and the grinding poverty they had suffered for years before the brief optimism of Bosch's rule. It showed in their eyes, a mix of anger, fear and resentment. The place had the feel of a powder keg with the fuse waiting to be lit.

None of what we were seeing from the windows of the embassy Ford fazed Val in the least. She waved to the kids playing soccer. She smiled at the old men and drew a toothless smile from them in return. And when she asked me which way to turn when we came to a T intersection and I told her I had no idea, she leaned out and asked a half dozen *Tigres* who were loitering there, '*Dónde ésta La Poza del Chino?*' The toughs were used to being feared and avoided by outsiders and were so taken aback by Val's blithe query that they went to extra pains to point us in the correct direction. She favored them with a wave, followed their directions and had us to the edge of the Chinese pool in two minutes. La Poza del Chino was a jewel in the trash heap that was Gualey, the water in the natural pond an inviting blue-green, the surroundings on all sides a verdant wall of vegetation and the air surrounding seemingly exempt from the burning garbage scent that overhung the rest of the barrio.

Val drove to the muddy entrance to the pool and parked, the Ford the only vehicle in sight. There were families and groups of boys and girls splashing in the cool waters. We drew a few stares of curiosity but no hostility. La Poza del Chino had the feel of neutral ground, a place of peace and respite amid the anger and struggle of the slum.

Val and I stepped out. I eyed the surrounding shacks, hoping to see an elderly woman on a stoop who might be Jaime's *abuela* or maybe even Jaime himself. No such luck. Val wasted no time, approaching a man just emerging from a dip in the pool with a young girl in his arms.

'Excuse me, señor. We are searching for a man named Jaime, who lives near here, possibly with his *abuela*. He works as a bartender now.' Val's Spanish was better than passable.

The man boosted his daughter higher on his hip. Val turned on the charm, a broad smile, and a nod to the little girl. It was enough to keep the man from dismissing the blonde Yankee outright. He thought for a long minute before answering, '*No conozco a nadie aqui con ese nombre.*'

That was the first in a long line of '*no conozco*' answers we received as we worked our way around the perimeter of the Chinese pool. Val gamely asked her question until she ran out of people to ask. It seemed that no one named Jaime had ever lived in the area. Or the good people of Gualey had a hearty mistrust of the two Yankees in the fancy car. If I were a betting man, I would place money on the latter.

Two hours by La Poza del Chino and the heat and humidity had me to the point of jumping in the inviting water. Val, on the other hand, appeared as if she had just emerged from the air-conditioned comfort of the embassy. 'I don't see anyone here we haven't spoken to, Henry. What's next on your agenda?' She asked the question like we were on an exceptionally exciting date and we were about to move on to the next nightclub.

'We knock on doors.'

'OK. I'll take this side of the pool. You take the other.'

'Ah, I think we had best stick together here.'

'You're the boss.'

The first hour of door-knocking went quickly, mainly because no one answered their doors. We were into the second row of dwellings beyond La Poza del Chino when an ancient lady, all of four and a half feet tall, answered her door and, in response to Val's now oft-asked question, said, '*Soy la abuela de Jaime.*'

THIRTEEN

Jaime's elfin grandmother was the consummate hostess, despite her poor circumstances. She seated us on the only two wooden chairs at her rickety table and bustled off to a gas single burner to make coffee. The floor in her one-room hovel was dirt. She slept on a mattress in the corner. She served our coffee in mismatched chipped cups and did not pour one for herself.

'Thank you, Señora . . .?' I said.

'Vargas. The same as my Jaime. Eliene Vargas.'

'I am Henry Gore and this is Valerie Spicer. I am a friend of Jaime's' – I hoped the exaggeration was not too extreme – 'I have lost touch with him. I am hoping to find him and speak with him about an urgent matter.'

Señora Vargas responded without questioning my statement, exhibiting the trust by the elderly found in almost every society. 'My Jaime was last here five days ago. He never stays away from his *abuela* for so long. I am concerned about him.'

Five days. The day before the bombing. 'I am concerned also,' I said. 'I saw Jaime at his job five days ago and not since. He did something very nice, very helpful for me on that day and I would like to thank him for his kindness.'

'Do you think Jaime was killed in the bombing?' Señora Vargas surprised me. She had not betrayed any knowledge of the bombing or Jaime's presence there up to this point.

'I do not know, Señora. The police have told me there was no trace of him at the site, though they did find and identify the bodies of others who were killed. I am also trying to locate another man who was at La Españolita that day.'

'What is his name?'

'Jerry Pleasants.'

'An American, like you?'

'Yes.'

'You feel that if you find Jaime, he can help you locate Señor Pleasants.' A statement, not a question. Her eyes were hard.

'Yes,' I admitted. I didn't see the value in mentioning that I thought the old girl's grandson might be the bomber. If anything, that might make her less likely to give me information on his whereabouts. And I really wasn't after locating the bomber so much as finding Jerry. The bomber was Cosme Salazar's bailiwick.

'Maybe this is so.' The *abuela*'s hard eyes softened not one whit. 'It matters not why you search for Jaime, only that you find him safe and return him to me.'

'We will, if we locate him,' Val interjected.

Señora Vargas sighed and went on. 'I will tell you what I know. My Jaime has no girlfriend. He does not chase them. He works hard, long hours, and then he comes home to take care of his *abuela*. He has friends, not many, and they never meet him here, so I cannot tell you a great deal about them. There is one, Carlos, a tall skinny boy with a pompadour haircut, and Julio, built like a bull, a brick-layer. I do not know their last names. Perhaps if you find one of them, they will lead you to my Jaime and he will, in turn, lead you to the American you seek.'

'Thank you, Señora Vargas,' Val said. 'We will do our best to find Jaime.'

I left my address with the old girl, now shamed into finding her grandson as well as Jerry Pleasants.

Once we were down the path from Señora Vargas' place, Val said, 'That worked well. Now you have two people to find and more people with one name and no address who can help you find the two you are searching for. It's like one of those Russian nesting dolls.'

'It's been a long day,' I said.

'Tired?' Val sounded motherly.

'Yes.'

'I'll take you home.'

FOURTEEN

I t was midafternoon when we arrived at my place, the drowsy, lazy midafternoon of most of the places in the Caribbean, a time of light breezes, strong sunshine and indolence. Camila had disappeared, gone in the way that housekeepers go when the dishes are done, the pantry is stocked with groceries and the usurping gringo woman seems to have the upper hand in the struggle for the affections of the boss.

We had not eaten during our long reconnaissance of Gualey. 'I'm famished,' Val said as soon as we arrived. She pawed through the cupboard and pulled out bread, butter, eggs, tomatoes, an avocado and a package of *queso de Hoya*. She attacked – yes, attacked – the ingredients like a blitzing army, stove firing, utensils banging and smells, sizzles and the clatter of plates in the air. She wasn't an artist in the kitchen like some women. She didn't display much finesse in her cooking but what she lacked in skills she made up for in enthusiasm, humming and smiling all the way, her blonde curls bouncing, her compact body swinging as if she heard a samba while she cooked.

'Have you got any beer?' she asked as she plated her masterpieces.

'In the icebox,' I said. The half-size refrigerator beside the pantry was a rarity in Santo Domingo, a little luxury I allowed myself.

'Presidente, huh? You have acquired a taste for the local stuff, Henry?'

'It's passable. And it's a long way to a Carling Black Label down here,' I said. 'What about you?'

'The cultural attaché drinks French white wine at all embassy events, just like Jackie Kennedy. Oh, and an icy gin martini, up, for relaxation. I thought about suggesting a pitcher for us since we are now in the relaxation mode but it seemed that the sun was not far enough over the yardarm for us to get *that* relaxed. And there is your delicate condition.'

'Nothing that can't be cured by a little nourishment. That smells great.'

'Fried egg, cheese, tomato and avocado sandwich. My roommate at Bryn Mawr, a California girl, taught me its magical properties. She said it was the cure for hunger, hangovers and horniness. Although I noticed that she only fed it to her boyfriend *after* they spent the afternoon doing the deed. Maybe I have things in the wrong order. What do you think, Henry? Are we doing things in the wrong order?'

Like I said, I'd like to think that I am a man of the world but that made me blush until the heat filled my ears. I've been on the receiving end of some fairly direct propositions in my day, but they were usually of a commercial nature – I had occasionally walked the streets at night in Batista-era Havana. But Val's bluntness put me off balance. All I could manage was: 'I think we could both use a little food.'

'First.'

'What?'

'We could use a little food first, before we, well, you know.' Val gave the slightest arch to the edge of a flaxen eyebrow.

I wanted to say, 'No, I don't know', when it occurred to me that would prompt Val to describe to me precisely what she had in mind. And that I really shouldn't do precisely what she had in mind. I don't know why I thought I should avoid spending an afternoon making slow, sweet love to Val. She was attractive, unattached and more than willing. But I was wary. She was probably CIA, or maybe DIA, although, in the world of espionage, DIA agents usually served as military attachés. It didn't matter. I thought she was a spy of some sort. My Air Force OSI training had ingrained that into me. But if she was a spy, what did she want with me? I was associated, loosely, with the democratic government of the deposed Juan Bosch. But if the CIA wanted information on Bosch and his government in exile, they could just ask him. The United States supported him. His exile was in Puerto Rico. They could just go knock on his door.

So maybe Valerie Spicer was attracted to me and just wanted an hour or two of illicit fun with a fellow American not on the embassy staff and free from any workplace repercussions. I couldn't tell. It made me uneasy.

So I temporized. 'Yes, food first,' I said.

'Try not to be so enthusiastic about what follows the meal,' she said, the words sarcastic, but her mien convivial. 'Eat up, gorgeous man. You'll need your strength.' She placed a sandwich and a dewy bottle of Presidente at each place at the table and sat.

'It can't be the housekeeper,' Val said. She watched as I ate, her egg sandwich untouched. 'A girl like that is a fling, not love.' She sipped her Presidente, holding the bottle by the neck. 'So who is it? Please don't tell me it's the girl back home.'

The afternoon sun streamed in, back-lighting Val so that she looked like some beer-drinking golden-haired goddess. I chewed, then said, 'No, no girl back home.'

'And no girl here?'

'No.'

'You're not a queer, are you, Henry?' Before I could answer, she said, 'No, you're not. You just need some motivation.' She swigged her beer, stood, pushed the small kitchen table away and straddled me. I opened my mouth to speak. I'm not sure what I was about to say but it didn't matter. I never got the words out. Val placed a finger on my lips and only removed it when her lips were an inch from mine. She kissed me gently, so softly her lips felt like a feather. I . . . cooperated.

'That's better,' she said and then her lips were full on mine, her tongue probing, her hands gripping my wrists and pushing my hands against her. She was less aggressive than insistent. And in the end she had her way, there, on the kitchen chair, and then in the big old four-poster upstairs as the late afternoon glow flooded the room. And again, as the last light fell and night enveloped the world. All wordlessly, silently, smiling but not speaking, the only sounds the gurgling and chirping of palmchats in the tree outside the window and the costermonger calling his wares in the street below.

I complied, then participated in and, finally, enjoyed the love-making. We lay in each others arms as the day went full dark, spent and thirsty, and Val finally spoke. 'See, Henry, that wasn't so bad now, was it?'

'Not at all.'

She laughed. 'Faint praise.'

'No. No. Not faint praise. It was marvelous. Fantastic. Wonderful. Mind-blowing.'

'I guess I'll take that as meaning you enjoyed it, despite your earlier reluctance. Maybe next time I'll let you drive.' Her voice was husky. 'I need a drink.'

'I've got rum, gin and I think a little tequila.'

'I was thinking more like water. Hydration, Henry. I don't need any intoxicating substances. My mind's blown too.'

'Sure, Val. I'll get us some water.' I pulled on my pants and went to the kitchen. Got two bottles of water out of the refrigerator. When I turned, there was Val. Dressed and looking like she had just stepped out of an embassy staff meeting instead of a visit to the favela, followed by hours of lovemaking.

I popped the cap off a bottle and handed it to her. 'Usually it's the man who makes the quick exit,' I said.

'Duty calls, Henry.'

'It's almost seven o'clock.'

'And there's an eight o'clock theater performance for the ambassador and the cultural attaché to attend with General Wessin y Wessin and the interior minister.' She brushed light fingers across my bare chest. 'Don't worry, Henry. We'll have plenty of spooning time in the future. And I meant what I said about letting you drive the next time, lover.' She planted a kiss on my cheek and was gone.

So much for keeping my guard up. So much for keeping my fly zipped. So much for honoring the memory of the woman I had lost so long ago. I really hadn't fallen for Val but I really hadn't not fallen for her either. I didn't know what I wanted. Maybe just a carefree roll in the hay. I didn't know what she wanted. It sure seemed like all she was looking for was a carefree role in the hay. Val appeared straightforward about her wants and needs. But things aren't always as they seem. Maybe there was more to what had started between us. I decided time would tell.

FIFTEEN

I t was Camila's day off. Val had probably had a late evening being cultural with the ambassador and the powers that be and I guessed wouldn't appear before noon. I lazed in the four-poster bed, watching the sun edge across the far wall and inhaling the lingering scent of Val's perfume on the pillow. Woodsy. And iris, I thought. Caleche by Dior. I had known a French woman in Port-Louis who had worn it. She was an artist and lived in a glorious house by the sea. Her paintings were all of island flowers and very bad. She had money, though, and viewed me as a project after my time in Cuba. I left the glorious house, the woman and the island after a week.

Deciding it was shameful to lie abed thinking about women while the rest of the world was up, working, fighting and engaging in the unending struggle, I tossed on some clothes. A café and some *yaniqueques* at the little place around the corner beckoned.

When I opened my front door, I saw a folded paper on the step. Unfolded, it read:

'CATEDRAL SANTA MARIA LA MENOR EL CLAUSTRO'. The first cathedral in the New World, Santa Maria la Menor was mere blocks from my home. But the note was lacking in vital details – time and date, if intended to suggest a meeting; the purpose of such meeting; and, most importantly, the author, who was presumably the person with whom I was to meet. At least the note specified the location of the meeting in the massive building – the cloister section on the south side, with the cells of canons adjoining. The open air structure was easily approached from the street.

My quandary was simple – do I go there? There was no explanation of what awaited if I did. My mind dredged up a memory of a short-notice meeting at an undisclosed location with the Directorio Revolucionario in Batista's Cuba, with no back-up and no weapon. It was against my AFOSI training but I hadn't cared then. Now maybe I did care but I couldn't think of a reason to be concerned. I wasn't involved in clandestine activities like I had been in Cuba. As far as I knew, no one cared what I did. The only thing I was doing that was out of the ordinary was my search for Jerry Pleasants. Maybe the note was a clue or a lead.

I decided to go. Within minutes, I stood before the gold-toned coral stone façade of the cathedral. A quick turn at the end of the building and I was on the shaded street adjoining the cloister. I stood on the corner opposite, pretending to read the day's *Listín Diario*. No one was present that I could see. Insects buzzed. A yellow dog trotted along the cobbled street, intent on a yellow dog mission of some sort. Or maybe it was like me, not knowing the exact reason for its sally but focused nonetheless.

I crossed, stepped over a low wall, through an arch and was under the roof of the cloister. I walked a few feet, listening and seeing no one. I was beginning to think that someone without much of a sense of humor had left the note and sent me on a wild goose chase. Then I heard my name called, almost as a whisper, from the far end of the gallery.

I caught a glimpse of a figure which quickly retreated into the shadow of a column. I stepped lively after the figure. It must have been the excitement of the sighting and the hunt that caused me to let my guard down. I was halfway along the colonnade when a cloth bag was placed over my head and my arms were pinned to my side from behind. I struggled but my assailants had the advantage of surprise and superior strength. My arms were trussed and the bag was tied loosely at my neck. I heard the sound of a car engine, unhurried, not revving, and I was pushed onto the rear seat of the vehicle. My captors moved from the curb and took me on a half-hour ride, twisting and turning, changing direction until I was disoriented.

We came to a stop, finally, after I'd had time to run through all the horrible possibilities that might ensue: a robbery; an interrogation by General Wessin y Wessin's SIM for some unknown transgression; the CIA tying up a Castro connection that had been a loose end for a long time and needed some neatening up; an unsuspected affront to someone powerful and patient at some point in the last eight years about to be horribly rectified; even someone finishing the job that the La Españolita bomber failed to complete. None of the scenarios were particularly rosy. Some, in my vivid imagination fortified by my time in Batista's Cuba, were downright gruesome.

I tried to stay calm as I was half-lifted from the car and walked a dozen steps to a building. I knew when I was inside because the world darkened through the bag and because I heard a door shut behind me. There were no stairs. We were on the ground floor, a dirt floor, as nearly as I could tell through my shoes. Rough hands shoved me into a straight-backed chair and tied my legs to the chair legs. My hands were freed, then re-tied, one to each arm of the chair.

The bag was whisked from my head. The room was dim but not dark. Light came from a single hanging bulb behind me. I felt a wave of relief; whoever had me, they were not professionals. Pros would've had the bulb in front of me, in my eyes and focused enough to be painful after the blackness inside the bag. Then I felt a wave of dread. Whoever had me, they weren't pros. Pros could be counted upon. They weren't nice but they usually played by some kind of rules or constraints. They had objectives and they knew how to attain them. And, if pros were going to do away with you, they usually did it quickly, efficiently. They didn't drag you around town and torture you first. That would be, well, unprofessional. So I was with amateurs, inexperienced, impulsive, maybe emotional amateurs.

My eyes adjusted slowly. There was only one person in the room that I could tell. I recognized the way the man moved first, though out of context I could not place him. Then his face became clear.

Jaime, the bartender from La Españolita.

SIXTEEN

'Señor Gore, you were asking after me?' Jaime Vargas, the maybe-bomber of La Españolita and the man whose note had saved my life, said. 'You and the spy lady.'

'Spy lady?' I said. 'I don't know who you mean, Jaime.'

'The lady from the American Embassy, who accompanied you to Gualey yesterday.'

'Miss Spicer? She's not a spy. She was just trying to look out for me, after I got blown up.'

Jaime lifted his chin skeptically and said nothing. What did he know that I didn't about the embassy's cultural attaché?

'Speaking of which, I owe you a debt of gratitude,' I said. 'You saved my neck, passing me that note.' I hoped reminding Jaime that he had once saved me would remind him not to harm me now. 'Thanks, my friend.'

Jaime ignored my appreciation. 'Why are you going around Gualey asking after me?'

'How did you find me?' I said. One test of whether you are dealing with an amateur in an interrogation is to see if you can control its direction. It's a good thing to find out early. In the right circumstances it can save your life.

Jaime immediately confirmed his rookie status. 'You went to my *abuela*'s house and left your address with her.'

'She said she hadn't seen you since La Españolita was bombed and didn't know where you were. I guess she wasn't telling me the truth.'

Jaime bristled at my attack on Grandma's veracity, another sign that he was an amateur. A good interrogator never betrays any emotion, other than empathy, to the subject of the interrogation. 'You do not open up to outsiders if you live in Gualey. We *Gualeños* have a long history of betrayal by those from outside the neighborhood, especially when they have an association with government. Especially the government of the United States.'

'Well, you and your *abuela* have no reason to be concerned about betrayal by me or Miss Spicer. We visited your *abuela* as part of a search for a missing American. My buddy, Jerry Pleasants. That's all. No ulterior motives.'

'Why do you search for him?'

'He's missing after the bombing. He's an American,' I said, as if that were explanation enough. It didn't feel like it when I said it. I thought about saying he was my good friend but I couldn't. He was a buddy, someone I had an occasional drink with because we were foreigners in Santo Domingo together. He wasn't someone I would have as a friend in the United States. 'That's all. No government, no ulterior motives, just one American looking for another American who seems to be lost.'

'Why don't you go to the police?'

'I have. They . . . lack interest.'

'The PND and SIM lack interest in everything except keeping control over the people and lining their own pockets.'

'Who am I to disagree?' I said.

Jaime became more conversational in his tone. 'You know that he saved both of our lives.'

'I thought you slipped me the note.'

'I did. After he warned me. I was getting stock for the bar in the store room, next to the *servicio*, when he came back. "Jaime," he said. "If you know what's good for you, you'll get your ass out of here. Pronto, because this place is about to go 'boom' in three minutes." Then he smiled at me. "I always appreciated the little bit of extra pour you gave me, *mi amigo*. Consider this a tip. The best tip you will ever get in your life."'

'That's it?' The roles in the interrogation has been completely flipped now.

'*Si*. Señor Pleasants walked right past the *servicio* and out the rear entrance. I wondered what to do. I thought he was joking at first, because we both know this was the kind of poor quality joke he made all the time. Well, not about bombs, but you understand what I mean – jokes about things that Señor Pleasants thought were funny but that really were not funny. Then I asked myself, What if it is not a joke? Do I want to die because I did not believe what he said?'

By then, I had stepped back behind the bar. You were not in your seat. I thought about losing my job if I left. It was a very good job. The pay was poor but the tips from the gringos, especially the *touristas* when they had had much to drink, were good. And one's mind does odd things under such stress. I thought about the customer who always left me the best tips. You, Señor Gore. By then a minute or more had gone by since Señor Pleasants had told me three minutes and "boom". So I wrote a note and put it at your place at the bar and I ran out the back way. I should have yelled for everyone to leave but the time was short and I was not thinking straight.

'I got about a half block away when the bomb went off. I was running next to a building made of concrete block. It shielded me from the blast and the shattering glass broken from all the windows. I didn't receive a scratch. I just kept running for ten blocks and caught a *carro público* back to Gualey.'

'Why didn't you go back to help after the explosion?'

'I was frightened. I didn't know why anyone would want to blow up La Españolita. I did know from the force of the blast that those inside would be dead and that some would be foreigners who had been drinking in the bar. The junta would feel pressure from the US and the other nations whose citizens were caught in the explosion to find the perpetrator of the crime. A bartender who knew to get out and then returned to the scene of the crime would be a logical suspect, made more so if that bartender was a follower of Juan Bosch.'

'And are you a follower of Bosch?' I asked.

'Are you, Señor Gore?' Jaime countered. 'I know that you worked with the government after he was elected.'

'I did.' I decided not to reveal my ongoing consulting work for Bosch's government in exile. 'But I am not a political man. And this is not my country.'

Jaime eyed me, considering whether he could trust the man he had tied up in this dark room in the bowels of Santo Domingo. If Jaime was simply a worried *Gualeño* intent on protecting his *abuela* and himself from wrongful suspicion for the bombing of La Españolita, my loyalties to the powers in charge or the former powers in exile really shouldn't matter to him. But his consideration seemed to be more nuanced. Or maybe my nose had spent most of the last decade in an atmosphere permeated by the odor of revolution and I now smelled one wherever I traveled.

'I am a Constitutionalist,' he said.

'And a serious one,' I said.

'How do you mean this?'

'Jaime, Gualey must be full of men sympathetic to Bosch,

concerned that the constitution is followed and the results of fair elections are honored. But I'm guessing that few of those men can muster a car, plan a public abduction and move the – no other way to say it – victim to a safe house without an organization in place.'

Jaime nodded affirmatively after a long moment.

'Cut me loose, Jaime. I'm not the enemy. And I'm not going to rat you out to the PND or SIM. I want to find Jerry Pleasants is all and I'll bet you do, too.'

'I want to find him. I'm not sure if I want to do so to thank him for saving me or to curse him for placing me under suspicion.' Jaime untied my left arm from the chair. 'Do not try to untie the other ropes until I have departed, Señor Gore.'

'Fair enough,' I said.

'If Señor Pleasants knew of the bomb, he was the bomber or associated with them,' Jaime said. 'You know him. Why would he do such a thing?'

'I don't know. Maybe he just knew, somehow, but had nothing to do with planning or carrying it out.' It sounded dubious as soon as I said it.

Jaime opted not to challenge me. 'It doesn't matter. The PND already said that they have solved the bombing and have stopped looking for suspects. I have no reason to be concerned about them. As long as you are not looking at me as a suspect, I have no reason to be concerned about you.'

'You don't have a reason to be concerned about me, Jaime.'

'Good.' He backed away into the darkness. '*Adios*, Señor Gore.'

'But, Jaime, before you go, do you have any idea where Jerry might be found?'

There was nothing but silence. Jaime was already gone.

SEVENTEEN

I 'm a right-hander. Jaime had untied my injured left hand so it took me a good ten minutes to get all my limbs free and then sit silently for another minute to size up my surroundings. By the time I stood and found a door that let me out of the deserted warehouse, Jaime could have been miles away. I walked a block until I found a taxi. It was noon before I was back at my place.

Val Spicer was in the kitchen when I entered, done up in an apron like a *hausfrau*, a skillet of chicken pieces braising on the stove. 'I let myself in,' she said, by way of greeting. 'You really should have a better lock.'

First kidnapping, then home invasion. It was shaping up to be a red letter day. 'I'll have it looked at,' I huffed.

'Well, aren't we grumpy today?'

'Sorry. Long day already.'

'You shouldn't start so early. It would have worked out better if you had stayed in bed a little longer. I was hoping to catch you there and continue where we left off last night. Now that I'm cooking, morning glory is going to have to turn into afternoon delight. I hope you can wait. I know I can't.'

'Someone kidnapped me this morning,' I said, I guess by way of excuse.

'Really? It wasn't Camila, was it? I wouldn't put her above that.'

'No, it was Jaime Vargas.'

'I guess he wasn't as elusive as we thought.'

'His doddering old *abuela* was not as uninformed as she led us to believe.'

'And he kidnapped you? From here?'

'No. From the Catedral Santa Maria la Menor.'

'What were you doing there?'

'Someone left an anonymous note on my doorstep to go there.'

'And you went? Forgive me, I am only a dewy-eyed cultural attaché and you're the former counterintelligence guy, but shouldn't you not go unaccompanied when you get an anonymous note to just show up someplace?'

'Well, when you put it that way, and in hindsight.'

'Are you OK? You don't look the worse for wear.'

'I was tied up but no harm.'

'Probably safer than you would have been in the four-poster upstairs.' A full on leer from Val. The chicken fricassee hit the plate. She pulled two beers from the fridge and sat me down. I didn't feel like talking to her. She didn't seem to notice or, if she did, to care. 'Did Jaime tell you where Jerry Pleasants is?'

'He didn't know.'

'So he said.'

'I believe him. He said Jerry tipped him off about the bomb. That Jerry had saved his life. And you know what that means? It means Jerry didn't feel the need to tell me about the bomb. To tip me off and save my life. He wanted to save Jaime and he was more than willing to let me die. Why?'

Val had dug into her lunch. She stopped now, fork in the air. 'I don't know, Henry. Maybe he was too busy saving his own skin. Maybe he really doesn't like you. Maybe he couldn't tell you why if you asked him. Why do you care? I mean, really, lover, why do you care anything about finding Jerry Pleasants and learning why he did, or didn't do, anything? There are better ways for you to spend your time. For us to spend our time.' She reached under the table and slid her hand along my thigh.

It made me angry. I was supposed to think with my dick or at least that was what Val was counting on. I brushed her hand aside.

'A less persistent lady would feel hurt, Henry,' she said.

'I'm not in the mood, Val.'

'Now I am hurt.' Val's face betrayed no hurt. It was clear she now viewed the situation of how we were to spend the afternoon as a challenge.

'Don't be. It's just that I can't let it go. We were friends. Why would he allow me to die? To think that when I believed he might be dead or injured or lost somewhere, I went out of my way to find him. Why would he be less concerned about me?'

'Some people are just that way, Henry. To be honest, he sounds to be a bit of a loser. Self-centered. Lazy. At loose ends. Unreliable. You really shouldn't expect much of anything from him. Forget him. Come here. I'll put you in the mood.'

* * *

I lay staring at the ceiling above the big four-poster bed. Val snored lightly beside me, nestled into my chest, not a care in the world. My mind, though, was filled with care that allowed no rest.

It all centered around Jerry Pleasants but it broadened out quickly from there. The questions about Jerry revolved around why he would warn Jaime Vargas, who he viewed as a mere servant, and not me, who he ought to view as a chum, a buddy, an *amigo*, a friend? Why did he take steps to save Jaime's life and not lift a finger to preserve mine? Then the somewhat broader questions – why would Jerry bomb or be involved in a plot to bomb or even just know of a plot to bomb La Españolita. La Españolita, while a nice enough bar if you liked your drinks poured with a heavy hand and a touch of tourist atmosphere, was hardly a worthy political target. It was just a bar. If the Constitutionalists and the *junta*, who called themselves Loyalists now – convenient how both sides used their names to claim the moral high ground, not exactly a first in the world of politics – wanted to rip and tear at each other, there were many more targets where the message would be clear. Bomb a party headquarters. Shoot up a rally. Assassinate a bigwig. What was it about La Españolita? Bombings are political. What was the political statement in bombing La Españolita?

And why Jerry, who if I had to pick one person in Santo Domingo to be least likely to be involved in the local machinations between the Constitutionalists and the Loyalists, it would be him. None of it made sense.

Something, though, did make sense. Much as I hated to admit it, Val's counsel to forget Jerry and his callous lack of concern for me was the best course for me to take. So I stared at the ceiling and told myself Val was right. And, admitting that, first, I felt hurt that Jerry would do what he'd done. Then I felt foolish for being so concerned about him, when he was so willing to cast me aside. But the final emotion I experienced, lying there beside the unperturbed Val, was rage. Jerry, that son of a bitch, was willing to let me die rather than inconvenience himself with a simple word of warning to me. I'd been through a lot in Cuba and since. I had seen brutality elevated to an art form but the personal nature of Jerry's callousness toward me awakened a seething anger in me. I had to know why he had done what he had done and to make him answer for it. I had to find him.

EIGHTEEN

You may wonder how an American expat, a relatively young man of thirty-five, passes his time in whatever island town or beachfront backwater he currently calls home, knowing that he is never truly home in any place washed by the bottle-green waters of the Caribbean. How are the days used, or spent, or frittered away, like so many showy petals of a Poinciana tree drifting away on the warm southeast trade wind? How are the nights survived in the humid stillness, the silver moonlight, the welcoming arms of a stranger? Is there joy, sadness, struggle, triumph? After what happened in Cuba, is there recovery, redemption, absolution?

The sad truth, friends, no matter what the images are in our collective dream of what it is to be young, in a beautiful place, with time and money enough, is that the life of an expat is less than glamorous, sometimes ordinary and often deadly dull, a life alone, without family or longtime friendships, and many times among local people who have no reason to trust you and many justifications to do just the opposite.

My life in Santo Domingo had certainly been that way. Not to say that there weren't some positive aspects: the pleasant house in the old colonial neighborhood; the affections of Camila Polanco, until things became entangling and complicated; the challenging work for positive change that I had done for the Bosch government. But now, many months into my time in Santo Domingo, the good work had been taken away and undone by the Wessin y Wessin junta, the romance with Camila had fizzled to dull acrimony on my part and unabated neediness on hers, and the historic streets of the city seemed decrepit, crumbling, faded to senescence in the unyielding tropical sun. The dullness gave rise to indolence and boredom, encouraging the day-drinking that had marked my recent time.

The day I embarked on now was shaping up to be more of the same. Val had departed early in the evening before; her embassy work schedule seemed to involve many receptions, parties, concerts and openings which took place between the hours of seven and midnight, all to which I had no invitation and none of which I minded. Camila had appeared early, deduced that the competition had been in the house the day before and was sullenly washing dishes and sweeping when I escaped in search of a breakfast venue where veiled hostility was not served along with the café and *pasteles*.

I landed at a nameless place a quarter mile's walk toward the Rio Ozama from my house. It consisted of a hole-in-the-wall brick oven that had probably baked *pasteles* and *pain* for Chris Columbus' younger brother, Bartholomew, when he was Santo Domingo's governor in the late 1400s, and a collection of mismatched wooden tables and chairs crowding the narrow sidewalk at the oven's mouth. The *café* was brewed on a brazier by a chubby boy who was the spitting image of the hefty baker running the oven. The boy was also the waiter, dusting off the chair with the least broken seat at the prime table closest to the street for me. I passed an hour, eating an air-light guava *empanada* and musing my way through three cups of smoky *café*. The boy-waiter was cheerfully attentive.

I had visited the tiny place before on mornings when my guilt and Camila's clinginess were too much to tolerate at home. The life of the city made a slow transit just outside the imaginary boundary between the street and the café. Laborers with shovels and pickaxes, dressed in little more than rags, talked cheerfully on their way to one of the perpetual repair projects in the 500-year-old city. Schoolgirls in uniform headed for the convent schools. Businessmen wearing black slacks and crisp, white shirts ironed that morning by their steadfast wives passed in twos and threes. Cleaning ladies with the tools of their trade, two-wheeled carts holding mops, brooms and pails, trudged along. My eyes followed the human procession as I idled the morning away. For a while, I cleared my mind, feeling the rising warmth of the day and the caffeine and sugar rush of the *café*. It was mental loitering, a skill honored in the Virgin Islands as limin', in Guatemala as *peluche* and in the Dominican Republic as *tranqui*.

Unfortunately, after a while, my *tranqui* evaporated as the anger at Jerry Pleasants from last night's sleepless hours resurfaced. To bury the anger, I tried to think pleasant thoughts. In my case, always, pleasant thoughts mean thoughts of home – as in the United States – and family. Family for me now means only my kid sister, Janet. My Uncle Tony and Aunt Ruth have passed and Mom and Dad are long dead, killed by a drunk driver while I was in the Air Force. Janet was a child then, the last time I had seen her, but now she is a wife and new mother, with a husband, George, who she adores, and a baby, Linda. While my status as *persona non grata* has kept me from visiting Jan in the States and her and George's new family prevents a visit to me, we have had a lively and ongoing correspondence since my earliest Cuba days. I enjoy her letters, hearing her excitement about love and marriage and motherhood, and hope she enjoys mine filled with tales of sun, sand, revolution and escapades on the half dozen islands on which I've lived since leaving the Air Force. I take special pride in her happiness. I made a sacrifice, not the ultimate sacrifice, but near to it, in order to ensure her future. Her letters extolling her domestic bliss made it worthwhile.

Thoughts of Janet and home always motivate me to visit the one place I associate with them, so I paid my breakfast tab and pointed my steps in the direction of the Palacio de Correo. I made it a stroll, killing time and hoping it would help me lose the anger that hovered at the edge of my morning. I arrived, tired, hot and sweating and left a few minutes later, disappointed with the window clerk's reply of '*Nada, señor*' when I asked after my mail.

The disappointment worked its magic on my suppressed anger at Jerry, dredging it up to float on my mind's surface like yesterday's garbage tossed into the stagnant Rio Ozama. I heard Val's voice in my head telling me to let it pass but I could not. I walked to the section of the post office where the telephones were, paid for one and was about to call Cosme Salazar when two PND officers approached me and placed me in handcuffs.

NINETEEN

'So good of you to join us, Henry.' Captain Cosme Salazar rose from the poolside table at the Hotel El Jaragua with his hand extended in greeting. His companion, who I had never met but recognized from newspaper photos, remained seated.

'Your invitation was rather difficult to refuse, Cosme.' For emphasis, I rubbed my wrists before shaking hands. The two cops, who had only removed the handcuffs when we were in sight of Captain Salazar, trailed behind me like obedient sheepdogs, making certain that I found my way directly to him.

'A misunderstanding, I assure you, Henry.' Cosme feigned joviality. 'Sending an order down the chain of command is sometimes like being the initiator in a game of Chinese whispers. It is almost guaranteed that one's words are completely garbled when they reach their ultimate destination.' To the two flatfeet, he said, 'I'll have a word with you officers later,' and tried to look severe. The playact told me that the beat cops had probably followed their orders with precision.

To prompt the introduction that Cosme seemed to be purposefully delaying, I nodded to the man at the table.

Cosme took the hint. 'Please, both of you gentlemen will excuse my poor manners. Henry, let me introduce Major General Leandro Vazquez, the *jefe* of the Policía Nacional Dominicana. *General-Mayor*, Mr Henry Gore.'

General Vazquez, to demonstrate his superiority over both the introducer and the introduced, extended a casual hand from his seated position. He was a short man, powerfully built, which had no doubt earned him his nickname of 'Bullito'.

'Señor Gore, please be seated.' A command rather than an invitation. I sat.

Cosme played host. 'Would you care for anything, Henry?'

'Just a reason why I got an un-refusable invitation to this soirée.'

'Because you were seen to meet with one Jaime Vargas,' General Vazquez said.

'I didn't "meet" with him, General. He, or somebody working

for him, kidnapped me off the street near the Catedral Santa Maria la Menor. I couldn't see who it was exactly since they put a bag over my head when they did it.'

Bullito was unmoved by my victim status. 'What did he discuss with you?'

'We talked a bit about his *abuela*.'

'Your friend is a little asshole, Captain Salazar,' General Vazquez said. 'This almost certainly means he is a Boschist as well.'

'I'm an American, not a Boschist, General,' I said. 'I guess that makes me a little American asshole.'

'If you think being an American will protect you as you seek to revive the illegal communist regime of Juan Bosch, you will find yourself sorely mistaken.' Bullito almost growled the words.

'You're sorely mistaken if you think I'm a communist. Or if you think I have anything to do with attempting to bring Bosch back,' I said. 'And, by the way, the last I and the good old US of A could determine, the "illegal" Bosch government was chosen by the people of the Dominican Republic in a free and fair election. I don't think Uncle Sam believes the same to be true about the current occupants of the National Palace.'

'And what is it that you believe about the current occupants of our most lovely building, Señor Gore?'

'I take pride in not having any beliefs, political, or otherwise. I find it keeps me from receiving invitations I cannot refuse. Usually.'

Cosme, seeing the friendly intelligence-gathering luncheon he probably had suggested turning to shit, intervened. 'Gentlemen, gentlemen, we should enjoy this fine day, this lovely facility, the beautiful ladies within sight, and each other's company. My friend, Henry, we certainly did not invite you here to engage in an acrimonious discussion of our republic's politics. Rather, we became aware that you had encountered certain elements who are, shall we say, somewhat unsavory. We simply wanted to warn you to beware of them and to make sure that you were not being subjected to . . . importuning.'

'Nice word, Cosme,' I said. 'It can mean so many things.'

'Take it as you will, Henry.'

Exasperation flowed through me like an electrical current. 'Look, Cosme – and General Vazquez – I'll lay it out for you. I had a negative reaction to getting blown up and having pieces of me separated from the rest of me.' I waved my almost-healed left hand pinkie stub to demonstrate. 'I suppose I could have eventually let that go but what I couldn't let go was that I had an . . . acquaintance, Jerry Pleasants, who was in La Españolita and who has vanished since the bombing. Jaime Vargas was the bartender at La Españolita. I thought he might be able to give me information that would help me to find Señor Pleasants. That's all. I asked around about Vargas, couldn't find him, but he found me. I'm not working with him, I don't know what he's doing that would be of interest to the PND and I frankly don't care if I ever see him again. Now, are you satisfied?'

General Vazquez gave a little snort, rose abruptly and walked away. He skirted the pool filled with Cosme's beautiful ladies and, by the time he reached the driveway, an unmarked PND car was there to spirit him away.

'That went well,' Cosme said.

'What did you expect, dragging me in like that?' I said.

'I don't think, Henry, that you appreciate how benign I was able to make your detention. General Vazquez wanted to snatch you from your bed at three a.m., take you to a special facility the PND has and allow you to spend a couple days there in a blacked-out room to make you feel more cooperative when he finally got around to speaking with you. Now I'm not entirely sure his method was wrong.'

'Come on, Cosme, you know you can't go around putting Americans, even Americans that America doesn't want like me, in underground prisons like you can one of the locals. And all you had to do was ask nice and I'd tell you everything. I've got nothing to hide.'

'And have you told me everything, my friend?' I hated it when Cosme dropped the 'f' word. I could never tell if he was my friend or not. 'I'm asking nice.'

'I was about to. In fact, when your two goons snatched me from the Palacio de Correo, I was just about to call you to meet.'

'To what purpose?'

'To tell you what I told you and the general. And more, since you asked nice. Jaime Vargas warned me to get out before the bomb went off. I told you that before. What I didn't know then was how Jaime knew about the bomb. He told me he was warned by Jerry Pleasants. Jerry told him that the bomb was going off in three minutes and that it was as a tip for being generous when Jaime poured drinks for him.'

'You believe this, Henry?'

'Jaime had no reason to make it up.'

'Really? If Jaime was the bomber, would he not want to throw suspicion onto someone else?'

'No reason to, Cosme. If you recall, the efficient and illustrious officers of the PND solved the crime and took a couple of Boschists into custody within forty-eight hours of the explosion. Jaime was off the hook as far as the authorities are concerned.'

'So you were about to call me to tell me we had the wrong men. And that Jaime Vargas ought to be considered as a suspect. Or Jerry Pleasants.'

'Something like that, Cosme. I thought you might do something about it. I thought you might bring one or both of them in and find out who planted that bomb.' And, unspoken, if the bomber was Jerry, why he didn't see fit to warn me as he had Jaime Vargas.

'The men in custody confessed to the crime, Henry.'

'Did you conduct the interrogation of them?'

'No. What difference does that make?'

'I know Cosme Salazar is one of the very few officers in the PND who wouldn't beat a confession out of a suspect. No, I'll amend that. He's the *only* cop in the PND who wouldn't beat a suspect for a confession.'

'I'm flattered for myself and appalled that you have that impression of the methods of the rest of the PND.'

'Don't blow smoke at me, Cosme. You know it's true. I'll bet my last *peso oro* that your two confessed bombers were beaten. I'll bet my next-to-last *peso oro* that, in your heart of hearts, you have serious doubts that they had anything to do with the bombing. Certainly enough doubt that a good cop would want to investigate further. And you're a good cop, Cosme. One of the few in the Policía Nacional.'

Cosme looked off across the pool at the beautiful ladies, made a slow and elaborate production of locating a pack of Nacionals in his pocket, lit one and took a long draw. 'Do you know what I love, truly and honestly love, about women, Henry? They will never come right out and tell you exactly what they want. They know exactly, precisely, unequivocally what they want, down to the last jot and tittle – a wonderful expression you English speakers do not use often enough. But they never come out and tell you. They hint, dissemble, whisper, cajole. It is in their nature, a kindness. Why is it a kindness? Because if you cannot deliver precisely what they want, this allows you to deliver something less, an-almost-but-not-quite, a close approximation. It allows you to provide the best you can, to save face, to remain the *macho hombre*. Men never allow this with their requests. They say what they want. If you cannot deliver it, they tell you that you have failed them. That you are no longer as virtuous as they once believed you to be. That you are no longer a friend.' Another drag on the cigarette. 'I hope, Henry, that you can still consider me a friend.'

Cosme scribbled his signature on the tab that the waiter had brought and stood. He saluted and walked away.

TWENTY

Bars are a home to guys like me and often a place of business as well. In the Air Force, the base officers club was where some, though often precious few, of the formalities and disciplines of military life were relaxed. It was also a place which played a role in one or two of the more serious cases I worked on in the OSI. Bars were the lifeblood of Havana in the Batista years and the place where my fledgling PI business first grew and then went to die. Then bars became a place for contacts with the sometimes hard to distinguish enemies and friends of my short-lived stint as a counter-espionage agent for the Republic of Cuba. Bars were few and far between in my time with Castro; we drank our rum in the forests and fields of the Sierra Maestra, when we could get our hands on rum and when no one was shooting at us or bombing us. After my beneficent expulsion from Cuba for being too much of a gringo, bars became more recreational for me. I saw many an island sunset and more than the occasional sunrise from a stool where the bar was made of bamboo and two by fours and the floor was sand. In Santo Domingo, the drinking joints were less rustic, though the theme of rum and dissoluteness remained the same as in the lesser islands. Then I got blown up in La Españolita, a bar.

After all that bar room experience, I should have caught on that maybe bars were not the right place for me. That I could benefit from the sun, fresh breezes and clear waters that could be found in such abundance in this part of the world. That I could get in trouble in bars, get beaten, shot at, lured into conspiracies and generally have bad things happen to me in them.

But I did not catch on. Indeed, after my disappointing meeting with General Vazquez and Captain Salazar, I sought refuge from my disconsolation in the clubby confines of the bar at El Jaragua. I probably could have stayed at the table by the pool and, with a little work, persuaded the waiter that I was still drinking on the PND's tab. But the dazzling sun, Cosme's beautiful ladies splashing in the pool and the pleasing trade winds there did not match my mood. I needed to crawl into a dark and cozy lair to lick my wounds; the sedate inside bar fit that bill.

The place was surprisingly crowded for mid-afternoon. There was a surfeit of sunburned tourist types, occupying tables away from the damaging rays and opting for internal rather than topical medication for their scorched skin. There was a clutch or two of shady types in corner booths, doing business that shouldn't or couldn't be done in the open air. And there was the usual cadre of maleness at the bar, husbands escaping wives, hard drinkers working diligently at their only vocation and the rejected washing away their rejection. I took one of the two open seats at the bar. I felt right at home.

I was leaning into my second glass of Ron Barcelo when a voice over my shoulder asked, 'Is this seat taken?' of the stool to my right. The question came in English, probably because even after all of my time south of the US, I had the unmistakable look of gringo expat about me. The questioner, though her English was flawless, was most certainly not an American. The accent was European but hard to place, not the romance language purl of French or Spanish, not the guttural hardness of German. Not Baltic or Slavic, either.

'It's all yours,' I said, turning to get a visual to help identify the accent. She was one of those women who gave the illusion of being tall, by the way her arms and legs appeared, well formed and graceful, though not actually long; and big, though not carrying any extra weight, but substantial. Her face was fresh, not because she was too fair to be tan but with the appearance of one who spent time outdoors. Her hair was pale red, almost blonde and her eyes the muted blue that often came with that kind of hair. She wore her hair cut short, in what might be described as a pixie cut but even shorter than that, almost boyish. She didn't smile when our eyes met, as strangers often do out of nervousness. Her face advertised that she was self-assured, serious but not dour, welcoming if you were not forward, closed if she perceived you as insincere.

She wore a white cotton blouse, buttoned to the next to last button and a long gray skirt. The color of the skirt was unusual for the Caribbean; of the rainbow of colors which exist here, gray hardly ever makes itself known. The cut and the length of the skirt reminded me of the ones worn by Marta, my long-ago contact in Havana, after her performances as the lead dancer at the Tropicana; it was not severe but it was most clearly reserved.

'Presidente, *por favor*,' she said to the barman. She took a long draught when the beer arrived, like she had just stumbled in from a hike in the desert.

The two patrons on her right were deep in conversation. I toyed with my glass of rum on her left.

'What are your troubles?' she asked after a minute.

'What makes you think I have troubles?' I said it without any challenge in my voice. I was truly curious how she could pick up on my mood.

'You are young man, here alone on a weekday. You should be at work or with your family. Or on holiday. And you're not on holiday because you are not dressed for it. You're not dressed like a Dominican either. So you are out of place. It is not too difficult to conclude you have troubles given those facts.' When she called me a young man, she said it in the tone of a middle-aged librarian or head nurse, her voice strong, like she would brook no challenge to what she said. This though she had to be all of twenty-five or maybe thirty years old.

'You are an astute observer,' I said, not about to tell this pretty, self-assured stranger my troubles. 'What troubles bring you here?'

'What makes you think I have troubles?' she said, turning my words back on me. Like me, her question wasn't a challenge but a genuine expression of curiosity.

'You are a young woman, alone, on a weekday. Away from home and family and, also judging by your clothes, not a tourist or a local.'

She smiled then, showing small white teeth briefly. 'Touché, Mr . . .?'

'Henry Gore.'

She held out a strong hand. 'Beatrijs Hagan.'

'And your troubles, Miss Hagan?' I saw she wore no wedding band.

'I have none, Mr Gore.'

'Call me Henry. Then you're here because . . .?'

'I like beer. And you're here because . . .?'

I thought about why precisely I was in the El Jaragua bar and finally said, 'I'm trying to figure out who my friends are.'

'This sounds difficult for you.'

'It's not as straightforward as liking beer.' That earned me another look at her reticent smile. I decided I liked it.

'It may be more straightforward than you think. In my experience, if you have to think about whether someone is a friend, they usually are not.'

'In my experience, recent and distant, some who appear to be friends are anything but and those who seem indifferent turn out to be unexpected friends.'

Beatrijs took another sip of her beer. It left a thin line of foam on her upper lip, drawing my attention to it. It was a very fetching lip, pink and plump, unadorned by lipstick. I felt, and dismissed, an urge to kiss it. She wiped away the lingering foam with the back of her hand, giving her every appearance of being an experienced beer drinker.

'What is it, Henry Gore, that gives you this troubling experience with friendship?'

I thought about her question. 'Homes without a heart. People who aren't trustworthy. Travel without joy. All things I have brought on my self.'

'That sounds incredibly sad, Henry.'

'I'm not sad.' I realized I wasn't, too. Pathetic, maybe, to an outside observer like Beatrijs Hagan, but not sad.

'That is good, Henry. If you are not sad, it means you are a good friend to yourself. You are your first friend, your best friend.'

'You know about friendship then. Can you tell me how to figure out who my friends are?'

'No. That knowledge must come from inside you.'

'Maybe that's my problem. What's inside me.'

'I don't think so, Henry. You have a warmth, a light inside you. I can see it.'

I think I blushed like a schoolboy.

'I predict, Henry, that you will find your problem with friends does not come from inside you. I suspect you have more friends than you believe. You have a new one today.'

'As do you, Beatrijs.' That brought the return of her shy smile.

Her tall glass of Presidente had been drained. 'Will you allow your new friend to get you another?' I said, waving a hand at the glass.

'No, thank you, Henry. I must be going.' She was up from her chair and tossed a single *peso oro* note onto the bar.

'Wait,' I said, my tone sounding too urgent.

'Yes, Henry.'

'Now that we're friends, Beatrijs, we should get together again. Have another beer together.'

'A friendly beer would be nice sometime.'

'Will you give me your number?'

'I don't have a phone.'

'Your address, then.'

'Where I live male visitors are not permitted. But Santo Domingo is really a small town if you're a foreigner. I'm sure we will run into each other again. We can have that beer then.' And, as I was about to make another try, she turned and was gone.

TWENTY-ONE

had gone into the bar at El Jaragua thinking about Jerry Pleasants, Cosme Salazar and the vagaries and pitfalls of friendship. I came out thinking about my chance encounter with Beatrijs Hagan and my relationships with women, including Camila Polanco and Valerie Spicer and love.

I took a cab partway home, to just outside the remnants of the old city wall and walked from there. I needed to walk to dissipate the haze remaining from the two Ron Barcelos I had consumed and to further consider the once one, then two, now three women occupying my thoughts. I wish I could say there was order and rationality in my musings about these three women in Santo Domingo, but the truth was my musings were anything but orderly and rational. Instead, as I walked in the shade along the narrow streets, a series of images popped into and out of my head. The nape of Beatrijs Hagan's neck, where her strawberry blonde hair met the smooth curve leading to her shoulder. Valerie Spicer, tangled in the sheets of my four-poster bed, asleep like a satisfied feline in the dappled morning sun. Camila Polanco, her dark eyes alight, laughing and teasing. Fanny Knutson in a sapphire blue evening gown in the spotlight at the Café Parisien in Havana on the night we met. Three women here in Santo Domingo, one woman gone so long ago. I was confused, emotional, unsure what my thoughts about these women meant and more unsure about their role in my future – even that of my long-dead love, Fanny – and my role in the lives of the three women still alive. Were they in love with me, any of them? Was I in love with any of them? Camila, to whom I had been, to give myself the benefit of the doubt, less than honorable? Val, so forward, so effervescent, so bold – could I be in love with her or headed that way? Beatrijs, so serene, so sure of herself, so enticing? Could any of them be the one to fill the hollow left in my heart after Fanny's death, to bring me back to living life instead of just going through the motions? How could I even know about Beatrijs after only one chance encounter? An encounter that ended with her walking out of the room and may be out of my life forever? How had things become so complicated? Were things complicated at all or just in my own mind? Had Camila written me off and moved on? Was it just a fling for Val until the next country, the next capital, the next diplomatic posting? Was I just a nice stranger, a one-time encounter in a bar, a brief connection of sympathetic souls never to occur again, to Beatrijs?

My wandering thoughts and rambling walk were interrupted by the noise of a crowd a block ahead. There were angry chants. Shouts of outrage. I was approaching Parque Independencia at the west end of Calle El Conde. The park contains La Puerta del Conde – the El Conde Gate – an original entrance to the city and the site of the Dominican Republic's proclamation of independence from Haiti in 1844. The crowd was at El Conde Gate, spilling out into the adjoining street. Men and women, seeming disorganized except for their chanting, called for the expulsion of Wessin y Wessin and his junta and the restoration of Juan Bosch as president.

I could see that the crowd was not being contained by the authorities. Indeed, there was an almost total absence of the authorities near the group or in the park proper. I saw one or two police officers, probably the regular patrol contingent used to keep loiterers and pickpockets tamped down, keeping their distance from the mob. They had removed their hats to make themselves less visible as police and probably would have ditched their uniforms if they had other clothes to change into. Someone in the crush produced a large red, white and blue flag of the republic, waving it vigorously and rallying the crowd. They began to head east, moving, like most mobs I'd seen, at a snail's pace.

The crowd had traveled less than a block when I heard the sound of sirens approaching from the east. The first police cars and jeeps appeared seconds later, halting a hundred yards away. The cars and jeeps pulled sideways in the street, creating a perimeter behind which the police assembled. Most of the officers had a ragtag appearance, dressed in civilian clothes rather than uniforms. Some had helmets but most were bareheaded and, if they had mixed with the approaching mob, would have blended completely. These first cops were outnumbered maybe twenty to one. They drew weapons, mostly side-arms and a few pump shotguns, and waited nervously behind their barrier of vehicles.

The mob stopped and milled about in the street, shouting slogans against the junta and taunting the police. The crowd was both young and old. There were boys, men and a surprising number of young women. I was caught in the space between the police and the protesters, close enough to see the anger in the eyes of the civilians and the white-eyed fear of the few police officers.

I ducked in the door of a mom-and-pop *colmada*, finding both Mom and Pop cowering behind the bottles of Coca-Cola and bags of rice that crammed the shop. Mom gave me a nervous smile and did not offer to wait on me. I returned the nervous smile and did not ask to be waited on. Pop busied himself removing paper pesos, American dollars and a few coins from the till box, dropping them into a slot cut into the floor on the non-public side of the counter, while Mom and I watched the confrontation through the front window. Neither of the proprietors made a move to lock the front door. They had apparently decided that their shop would be shelter for any protester who entered. The police would never risk holing up inside a store in a hostile area, which was decidedly the character of this neighborhood.

Outside the window, the confrontation entered the new stage. On the protesters' side, the chants ended and a young man in khaki pants and a dirty singlet stepped up on a crate in the middle of the crowd. He began a harangue about the wrongs perpetrated by the junta. He was a dynamic speaker. In minutes, the crowd was in a frenzy. The young man began a series of call-and-response chants, in the best style of a good old southern Baptist preacher in the US. But, unlike a group of Sunday parishioners, the mob was moved to more than verbal action. Stones from the cobbled street were pried up. By the force of dozens of hands, a section of the park's wrought iron fence was pulled apart and fashioned into makeshift clubs.

The initial phalanx of police had done their job. While the mob spun itself up, the first cops were supplemented by more of their compatriots and two deuce-and-a-half trucks full of soldiers. The police stepped into the open territory beyond the line of police cars and jeeps, while the soldiers, bayonets fixed, formed a line behind them.

The air outside the *colmada* was electric with tension. A piece of cobblestone flew through the sky, falling short of the police line. It was followed by a rain of stones. An officer fell, his head bloodied. The police popped a half dozen canisters of teargas and lobbed them into the ranks of the mob. Several in the crowd risked burning their hands and hurled the spewing gas canisters back at the police.

Neither the police nor the protesters had gas masks. Soon both sides were vomiting and crying, the air filled with a smell akin to bleach or acrid vinegar.

The young man in the singlet shouted, 'Viva Bosch!' and charged the police line. The mob followed fearlessly, throwing rocks at the cops and soldiers. There was apparently no more teargas; the next move of the authorities was a volley from the soldiers aimed above the heads of the protesters. The crowd faltered at the gunfire but the young leader, alone in the gap between protesters and police, used the silence after the fusillade to urge them on. They regrouped and continued toward the guns, tossing rocks and waving the wrought iron fence rails as weapons.

There were no outward signs that I can describe but the crowd underwent a change. The hesitation was gone. The mob gave itself over to battle, running forward where it had tentatively milled before. The few policemen with shotguns stepped to the front of the line and fired as one. The pellets were aimed low into the crowd this time. A dozen protesters fell, clutching their legs and lower bodies. The police had used birdshot. The injured howled in pain but it was clear none of them had suffered serious wounds.

The shots into the crowd broke its charge. Some tended to the injured. Others hurled rocks and insults at the police from a distance. Then a new sound came from the west, behind the mob, an amplified bullhorn wielded by a uniformed PND captain, ordering the protesters to disperse. No sooner was the order given that another volley of shotgun blasts rang out from a squad of cops behind the captain. More protesters, mostly at the rear of the crowd, fell to the ground.

The result was immediate. Before, with their police enemy to the front, the crowd was aggressive. Now, caught between the two police lines, confusion and fear reigned. Women screamed. The wounded bled and shrieked for help. The loose organization in the ranks of the protesters was replaced by chaos, people running hither and thither, seeking shelter and finding little.

The police shotgunners set to work in earnest, firing at will, as rapidly as they could reload. The man in the singlet went down, hands to his face as blood gushed between his fingers. A woman who rushed to help him went down as well and did not move. A cacophony of noise, gunshots, screams, angry oaths and running steps filled the air. The acrid teargas odor was layered now with the metallic smell of blood and the animal scent of sweat.

A woman ran through the *colmada*'s door, then another, dragging a child. Who brings a child to a protest almost certain to end in confrontation, I wondered before realizing they may have been innocently caught on the street between the police and the protesters, the collateral damage such confrontations often begets.

The women and the child were terrified but uninjured. I moved to the door, to what purpose I'm not sure. A man sheltered from the gunfire in the doorway, trying to make himself small in the tight space between the recessed door and the sidewalk. I recognized him through the store window. It was Jaime Vargas. I opened the door and pulled him inside.

'*Dios mío!*' he cried. Then: 'Señor Gore?'

'The same, Jaime. Are you hurt?'

'No. What are you doing here? Are you part of the protest?'

'No, just in the wrong place at the wrong time. And you?'

He ignored my question. 'It was supposed to be peaceful. That damn Jhonny. He wanted a fight. Well, he got one. People have died.'

'Who is Jhonny?'

'A hothead. The boy who took the lead of the protest from the front. The one shot in the face. I doubt he will live.'

I glanced out the window. The cops to the east had waded in with new reinforcements wielding long clubs. The police and soldiers to the west waited as the disorganized remnants of the protest were driven toward them like sheep. Whenever the police caught a protester – man, woman, or child – they beat them senseless and moved on to the next, not bothering to arrest or detain individuals, dispensing instant and brutal justice in the street. I knew that there would be arrests later on. I would bet there were informants in the mob. In my experience, no violent crowd or peaceful march escapes having a snitch or two in its ranks.

It was only a matter of time before the cops and soldiers would begin a mopping up operation to look for stragglers, which was sure to include entry into the shops and residences fronting the street.

'We need to get out of here, Jaime,' I said. 'Is there a back way?'

There was an exchange in Spanish between Mom and Pop and Jaime. 'There is a back door which opens onto an alley,' he said.

'Good. Let's go.'

'The women and the child must come with us.'

'They'll slow us down,' I said. 'The cops won't bother with them.'
I started toward the rear of the store.

Jaime grabbed my arm. 'You see what is happening in the street.
The police will beat them.'

He was right. 'OK, bring them. Let's go, now!'

Jaime spoke to the women and shepherded them to the back of
the shop. With a quick '*Gracias*' from me to Mom and Pop, we
were out the door.

TWENTY-TWO

The alley behind the *colmada*, like its fronting street, was paved with cobblestones that had come from Spain as ship's ballast in the colonial period. It was one horse wide, with the rear entrances of the shops on Calle El Conde on one side and the backs of the houses on the adjoining street hard on the other. Like all alleys everywhere, it was the collection point for the detritus of the neighborhood, almost blocked in places by crates and boxes, stinking of garbage and teaming with skittering things that I didn't want to look at too closely.

Jaime chose our direction of travel, moving eastward to skirt the police line on Calle El Conde. The child, a girl of three or four, couldn't keep pace. I picked her up and we all moved down the alley at a sprint for a hundred feet, then stopped for a breath and to listen for any sounds which might tell us where the cops were. Then we sprinted again. We repeated this several times, running and then stopping to look and listen. I began to think we might be in the clear.

'*Alto! Policía!*' The words were shouted behind us. I looked back. There was a uniformed PND officer and a second man in plainclothes. The plainclothes man had a revolver in his hand. He called, '*Alto!*' again.

We kept running. The plainclothes cop fired a single shot. The woman who had first ventured into the *colmada* just minutes before stumbled and fell to the cobbles. The little girl's mother, running beside me, screamed in terror. Jaime scooped up the injured woman in a fireman's carry. She was unconscious and bleeding from her mouth. The blood trickled down Jaime's back as he ran forward. I grabbed the hand of the screaming mother, pulling her while I carried the child.

The two cops came on but did not fire any more shots. They must have been confident that they would catch us without any more shooting and they were right. I scanned the alley ahead for an escape route. The block or two we had traveled had taken us into a nicer neighborhood of old colonial homes. The alley was neat, no boxes or garbage, the rears of the homes a blank wall flush to the alley with the occasional plain door, in the old Spanish style. There was no place to hide. The injured woman desperately needed medical attention.

'Jaime, we can't go on.' My words came out as a gasp. I was gassed from running and carrying the child. Like me, Jaime surely couldn't continue far carrying the injured woman.

A plain green door in the alley flew open. A well-dressed man stood in the doorway and hissed, *'Ven por aquí,'* in Spanish and 'This way' in English for good measure. Jaime ducked inside without hesitation. With no good alternatives, I followed.

The door opened directly into a courtyard hung heavy with bougainvillea, with a fountain in the center. 'Speak English?' said the man.

I guess the American expat look was pretty obvious. 'Yes,' I said.

'Quickly, in here.' He led us across the courtyard into a well-appointed room, a kind of gallery, with chairs and sofas arranged along its length.

'She is wounded badly?' the man asked. Not waiting for an answer, he said, 'I am a doctor. Put her on that chaise.'

Jaime did as instructed. The doctor conducted a quick examination and turned to us. 'Who is with this lady?'

'None of us,' I said.

'You do not know her?'

'No. We fell in together, trying to escape the . . . commotion.' I selected the most neutral word I could come up with.

'She is dead. The police will be here in seconds. You must leave now.'

'The police will not treat you well if you are found with her,' Jaime said.

'I am a physician. She was brought to me for treatment, which my oath does not allow me to refuse. That is all the police need to know. I am not a peasant. They dare not harm me. Go now, by the front door, before they arrive.' The doctor unbuttoned his shirt and handed it to Jaime. He motioned for Jaime to give him his bloodstained shirt. 'I will tell him I got bloodied treating her. Go now.'

The sound of pounding on the rear door spurred us on. We emerged onto Calle Arzobispo Nouel in the midst of an ordinary day. Businessmen and laborers walked in twos and fours. The police were nowhere to be seen, apparently concentrating their efforts on Calle El Conde.

'We should split up,' I said.

'Yes,' Jaime said and explained to the woman that we would be parting ways. She accepted her child from my arms with a nodded thanks and set off along the street to the east.

Jaime and I walked to the nearest corner and turned south. 'I am grateful, Señor Gore, that you pulled me into the *colmada*. You may have saved me from injury or worse.'

'*De nada*, Jaime. Just remember that next time you decide to kidnap me.'

'For that I am sorry, señor. When I did that, I did not know the reasons for your inquiries or where your loyalties lie. After today I have a better understanding.'

'After today, you should have all the understanding you need that my loyalties are with saving my own skin.'

'If that was your only motivation, there was no reason for you to drag me out of harm's way or to carry that girl child with you while fleeing. Those two acts tell me your motives are not purely selfish.'

'More spur of the moment reaction than any altruism, I can assure you, Jaime.'

'Altruism? What is this?'

'Just something I, and most of the world, do not possess. You apparently do, taking the side of justice in your politics.'

'I don't know what you mean, Señor Gore.'

'Don't play coy with me. You were involved in leading that protest, at least until your hotheaded compatriot Jhonny took over, God rest his soul. And, just so you know, after our little forced meeting, I had a visit from the PND. They knew that we had met, although they didn't have all the particulars. I don't know exactly what you're up to for the Boschists and I don't want to know. Just understand that you are being watched by the PND.'

'I was not aware of this. I shall be more careful. There may be one among my group who is disloyal. *Gracias*, again, Señor Gore. I owe you doubly now.'

'Maybe I should take advantage of your gratitude. Maybe now you will be more receptive when I ask about Jerry Pleasants.'

Jaime smiled. 'You certainly are fixated on Señor Pleasants. In candor, I have already told you all I know about him or his whereabouts. But I will do this. I will keep my eyes and ears open. I will make discrete requests to certain persons in Gualey. If I learn anything, I will let you know.'

'And if I need to contact you for any reason?' I said. 'Do I go back to your *abuela*?'

'No, señor. I'm sure you understand that I wish to insulate her from any . . . intrigue as much as possible. If you need to contact me, there is a blind man who makes his living selling candies, trinkets and gum at La Poza del Chino. He goes by the name El Pâjaro. The Bird. Tell him you are the man from the country of snow – *el pais de la nieve* – and give him your message or tell him where and when you wish to meet me.'

'The man from the country of snow?'

'It is the barman's secret, Señor Gore. We hear all conversations, say nothing and remember everything. *Adios.*'

TWENTY-THREE

'Señor Henry, you look awful. Are you injured?' Camila's greeting made me take stock of my appearance in the mirror in the entry hall of my house. Sweaty, dirty, hair tousled. Blood smears on one arm of my shirt. Hollow eyes. She was right, I looked like hell.

'I'm not hurt, Camila.'

'*Dios mío*. What happened? Were you in a fight?'

'I was in a riot. By accident. I was walking down the street and ended up in the wrong place at the wrong time, between the rioters and the police.'

Tears in her eyes, Camila placed her hand on my cheek. 'You poor man,' she said and hugged me. Close. And long. Uncomfortably long.

'I saw the door was open and let myself in . . . oh!' Val Spicer said from the doorway. 'I hope I'm not interrupting anything, Henry. And Camila. But it certainly appears that I am.'

I managed to extract myself from the embrace of the teary Camila. 'Val . . . er, hello.'

Val rebounded quickly. 'Don't be embarrassed, Henry. We are all free and over twenty-one. If you want to play the field, I'm prepared to beat the field.' She leveled a look at Camila that appeared to be neutral until you saw the venom in the depths of her blue eyes, the tiny nub of hate there like a predator swimming in a fair sea.

'I'm not playing the field,' I said. 'I was just caught up in a riot while walking in the street. And before that, I was arrested. I'm having a bad day. When I come back to my own home, I expect some peace and quiet.'

'Things appeared very peaceful when I stepped in the door just now,' Val said, her version of the evil eye boring in on Camila again. The housekeeper, defeated, retreated to the kitchen.

'Val!' I said.

'Henry, sweet,' Val cooed. 'Are you hurt? No? Good. Maybe you need a shower and some clean clothes. And a drink. Why don't you go upstairs. I'll bring you a drink up in a few minutes.'

Part of me wanted to order Val out. Another part found the idea of a shower and clean clothes an enticing avoidance of confrontation with the woman problem I seemed to have right in my own house. 'I'm going to take a shower,' I said.

The door to my room gave a telltale squeak a few minutes later, just as I stepped from the shower. I wrapped the largest towel I could find around me and stepped out. Val sat, or rather lounged like a satisfied cat, on the bed, a drink in her hand. 'Feel better?'

'Human.'

She patted the bed beside her. 'I brought you a rum. Come, sit down and tell Val all about it.'

I sat a foot away from Val. 'First thing is, Val, you need to ease off Camila. She's just my housekeeper, nothing more. Don't keep trying to frighten her away. Please.'

'If I was trying to frighten her away, Henry, she would already be gone. I'm just trying to establish some much needed boundaries. It appeared just now that she was not performing housekeeper duties and I wanted to set her straight, that's all. I've got her back to work, preparing dinner for two. You'll be hungry soon. I even had her put a couple of bottles of wine in the refrigerator.'

'A couple? Isn't that a bit much?'

'You've had a hard day. You need to relax. And I'm here to help you relax.' She slipped a hand under the edge of my towel and glided it along my thigh. My body reacted as she had planned.

'No, Val.'

'Your lips say no but the important part of you has other ideas. And so do I.' She leaned in to kiss me.

I drew back. 'Not now, Val.'

She smiled at me. Happily. 'All right, Henry, when?'

'Not today.'

'What about me has my man so put off?'

'It's not you, Val.'

'That . . . housekeeper?' Her eyes danced merrily when she said it.

'No. It's this place. Santo Domingo. It's becoming . . . difficult for me to be here, to live here. I want a quiet life. Peace. But since the bombing of La Españolita, peace and quiet seem pretty elusive.'

'You mean you can't sleep all morning and stay buzzed all afternoon like before?'

'Yes. Exactly. That is exactly how I want to pass the time as long as I'm stuck here, away from the States.'

'You miss home.'

'Damn right I do.'

'Go back.'

'I can't. You probably already know this.' As cultural attaché-cum-spy.

'Explain to me.'

'I was in Cuba before Fidel was in power, during Batista's reign. I was fresh out of the Air Force. I was trying to get a private detective agency started and I stepped on some mob toes. They effectively shut me down. I was pressed for cash. About to starve, actually. Batista's lackeys used that to get me to work for them. Counterintelligence stuff. It got a lot of people, good people, killed and locked me in even tighter. They sent me after Castro next, to infiltrate his operation. They were bad people, Batista's guys. Castro was no angel but he had the Cuban people's interests at heart and he was no commie. At least then he wasn't, that I could tell. I flipped the script, Val, and joined up with Castro. I became useful to him and rode into Havana with him. I was part of his government for a short – a very short – time, until it was inconvenient to have a *yanqui* down the hall from El Comandante. I was ushered out the back door with a hefty severance and Fidel's thanks.

'What I did in Cuba made me *persona non grata* in the US. They didn't have any crimes to pin on me but the State Department made sure I couldn't return. I've been bouncing around the Caribbean ever since, living on Castro's largesse and money from odd jobs. I'm sick of it, Val. I thought I'd found a home here in the Dominican Republic but not now. The streets are simmering just below the surface, just like I saw in Cuba. There's gonna be a war here and all I want to do is go back to a quiet house in the suburbs, mow my lawn and have barbecues on the weekends with my sister, Jan, her husband, and my new niece. They're the only people I've got in the world.'

'You've got me.' For the first time since we had met, Val dropped the façade of unrelenting cheeriness and was serious. 'We could make something together.'

'Really? Do you think so? The career diplomat and the vagabond ne'er-do-well with "commie" tattooed on his forehead, at least as far as her bosses are concerned? Do you think they'd let that happen? Do you think you could afford to let that happen, Val?'

'I don't know, Henry. We could take it one step at a time. See what happens. Maybe work it out with State. If they thought you had been wronged. If you did something that would redeem yourself in their eyes.'

'Like what? And how would State even know?'

'I could help.'

'How?'

'I have contacts. I wasn't always a cultural attaché.'

No, you weren't, Valerie Spicer, I thought. You were a spy, probably still are a spy. Most likely, CIA. And you're recruiting me, right now. Has that been the plan all along, ever since the day you were sent to sit at the side of my hospital bed until I woke up, so grateful for your concern? Or maybe that wasn't the plan then. Maybe it was just a matter of ordinary concern for a US citizen, injured in a foreign land, that brought you to me and it was only later that you saw a chance to recruit. Was it before or after you jumped into my bed?

'No. No,' I said. 'I can't redeem myself in the eyes of the United States. And you shouldn't risk your career to help me.'

Val, either good asset recruiter, good woman, or both, said, 'OK, Henry.' She knew not to push the matter. But she had planted the seed. She was patient enough to see if it would grow. 'Let's eat.'

TWENTY-FOUR

Every town in the Caribbean is a small town in personality. All the locals, even in places as big as Kingston, Fort-de-France, Bridgetown and Port of Spain, seem to know each other and each other's histories. This was true in Havana when I was there and it is true of Santo Domingo. The small town effect is multiplied exponentially in the communities of non-locals. Every diplomat in the British Embassy knows all of the French, Spanish, US and Dutch Embassy staffers and their spouses, and vice-versa. This is, in part, due to the endless round of parties and receptions to which they all receive invitations and the limited pool of acceptable guests for such affairs, and in part because of the inevitable hang-together mentality that being foreigners in the same profession in a foreign land inevitably fosters. For expats not in a foreign service, or otherwise employed in a segregating profession – oil drilling in the jungles or running mining facilities in remote locations – a similar rule applies. We frequent the same, better-than-average bars, shop in the higher quality markets, eat in the same restaurants, swim at the same beaches. The same servants see to our needs, the same cobblers repair our shoes, the same seamstresses stitch our threadbare clothes. Even in a city the size of Santo Domingo, I can go to one of the establishments on the expat-approved list and expect to see several non-locals who I know, and who I will see again next week and the week after in the tight circle of expat haunts.

That is why it was not a complete surprise when a European-accented voice of indeterminate origin said, 'Hello, Henry Gore,' behind me at the cobbler's shop on the morning after the riot.

Hearing the voice, I knew that I would turn to see Beatrijs Hagan. I was not disappointed. She was in the same conservative attire as when I first met her, a well-used, well-pressed white blouse, gray-green skirt that fell below the knee and black flats. She had another pair of identical flats in her hands, with a hole in the sole of the right shoe and a Mona Lisa smile on her lips. The smile was so subdued that it was difficult to tell if she was pleased to see me or just glad she was getting her shoes fixed. I hoped that it was the former, that I was not outdone by the prospect of new soles.

'Hello, Beatrijs.' I smiled warmly. I knew it was warmly because I flushed like a schoolboy when I said it. 'I see we both . . . walk.' Really, Henry, how suave.

It was such a lame comment that Beatrijs laughed, an open, hearty, infectious laugh that made me start to laugh, too. Soon we had both dissolved into a fit of silly giggles. The cobbler behind the counter was not an English speaker and could not understand the source of our amusement. He looked on us with the knowing look that a man gives when he recognizes two people on the verge of romance. I saw it in his eyes. I glanced at Beatrijs and realized she saw it, too, and wasn't bothered or embarrassed by it.

I allowed her to step ahead of me with a 'Ladies first'. She rewarded me with a smile that crinkled her lovely blue eyes at the corners. After she was done, she waited while I concluded my transaction. The cobbler sent us on with a muttered blessing that I did not quite catch. Beatrijs responded with flawless Spanish, which again I was too slow to translate. The cobbler had a final word or two.

Outside, she said, 'The old man said, "God's blessing on you and the señor, and on all young lovers." I explained that we were not lovers, that we were barely acquainted. He said, "Just wait."'

'Maybe the shoemaker knows something we don't.' That was rather forward of me but it didn't feel forward when I said it. It felt like something I would naturally say to my girl. In those few seconds in the shop, laughing together and being viewed as lovers under the cobbler's assumption, I felt like Beatrijs could be my girl. Like we could go out in public and laugh together. Like we could walk in the sun holding hands and basking in each other's company. And I liked it.

Beatrijs ignored my remark but she didn't leave. We stood facing each other outside the shop and then she said, 'I'm thirsty for a beer, Henry.'

'There's a place nearby,' I said. 'Not a class joint like the bar at El Jaragua but it's quiet and the Presidente's cold. It's just down the block and around the corner.'

We walked the short distance in silence. I wanted to touch her hand, to hold it, but I did not. I cast a sidelong glance at her profile, the strong nose, the red-blonde hair that twined along her neck. A few steps more and another stolen look in which she caught me. She met my eyes and said nothing.

The place we entered, like so many spots in Santo Domingo, had no name, at least, not that it advertised with any signage. It was a beer garden in a courtyard, away from the street. There were three tables with three chairs each, a crumbling fountain that hadn't seen water in years and a cobblestone floor that matched the street outside. The only adornment was a potted Valença orange tree, its white spring blooms scenting the air with sweet promise.

I had been introduced to the place by Camila during our short-lived romance. The proprietress then was a chunky woman with black hair shot with gray. She was still on duty when Beatrijs and I entered. If she recognized me, she betrayed nothing as she steered us to one of the tables. '*Dos Presidentes, por favor*,' I ordered. The proprietress scooted away.

Beatrijs looked at me directly, almost unnervingly, in the eye. 'The way you looked at me as we were walking . . .' she began.

'I'm sorry. It's just that you are so beautiful.'

She seemed neither troubled nor flattered by the remark. 'You don't know me,' she said.

'I don't mean to push.'

'We must be friends. Only friends.'

'There's another man?'

'You could say that.'

She wore no wedding ring. That, I assumed, meant I had a chance. 'Yet you're here, having a beer with me, a man you barely know.'

'Henry, it's 1965. A girl can have a beer with a friend. A girl can do lots of things now that couldn't be done even a few years ago. It's a modern world. There's change afoot.'

'So that's what we are, friends?'

'Yes, Henry, that's what we are. And barely that. I barely know you. You barely know me.'

'I'd like to get to know you better.'

'Good.' The beer was delivered. Beatrijs took a long drink. 'Ask away.'

'Where are you from?'

'The Netherlands. I grew up in Nijmegen.'

'What brings you here, to Santo Domingo?'

'I came to serve. I do it by teaching poor children.'

'Where?'

'In the countryside. To the north east, in a small village.'

'Do you have family back home?'

'Back home? Yes. And here. Everywhere.'

OK, I could go with that. I had heard about some of what was going on back in the States and in Europe, that there were these modern women who were moving away from traditional roles, who saw the world as their home and everyone as their family. I had just never encountered one until now. I was intrigued.

'What do you want? In life, I mean.'

'To help the world, Henry. The world needs so much help. To love and spread love and peace.'

'Noble goals,' I said.

'And you, Henry? What do you want?'

'To go home.'

'Where is home?'

'I'm not sure now. It used to be Indiana in the United States. I can't say where it is now. Maybe it's where I find someone.'

'Someone?'

'Someone nice. Someone to settle down with. Someone to love. Like you.'

'I didn't say I was looking for someone to love, Henry.'

'That guy has quite a hold on you,' I said.

'No. I mean, no, I'm not looking for someone. I have someone. My goal is to love.'

I was confused now and my face must have shown it. Beatrijs placed her hand on mine. It was warm and soft and light. 'I don't mean to confuse you. Let's just keep it simple, Henry. I'm not for you. I am already committed. Just drink a beer with me and enjoy this beautiful day with me, my friend.' Her shy smile reappeared. Her warm hand was removed. We drank our beers in silence and parted afterward. Parted as friends, much to my disappointment.

TWENTY-FIVE

I t was only after we had said our goodbyes on the street outside the beer garden that I realized I had not learned where Beatrijs lived. It was like she cast a spell, a mesmerizing trance, over me when we were together. I knew how to get a girl's phone number, a girl's address, how to romance my way out of being just a friend. I was no Romeo but I had been around the romantic block a time or two. But I could not solve Beatrijs. I could not crack the façade. I could not really think straight around her, not even straight enough to get her address or ask if we could meet again and arrange a time to do it. And because of that selfsame time or two around the romantic block, I thought I could read receptiveness and interest from a woman. I had received those unspoken vibrations from Beatrijs but, as in my first meeting with her, I got nowhere. I was enticed beyond enticement, frustrated beyond frustration and wondering what to do about Beatrijs Hagan. If I ever had the good fortune to see her again.

It was evening when I returned home, to be greeted by the steadfast, good-looking and domestically capable Camila Polanco. Camila, much to my chagrin, loved me or at least saw me as the man she wanted more than any other in her life. Almost every guy I know would be overjoyed to have a woman like Camila seeking his attention. But not me. I was busy chasing shadows and women I couldn't have.

Camila had food on the stove. The smells told me garlic, red beans and *licrio de molleja de pollo* – rice and chicken gizzards – were on the menu. I used to detest chicken gizzards when I was a child, the gamy, chewy meat too strong for a kid's palate. Since Camila first made them for me and told me only the dish's to-me-indecipherable Spanish name, I had become a fan. The meal was now a favorite, the green olives and cilantro a perfect counterpoint to the earthy organ meat. She made it often, I suspect operating on the theory that the way to a man's heart is putting his favorite food in his stomach.

It was late, an hour past my usual dinner time. I had spent the afternoon and early evening wandering the quiet side streets of Santo Domingo and pondering my relationship, or non-relationship, with Beatrijs Hagan. There were no conclusions reached, only questions, and I had arrived home tired and grouchy.

Undaunted by my mood, Camila placed a plate of food before me and sat. This usually signaled that she wanted to make small talk in the way that couples do, the kind of how-was-your-day-dear intimacy hoped by her to blossom into something more than our current employer-employee relationship. On this day, though, she seemed agitated and uneasy. 'Have you heard about the children, Henry?'

'The children? No. What children?'

'There was a bus crash, at the Presidente Peynado Bridge to the north of the city. A bus full of children, students at a rural school, returning from an excursion to a medical clinic in Santo Domingo, went into the water off the bridge over the Rio Isabela. There were many killed and more injured. Maria says there was an explosion, maybe a bomb.'

Camila's friend, Maria Matos, the cook for a widowed lawyer down the street, was prone to exaggeration. 'That sounds horrible,' I said. 'Are there any news reports?'

'The radio has been filled with reports since four this afternoon.'

'The food is wonderful, by the way, Camila. Could you turn the radio on, please?'

Pleased with the compliment, Camila was quick to dial in the small portable. The Spanish was pretty fast for me but I was able to keep up with the gist. An explosion, believed to be a bomb or a mine, had destroyed most of the front of the bus full of Catholic schoolgirls returning to a rural area north of the Rio Isabela. The bus was in motion at the time of the blast and its momentum carried it over the guard rail and into a deep pool of the river. Despite the efforts of passersby, fifteen children and the bus driver perished and another twenty children were injured. Many of the injured were not expected to live. A PND captain on the scene was interviewed and declared that the explosion was not an accident and was probably the work of Boschist elements which, despite the best efforts of the PND, had a strong presence in the countryside north of Santo Domingo. The police were making a sweep of the area for suspects even as operations to recover bodies of the victims went on. The radio station, like all public media, was in the control of the junta; the broadcast concluded with a stream of invective against the followers of Juan Bosch and a vow from the PND officer to hunt down and bring to justice all of the perpetrators of this most heinous of crimes.

Camila began to cry quietly across the table from me. I snapped off the radio and sat, my half-eaten dinner before me, listening to Camila sniffle and wondering if the turmoil I had survived in Cuba had now found its way to Santo Domingo.

TWENTY-SIX

I sat in the back of the police car and pondered if I should get a telephone. I hadn't had one since the line that went into my old detective agency, Mercado y Gore, back in 1957. After that, I had decided that phones were unnecessary, at best and, often, downright counterproductive. If someone wanted to reach me they would find a way to do it without a telephone. My kid sister wrote letters. My friends, acquaintances, creditors and lovers had been able to reach me for the last eight years through drop-in visits, telegrams, dunning letters, whispered imprecations and various other non-telephonic methods. On all the islands I had visited since Cuba, a telephone was not a part of my furniture. But now I reconsidered. If I'd had a phone, maybe Captain Salazar of the Policía Nacional Dominicana might not have sent the two officers in the front seat of the police car to sort-of arrest me for the second time in two days. He could have just called and asked me to come in, if I had a phone. And I wasn't really under arrest.

The two gendarmes in the front seat had done a convincing job of making me believe I *was* under arrest. They broke down my front door. They came into my bedroom with guns drawn and rousted me out of bed. They barely let me dress before leading me to the police car, although they dispensed with the handcuffs. That should have been my clue that Cosme was just extending an invitation to come to his Investigation and Identification Squad office for a friendly chat.

Cosme certainly considered it as evidence of his good intentions. 'I'm shocked, quite shocked, that you are offended, Henry,' he said, channeling Captain Renault's sentiment from *Casablanca*. I wondered if he'd seen the movie and decided he had not. If he had, he would've quoted Renault's lines precisely.

'Maybe I should get a phone so you could just call me to come in instead of having your boys kick down my door and drag me in by the hair,' I said.

'Capital idea, Henry. Coffee?'

'Well, now that I'm up,' I said.

Cosme poured two cups from a pot on his desk. 'The reason I asked you in—'

'Asked?'

'Why, yes, asked. Surely you didn't believe otherwise, did you, Henry?'

'Oh, my, no.'

'Good. The reason I asked you to come in is this horrific Peynado Bridge bombing.'

'What about it, Cosme?'

'Well, first, and singularly as a matter of formality, you understand, where were you yesterday afternoon?'

'Cosme, I am hurt that you would even entertain a thought that I had something to do with it.'

'As I say, a formality. Although being at the scene of the La Españolita bombing . . .'

'I was blown up in it, as I recall,' I said. 'I didn't light the fuse.'

Continuing on, Cosme said, 'And keeping company with the notorious Boschist leader, Jaime Vargas, would raise questions in the mind of one not as well acquainted with your sterling character as me.'

'Sterling character. I feel better already.'

'Good. Now, where were you?'

'If you must know, I was drinking beer. In the company of a lady.'

'Her name?'

'Can we not involve her, Cosme? I'm hoping to convince her to continue keeping company with me. A visit from the police asking about me might have a deterrent effect on that.'

'Fair enough. Where were you doing your drinking?'

'A joint without a name over on Calle Santa Rita.'

'I think I know the place,' Cosme said. 'The woman who runs it carries a bit of weight and has gray streaks in her hair, doesn't she? It's in a courtyard with a dry fountain.'

'That's the place.'

'Good. We'll check with the proprietress. Due diligence, you know.'

'I would expect nothing less, Cosme.'

'Now, let me have your thoughts on the crime.'

'It's a tragedy. Murdering children. That's an atrocity.'

'I was hoping for something more specific, Henry.'

'Such as?'

'Such as who you think did it.'

'I haven't given that much thought, Cosme.' And I hadn't. It was no business of mine.

'Was it Jaime Vargas?'

'He doesn't seem like the bombing type to me but how should I know?'

'You saw his operation.'

'I saw the inside of a dark warehouse. While tied to a chair. I didn't do a great deal of looking around.' I considered Cosme to be on a need-to-know basis, given his ambiguous status with the junta. And he certainly didn't need to know of my second encounter with the bartender-cum-opposition operative at the El Conde Gate riot.

'You saw nothing and no one?'

'It was dark.'

'What did you speak about?'

'He wanted to know how I knew his gray-headed old granny.'

'Really, Henry, I thought you could come up with a more clever story than that.'

'It's the truth, Cosme. And then we talked local politics. He asked after my views and I asked after his. Our discussion was inconclusive. And then I asked where I could find Jerry Pleasants.'

'Still him, eh?'

'Still him. Call it an obsession.'

'And nothing about the bombing or rebel operations.'

'Oh, they're rebels now? Just a few moments ago they were Boschists, supporters of the last duly-elected president of the Dominican Republic.'

'Why are you being so coy about all this, Henry?'

'Unexpected rides in police cars make me cantankerous.'

Cosme leaned forward across his desk. The cynical smirk he wore as his customary expression disappeared. 'Children were killed, Henry. Young schoolgirls on their way home from an excursion. If you know anything . . .'

'If I knew anything, I'd tell you, Cosme. Do I suspect something? Yeah. I suspect Jerry Pleasants blew up La Españolita. I have no real evidence of it. Hell, I don't even know if he's alive. And maybe it wasn't him; maybe it was Jaime Vargas. Did either of them have something to do with bombing the bridge? I don't think so, but the one thing I know is that I don't know anything. If I find out anything solid, you'll be the first to know.'

'Good. Now, you mentioned you were with a lady at the time of the bus bombing. It wasn't the enticing Miss Spicer from the US Embassy, was it?'

'No. It wasn't. You seem to have an abiding interest in Miss Spicer.'

Cosme cocked an eyebrow. 'I do, old friend. And I take it that, since you were with another, the field is clear with her as far as you are concerned.'

'The field is clear.' I felt a qualm as soon as I said that. Val had been in my bed in what seemed like only hours before. How could I cast her away so quickly? She had been very . . . accommodating of my needs while satisfying hers. The strong attraction I had for Beatrijs Hagan overrode gallantry. Besides, Val was a big girl. She knew the score. She'd recover. Maybe she'd recover more quickly in Cosme Salazar's arms. 'But, please, Cosme, treat her with respect.'

The smirk returned to Cosme's lips. 'Oh, I shall, Henry. I shall. Perhaps our little meeting has not been a total waste after all.' He practically licked his lips.

No one at PND headquarters, including Captain Salazar, offered me a ride home but the day was fine, with big, puffy clouds and a steady trade wind pushing the heat away, so I walked and thought. I thought about Jaime Vargas and why I had concealed information about him from Cosme Salazar. I thought about Valerie Spicer, about how much she seemed to care for me and what a heel I was for not reciprocating and tossing her to Cosme like used goods. I thought about Beatrijs Hagan, thought about the attraction she had for me, the mystery and self-assurance she exhibited, thought about her hair, her neck, her milk-white skin and her soft blue eyes.

And then her eyes were there, directly in front of mine. 'Henry, what a nice surprise. We seem to have mastered the chance encounter.'

I took her hand in mine. 'Hello, lovely Beatrijs.' Her hands were warm and soft. She didn't pull away but she cast her eyes down. 'What is it, Beatrijs?'

'The children. Those schoolgirls. You've heard about them?'

'Yes. It's horrible. A tragedy.'

'They are mine.' She raised her eyes to mine. 'I should have been with them but there was not room on the bus for another chaperone.

The teachers, we all drew lots to see who would get the afternoon off. It was me. It was God's will that I was not on the bus. God's will that so many innocents were killed and maimed and I was spared.'

We stood in the street, hand in hand, facing each other and didn't speak for a long minute. Then I said, 'It wasn't God's will. Someone planted a bomb.'

'The police told me that. I went there, to the place where it happened. They said that the supporters of Juan Bosch had planted the bomb, detonating it when the bus drove over it, on purpose. To kill the children.' Her fair eyes flashed with anger for the first time since I'd met her, like a thunderstorm on the horizon of an otherwise perfect day.

'There are evil people in this world,' I said.

'It was not them, the Boschists. I know it was not them. Our school is north of the Rio Isabela. The area is poor. The people there were overjoyed by the election of Juan Bosch. For the first time in their lives, they felt as if they mattered, felt as if they had a voice in their own destiny. They still hope for his return. Some now believe that force should be met with force, that the junta should be forcibly removed. But even those who believe in force would never engage in random violence and would certainly never harm their own children. So, yes, Henry, there are evil people in the world. But those the police are blaming are not the evil ones.'

She had fire in her soul. When she mentioned that the children who had been killed were hers, I had expected tears to follow. But none had. I wanted to explain to her that the police would never be convinced to actually investigate who had killed the children. Blaming it on the followers of Bosch fulfilled the primary police mission under the junta to prop up Wessin y Wessin and his henchmen and to tear down the Bosch Constitutionalists. If the deaths of a few children went without proper investigation in the process, it was considered an unfortunate but small price to pay. I wanted to explain this to Beatrijs as we stood hand in hand. She didn't give me the chance.

'The truth must come out, Henry,' Beatrijs said. 'Those dear children sit now at the right hand of our Lord and there is little beyond prayer we can do for them. We can provide solace to their families. I and the other teachers will do that. Someone, though, must find out who did this, if the police will not. That someone is you, Henry.' Beatrijs delivered this last line with a certitude not to be questioned. It was as if she'd declared a mission from God for me.

God was not someone who had figured prominently, or even peripherally, in my life of recent. I have experienced my share of pain and misfortune – the death of my parents and the woman I loved, the loss of many others in Cuba because of actions I put in motion. I had killed, which, for those of you who have not done it, brings its own reward of sleepless nights and soul-searching. But God had made no appearance in any of those instances.

Now, though, Beatrijs's declaration of what I was to do seemed somehow to have come from the Almighty. At least, I was left with that impression. So, instead of objecting, instead of explaining to Beatrijs that I didn't have the skills, that I wasn't the man for the job or that I just plain didn't want to do it, like a damn fool I said, 'I can do that.' That response got me a hug, a peck on the cheek and an address for Beatrijs in a village that I had never been to. I promised I would keep her updated on important developments as they occurred. We agreed to meet in two days at the beer garden on Calle Santa Rita. We parted, both solemn, Beatrijs with her loss and I with my fool's mission.

What had I gotten myself into?

TWENTY-SEVEN

I closed the door to my house and leaned back against it, listening. Silence, save for the calls of a flock of Antillean grackles in a tree down the street. No Camila. No Val. I needed the peace of an evening alone, time to decompress and absorb the events of the recent days. I needed some perspective.

Camila had left me a supper of *riki taki* sandwiches in the fridge. It was early for dinner, but I was famished as my wanderings, forced and unforced, had not allowed time for anything to eat since dinner the night before. The burst of flavor from the vinegary tomato, cabbage and adobo topping the ground beef between the pressed bread revived me. I ate with gusto, alternating savory bites with sips of Presidente. For a moment, all seemed right with the world.

Until a strong hand clasped over my mouth from behind. I tried to bite but my mouth was full. I twisted in my seat, bringing my right arm up as I did.

'Señor Gore, it is me, Jaime,' a voice said in a loud whisper, just as I broke the grip over my mouth. Food spewed across the table.

I spun to face Jaime. 'What the hell?'

'I am sorry, Señor Gore. I did not want you to cry out when I approached you.' Jaime rubbed his arm where I had broken his grip.

'Well, I didn't cry out, I'll give you that. There are places in this world where you'd have a bullet in you now, though. I guess that would've made too much noise, too. Good thing I don't have a gun.'

'I am sorry. I needed to see you.'

'You could try knocking on the front door. I have been known to open it without violence to the person knocking.'

'I could not linger on the street. The police are after me.'

'Let me guess. The bombing on the Peynado Bridge. They've already dragged me in and explained that it was a Boschist plot. I was just too American and too ambiguous in my Bosch affiliations to arrest out of hand.'

'The PND have come in force to Gualey, searching for me and any other known Constitutionalists. I was able to hide at *mi abuela*'s house.'

'That place isn't big enough to hide a peanut from a squirrel.'

'*Mi abuela* made a special place in the roof rafters for me.'

'Every fugitive should have such a granny.' Jaime gave me a quizzical look. I guess the word fugitive was too much for his otherwise stellar bilingual vocabulary. 'Forget it, Jaime. Why are you risking your neck to see me?'

'The streets are a powder keg, about to blow up,' Jaime said. 'The people are angry. They want justice for the children who died and for those who were hurt. They want the PND to find the person who did this terrible crime, have him tried and made to answer. But the PND doesn't search for the true offender. Instead, they use the crime as a cudgel against the Constitutionalists. If they continue to do this, the real villain will go free and we will have more riots like the one at the El Conde Gate. Many will die needlessly.'

'If you expect me to talk to the police and change their minds, you're living in a fantasy world. I don't have that kind of influence and the cops don't have the inclination to look for suspects who aren't enemies of the regime.'

'I don't expect you to influence the higher ups of the PND to refocus their investigation, though you do sit down to lunch with them,' Jaime said.

'You don't miss a trick, Jaime. How . . .?' I said.

'Let us say that there are special waiters serving at El Jaragua when the junta has lunch there. As a result, we know how little, and how much, influence you have. So little that you cannot force them to do justice but just enough that they cannot ignore you if you present them with the true perpetrator.'

'You want me to dig up the bad guy and drop him in their laps?'

'In a manner they cannot ignore.'

'Even if it's Jerry Pleasants?' Jerry had saved Jaime and I wanted to be sure.

'You believe it is him, too?' Jaime said.

I gave a slow nod and he said, '*Si.*'

'You know, Jaime, you're the second person to ask me to do that this afternoon.'

'And were you persuaded by the other person?'

'To your benefit, yes. And it's a good thing for you. If it was just you, the answer might have been no.'

'I congratulate the other for their influence on you. My colleagues and I will be happy to ride on the coat-tails of that individual.'

'"Ride the coat-tails." Very good, Jaime. We'll make a Yankee of you yet. All right, I'll let you ride the coat-tails. And I assume I'll have your information and help whenever needed.'

'Of course.'

'And to get in touch with you, still El Pâjaro?'

'Of course.'

'It's almost dark. It should be safe for you now.'

'Yes, Señor Gore. And thank you.'

He was out the door and into the twilight. The rest of the evening passed without any further visitors. My time for decompression was spent, instead, on planning my investigation for my two taskmasters.

TWENTY-EIGHT

'**D**o you even own a decent suit, Henry?' Val rifled through the under-sized closet that held all the clothing I owned. Since she had achieved admission to my bed, she assumed she also had an entry pass to my closet.

'I thought they were all decent. Most of them fit pretty well. Most of them are somewhat clean. With the touch of an iron on the pants and a brush down, they're all serviceable.'

I had had the morning to ponder how to learn who had bombed the Peynado Bridge. I'd thought about some Bosch connections I could tap, a shady expat or two I'd met who might know someone who knew someone, a crooked politician I had turned informant in my days as Juan Bosch's law enforcement consultant. I planned to start that afternoon. Then Val invaded.

'This is an embassy event, Henry. You just can't stroll in wearing a shabby suit.'

'I thought you said it was, and I quote, "a small gathering for a friend who has taken a new job back home."?'

'The friend is the French cultural attaché. Andre has served his time here. He's been called back to Paris, to a promotion in the ministry.'

'You said a garden party.'

'It is. At the French Embassy. All the attachés will be there. And the French ambassador and chargé d'affaires, of course. And spouses and significant others.'

'Well, if it's a garden party in this heat, any suit will look like a wilted lily in fifteen minutes.'

'Ah, at last. This will have to do.' Val pulled out a blue-striped seersucker suit. It had a stain on its front that the lapel mostly hid, that she didn't notice. Looking over her shoulder in my closet, I had to agree that it was the best choice.

'And this dark blue tie,' she said, choosing between the blue, brown and black one hanging on a wire coat hanger. 'Put it on after you shave and let's go or we'll be late.'

Minutes later, we were on our way in Val's embassy Ford. The day was hot and the seersucker was already limp. Val was doing her best Doris Day in a yellow sundress with blue *lunares* that matched the color of her eyes. It was a certainty that she and the dress would never wilt in the blistering sun.

We met this Andre character first thing. He was dressed to the nines. He spoke in French to Val, gave my hand a perfunctory shake and moved on. I couldn't figure if he was one of Val's previous conquests, a fellow spy, a homo or all three. It didn't matter. Val introduced me around, made some small talk with the right people and then had me off to a shaded corner of the embassy garden. A waiter brought champagne on a tray. It was all so civilized. I felt I was there for a reason. Finding out the reason didn't take long.

'Have you heard about that horrible bombing with the children?' Val stared off across the garden as she asked, gazing out on the knots of beautiful people and circulating waiters standing on the lush lawn seeming as if they had never heard of bombings, or dead children, or any other unpleasantness.

'Appalling that a human being would do that. Sick,' I said.

'Who did it?' Val's question had a light tone, like 'who wrote that book, who did that painting?' Not like 'who committed that atrocity?'

'The PND said it was the Constitutionalists.'

'Do you believe that?'

'These days I don't know what to believe. Do you believe it?'

Val dodged on her personal beliefs. 'The word at the embassy is that the junta might have done it, so that Wessin y Wessin could pin the blame on the Constitutionalists.'

'Why do that?' I asked.

'It gives Wessin y Wessin's SIM and the PND an excuse to crack down on the Boschists. Who is going to say they don't want child-killing terrorists brought to justice?' Val said. 'State thinks it's a ploy, a way for the junta to use the kids' deaths to its own ends.'

'Anything solid on that?' I thought I might as well use this opportunity to get what information I could. Maybe Val had something that would give me a start on my investigation for Beatrijs and Jaime. Besides, I had a sneaking feeling Val was about to ask me for something.

'Nothing,' she said.

'You don't have any assets in town with the real scoop?'

'A cultural attaché doesn't have assets, Henry.' Val stared straight ahead, a half smile on her lips. She enjoyed telling some guy she was trying to make one of her assets that she had no assets. 'Do you have anything on that?'

'Is that why we're here, Val? So you can find out what I have on the bombing?'

'No, Henry, that's not why we're here. I wanted us to have a pleasant time. I wanted to give you a look into my world. I wanted to show you off to some of my friends. I wanted to spend some time with you where we aren't in the sack, despite my abiding need to rip your clothes off and fuck you every time I lay eyes on you and despite feeling that way right now. So, no, we're not here for me to get information from you.'

'Val, I'm sorry . . .' I began.

'I know you don't have information. If you did, you would have gone to the PND with it, probably to your friend Salazar. And if he did nothing with it, you probably would have brought it to me, to pass on through other channels, to bring pressure to bear on the junta to do the right thing. So I'm not here with you for information on the bombing. I'm here for those things I just told you. And I'm here to do my job. I'm here to recruit you. So there's no need to say you are sorry.'

That took a minute to absorb. Then I said, 'What are you, Val? CIA? DIA? Some other set of initials I'm not even cleared to know?'

'Do the initials matter, Henry?'

'No, I guess not.'

'I hear the disappointment in your voice,' Val said. 'Just understand that everything I've said to you here is the truth. Everything. But I have a job. America has a need. The Kennedy administration supported the elections here, made sure they were free and fair. After the election of Juan Bosch, America sent aid and support to his administration. When the junta deposed him, we gave him safe asylum in Puerto Rico. We would like to see him come back. But he has to get here on his own. After the Bay of Pigs, my bosses are gun-shy about direct interference. But they're not gun-shy about the truth and helping true information into the light of day. They think the junta is behind the bombing and the Constitutionalists are being scapegoated. All they want is for the truth to come out.'

'So you want to recruit me for some alphabet agency to find the truth about the bombing?'

'Yes. Just the truth. We think the truth is that the junta is responsible.'

'Why me?'

'Do I need to recite your credentials for you, lover? OK. You've been on the ground here in Santo Domingo longer than any of our other assets, few that they are. You've been in the business before, trained by Uncle Sam. You have background as an investigator, in the Air Force, and in your private eye business in Havana. You have a knack for getting into places you shouldn't be able to get into – Batista's SIM, the Cuban Directorio Revolucionario, Castro's rebels. You have Boschist connections but you also have connections in the PND which might be sources for this mission. And you have a need.'

'A need? A need for what?'

'You need to return to the United States of America. I would say that you *want* to return but it's really much stronger than that. You've been away for nine years, bouncing around the Caribbean and you're desperate to get home to country and family. Don't deny it. But you have a problem, dear one. You helped Fidel Castro, America's biggest enemy in the hemisphere, to get where he is today. You fought with him, entered Havana in triumph with him and served as a minor player in his government.'

'All before he was an enemy of America.'

'Maybe. Maybe he wasn't a communist then but he certainly was short months after those events and he was one when he sent you packing with a hefty paycheck, when people a lot more loyal to him were repaid with a bullet. This has caused the State Department, in its wisdom, to label you with a scarlet "C". Rightly or wrongly, Uncle Sam considers you a communist and you're never coming home to the US as long as that's in your files. You need to make that label disappear. You doing this for Uncle Sam helps to reestablish your loyalty to the US. It's your ticket home. And, who knows, if this goes right maybe my next posting will be back to Foggy Bottom. I'm due for a stint in the States. We could continue what we've started here.'

Val had been looking out across the flawless lawn of the French Embassy as she spoke but she turned to me when she said the last. There was a look in her eyes different from the saucy challenge or the pleasure-seeking hunger I had seen there before. It might have been love. Or a practiced imitation of love. Either way, I was wary.

I did not love Val. After meeting Beatrijs, I understood this. But right then, at that moment, Val wasn't asking me for love. She was asking me to do what I had already committed to two other people to do. Each of them had their own reasons for asking me, but the mission, if it could be called that, was the same. And if I said yes to Val, if I committed to do nothing more than I had already committed to do, I might be able to remove the scarlet letter that had followed me from island to island around the Caribbean for almost a decade. I might be able to go home.

'All right, Val. I'll do it.'

She brightened and kissed me. 'Let's get out of here, Henry.'

TWENTY-NINE

The scene of the crime is where all investigations, good or bad, successful or botched, genuine or sham, start. That is the really easy part which those who are not professional investigators don't understand – that every investigation has the same beginning and the same end. Visit the scene to start. Capture the guilty party to end. And let the facts fill in the middle. Congratulations. You are now a graduate of the Henry Gore School of Investigative Technique.

I took a cab out to the Presidente Peynado Bridge first thing in the morning, hoping to get a look at the scene before the heat of the day. When I arrived, I realized missing the heat of the day was not a possibility, even if I got there at dawn, dusk or the middle of the night. The Rio Isabela shimmered languor and humidity upward from its surface. There was deep green jungle on each end of the bridge, a perfect hiding place from which to watch and time a detonation. The bridge itself was remarkably intact, with just a few planks from the wooden driving surface disrupted and the iron skeleton of the structure fully intact. Whoever had set the charges was experienced. They had made sure the bridge wouldn't be significantly harmed and that the force of the blast was directed upward for the maximum effect on the bus full of children. So, the bomber was both experienced and without a soul or a heart. Was that Jerry? I really couldn't tell. Was he experienced with explosives? Nothing I knew about him gave me a clue. Could he be that cold? Even after my time with him, I couldn't say one way or the other.

The place was crawling with cops. PND cars blocked the bridge entrance on both sides of the river. I had my cab drop me a couple hundred yards back from the action, figuring if the cab drove all the way to the roadblock it would just get sent away and I would only get a quick look. By walking in, I could eyeball the place during my leisurely stroll up to the barricade before I was turned back.

I needn't have bothered. When I approached, all eyes were focused on the gray-green waters of the Rio Isabela. With a couple ragged tow trucks and some cables and winches attached to two towering mahogany trees on the south bank, the authorities were pulling the bus out. The front of the bus where the driver had sat was obliterated, a tangle of twisted metal. The windows were broken; as the wreck was dragged up the bank, water flowed out at eye level, carrying with it books, a stuffed toy, a torn skirt from a school uniform. The police had not bothered to chase the locals away. When the vehicle surfaced, a cry of anguish, an animal wail of grief, rose from the massed peasants.

'I don't see you for months, Henry, and now I see you more than both the girl who believes she is my fiancée and the girl with whom I am cheating on the girl who believes she is my fiancée.' Cosme Salazar stood at the corner of a police car which formed part of the barricade. 'We should have dispersed the crowd before we pulled the bus out.'

'I'm surprised you didn't. This isn't your first rodeo, Cosme.'

'I am not in charge of the scene. My suggestion was overridden.'

'General Vazquez himself on the case?'

'For today. To have his photograph taken directing the operation. To make sure that the crowds are not dispersed and the people are inflamed against the Boschists who perpetrated this atrocity.'

'You already caught the guys?'

'Of course not. But the PND knows that the guys, as you call them, should be Boschists.'

'Does the PND that knows this include you, Cosme?'

Cosme made a sour face but didn't answer, turning back to the spectacle. The bus was fully out, perched on the muddy bank, with PND officers crawling over it, shouting instructions and pulling away bits and pieces of the devastated vehicle.

'Your crime scene is getting contaminated, Cosme,' I observed.

'It doesn't matter.' Cosme's mien was one of dejection. He knew he was participating in a charade, a kabuki theater version of a real investigation. The policeman in him rebelled at the thought.

'Captain Salazar, what is this man doing here?' Major General Leandro 'Bullito' Vazquez approached us from the river, his leather boots muddy and the cuffs of his uniform pants stained. 'He is not to be here. Have him removed. Immediately.'

'A cheerful good morning to you, too, General Vazquez,' I said.

Bullito, red-faced from anger or the steep climb up the riverbank, said, 'You are still disrespectful, Señor Gore. I do not like you. You stick your nose in where you do not belong. I warn you, do not go near this investigation. This is a matter of national importance. Interfere and you will be deported. Across the border to Haiti, which is not a very nice place these days.'

'I wouldn't think of interfering with your investigation, General. And I use that term in its loosest sense,' I said, leaving him to figure out if I was referring to his investigation or his general officer rank.

A tiny body was brought out of the mangled bus, prompting another chorus of keening from the onlookers. It set General Vazquez off. 'Remove him and arrest him if he returns, Captain Salazar,' he sputtered.

'*Si, mi general.*' Cosme snapped to attention. 'I will remove him personally. Señor Gore, you will come with me.'

Cosme led me to an unmarked PND Chevy. As we drove away, I said, 'So the fix is in. Are you even allowed to participate?'

'No, Henry. We were here at the start but my entire unit has been removed from the investigation. We are present today only for crowd control.'

'Too bad. We could have worked together. I saw some interesting things in just the short time I was there. The way the blast was set up, so it didn't injure the bridge and pushed upward into the bus. It had to be some kind of a shaped charge, not just some sticks of TNT. And to make whatever explosive that was used to do that, means it wasn't some amateur with a bomb-making cookbook. It had to be a pro.'

'C-4.' Cosme said.

'What?'

'You are right. The explosive used was not TNT. It was C-4.'

'The same explosive as in the La Españolita bombing,' I said. 'Who has C-4 in Santo Domingo?'

'No one that I know of. None of our military branches uses it. Civilian mining and engineering operations use TNT. It is what they are used to. There is no reason for C-4 to be anywhere in the Dominican Republic.'

'But it is here. Can you put some of your boys on locating it, Cosme?'

Captain Salazar heaved a dejected sigh. 'Not really, Henry. There are many loyal to the junta in my unit, some overtly and some, I suspect, more quietly so. It is difficult for me to know who I can trust. I am certain, though, that if I sent officers out in the field with orders to find where the C-4 came from, word will make its way back to General Vazquez. And he would not be pleased. I cannot risk it. I am sorry.'

'That's all right, Cosme. I understand.' And I did understand. Cosme wouldn't risk his rank, his position, his cushy, womanizing lifestyle, on such a thing as an overt display of principle. Not for some gringo, no matter how well he liked me. Not for a bus load of dead schoolgirls, no matter how much he was repulsed and horrified that someone would do that to children for political gain. That was what the junta, what Batista and Castro and people like them counted on and how they thrived.

'I guess I'll just have to find the source myself,' I said.

THIRTY

P olitics in the Caribbean basin in this enlightened year of 1965 is a strange mix of past and present. For the present, there is a new wave of progressive politicians who believe in service to their homeland, policies to benefit their constituents and a new approach to solving the problems of their countries and the region. These Juan Boschs seem determined to be the future.

In the past and lingering on into today, many of those in government were in it for themselves. They lined their pockets while claiming to be patriots. They would bounce into power on the wings of a coup or a crooked election, an army sergeant or a minor municipal official one day and, with the right palms greased and a few rifles standing behind them, *El Jefe* the next. This system bred a whole host of lesser officials who didn't aspire to be *El Jefe* but were content to have their own minor fiefdom where they could comfortably engage in petty graft, small fish in the larger pond, who weathered regime change with aplomb, their cash flows uninterrupted, displaying absolute loyalty to the guy at the top and a willingness to shift that loyalty to the next top dog on the turn of a dime.

Porfírio Melo was one of those lesser fish. His nickname, Grasso, reflected both his state of hygiene – greasy, looking as if he never bathed or washed his long black hair – and his dealings – slippery, shady and skimming some of the fat from every transaction falling within his purview. His ostensible business was wholesaling cocoa. He operated from a warehouse filled with bags of unprocessed beans. Trucks ferried beans in and out all day. Rumor had it that the trucks also ferried other items – untaxed cigarettes, marijuana and looted Incan and Mayan antiquities. If the rumors were true, Grasso was good at not being caught. He had never even been charged. A possible reason for this was that successive regimes, beginning with the dictator Trujillo, had appointed him to a variety of minor port inspector and customs jobs. Even Juan Bosch had followed the pattern, not wanting to upset the apple cart. Another reason was that Grasso held tight political control over a key industrial area of

Santo Domingo. When the strong man of the minute felt the need, due to international political pressure or ego, to hold an election, Grasso was able to deliver votes by the bushel, sometimes by stuffing literal bushels of ballots into the voting locations he controlled. In short, he was connected. He knew where all the bodies were buried in Santo Domingo. If anyone knew how the C-4 that had blown up the La Españolita and the Peynado Bridge had found its way into the country, it would be him.

'Henry Gore, are you still in Santo Domingo?' Grasso greeted me when I knocked on the door of his dingy office at the back of his warehouse. The place smelled of cocoa, the only attractive feature of meeting with Grasso. I had met with him many times. When I was consulting on police corruption for the Bosch administration, Grasso had been only too happy to rat out a bevy of corrupt cops for a price. Now those same cops were back with the PND but the slippery Grasso remained untouched.

'Juan Bosch left but I stayed,' I said.

'And the junta hasn't pitched you out? Or into the sea?'

'I am of too little consequence to be noticed, Porfírio.'

'Ha! Beware the midnight knock on your door, Henry. Is there something I can sell you? Cocoa? Information? Some works of art, perhaps?' Grasso was never subtle.

'Information. But I cannot afford to buy.'

'Information is the most dear commodity I sell. Still, Henry, you have been a good customer in the past. Perhaps you are entitled to a *regalo de promoción*, how do you say, a freebie? Just remember me when Bosch returns. Now, what information do you seek?'

'I need to know who could bring in C-4 to Santo Domingo.'

'C-4? The explosive?'

'Right. It was used in the bombing of the Peynado Bridge.'

'Those children.' Grasso's eyes brimmed with tears. *I'll be damned, he did have a heart.*

'I'm trying to find who killed them, Porfírio.'

'I do not know anything about the bombing, Henry, or I would have told the PND. For free. As for who might have C-4 or be able to get it, there is a man. An American. He claims to sell arms. He approached me some time ago to broker through me. I told him that I was not interested. I sell many things but I do not sell death. His name is McCarthy.'

'Does he have a first name?'

'McCarthy. His first, last and only name, as far as anyone knows.'

'Where do I find him?'

'He frequents Club El Pulpo. Ask German, the bartender there. Tell him that I sent you.'

'*Gracias*, Porfírio. I owe you.'

'You can make it up in the next regime.'

THIRTY-ONE

Club El Pulpo was new to me. I had to ask a cabbie where it was. Turns out I had been by it dozens of times on the shoreline drive along Avenida George Washington. It was well hidden in a plain storefront, its windows painted black. A small placard beside the door was the only clue to its location. It looked like a private club. I pondered how to talk my way in but when I approached, the door was flung open by a mini-skirted woman with a beehive hairdo. A tsunami of pop music, played badly, washed over me from inside. The woman asked no questions; she was, I guess, just there to open the door.

I stepped inside. The air was close; there seemed to be no ventilation. The walls were all painted black like the windows. The only relief to the nightmare noir was a red neon octopus on the far wall, above the bar. There were tables arrayed around a wooden dance floor, with smartly dressed Dominicans and expats seated at the tables and gyrating on the boards. I found the source of the badly played music – a Mexican mariachi band just finishing up 'I Want to Hold Your Hand' segued into 'Oh, Pretty Woman'. They played both tunes with a mariachi flair that butchered the music. The dancers and the couples at the tables didn't seem to care.

I made my way to the bar presided over by German. His hair was cut in a Beatles mop-top, which he jounced to the beat of the bad mariachi-rock.

'*Presidente, por favor,*' I ordered. There were no other patrons at the bar. German decided to chat me up, hoping to practice his English and enhance his tip.

'You like the Beatles, man?' he said.

'Sure. I like all the British invasion stuff. The Hollies, the Stones, the Zombies, Yardbirds.'

'"I Can't Get No Satisfaction" *es bueno.*'

German and I bonded over music. I had a second Presidente and placed a portrait of Andrew Jackson on the bar. 'If you can point me to McCarthy, you can keep the change,' I said.

German gestured without hesitation to a table in the corner, causing me to question whether I could have gotten away with laying a ten-spot on the bar instead of the dub. Too late, I told myself and made my way over to the mononymous McCarthy.

He was wearing a purple velvet jacket, white T-shirt and white pants despite the heat generated by all the dancers. As I approached, he held open the jacket to show me the butt end of a Colt 1911 in a shoulder holster. I continued to walk up to the table.

'What do you want, pilgrim?' McCarthy tried to sound as menacing as his gun appeared but his voice squeaked like a rodent and he couldn't carry it off.

'Just some friendly conversation, Mr McCarthy.'

'It's just McCarthy. No mister. And I ain't friendly and I don't like conversation.'

'OK, let me try it this way,' I said. 'Did you hear about that bus full of little girls that got blown up?'

'Who ain't? Yer point?'

'My point is that what blew the bus up was a block of C-4.'

'You some kind of a cop?'

'No.'

'What's yer interest?'

'The kids' teacher asked me to find out who killed her students.'

'Weren't me.'

'I know. But you sold the C-4 to the man who did it, didn't you?'

'You expect me to answer that?'

'How about you do and I walk out the door and forget we ever had this heartfelt talk?'

'How 'bout I plug you where you stand and German and I drag yer carcass out to the back alley and feed it to the rats.'

'That would be noisy and there are all these people around. Do you think they wouldn't notice? I know, it's dark in here and that mariachi band is playing but it ain't that dark and the band is just bad, not loud. Lots of witnesses here and I am an American. The embassy would raise a stink and the PND would chase you down.'

'OK. Yer persistent. C-4 ain't illegal to sell here. Just tough to get. What if I told you I didn't know who I sold it to?'

'I would find that hard to believe.'

'Believe it. I'll tell you everything, because it's kids and then yer gone and never come back. I didn't know it was gonna hurt kids or I never would've sold it to that slug.'

'You tell me everything straight, you'll never see me again,' I said.

'And my name stays out of it?'

'Your name stays out of it. How did you sell C-4 to a guy without knowing who it was?'

McCarthy kicked a chair out from under the table. 'Here. Sit.'

I sat.

'One day a month ago, German comes to me with an envelope. Says a street kid brought it in for me. German's no fool. He asked the kid what the one give it to him looked like. Gave the kid ten centavos. The kid described another kid, which could've been any street kid. So I read the note in the envelope. Says the one writing the note wants C-4, two kilos of it. I would've thought he was some crackpot but the note was full of technical information on remote detonators to go with the explosives. The guy knew his stuff.'

'Guy?'

'I just use the word to describe a person. The note was signed "X". Coulda been a man or a woman.'

'OK, go on.'

'I don't have the stuff but I can get it. So I write that on the back of the note and give it back to the kid. I also write on the price, which I set damn high because it's going to come from Haiti and it's going to cost me a pretty penny to get it. The next day, another kid, street kid again, comes in. This kid's got a sack of American greenbacks, all different denominations but it adds up to the number I'd given on the note back to Mr X. I asked this kid who gave him the sack to deliver. Again it's another street kid who the first kid don't know. Then I ask him why he didn't just steal the sack. Kid says the one that give him the sack told him he'd be followed to see that he done what he was supposed to do. And he'd be killed if he didn't do as he was told. Turns out the bag had been passed kid to kid, six kids total, before it was delivered to me. I'm guessing even if you find one or two of the kids, you'll never get back to the one who actually met Mr X.'

'Where can I find one of those kids?' I asked.

'Hell if I know. On the street, I guess. Couldn't describe either of the two who came in here. They were just street kids, ya know?'

I knew. I remembered Benny from my Havana days. Like all street kids, he seemed to be invisible until I got to know him. Until I was ready to lay down my life for him.

'They didn't say anything about this Mr X? That he spoke a certain way? What he looked like? Where they met him?'

'In my business, you don't ask, pilgrim. In my business, the less you know about the customer beyond that he can pay, the better. Wait . . . there is one thing. The kid that brought the first note, he said the kid that give it to him said the one sending the note was a gringo.'

'An American?'

'Maybe. Maybe a Brit. Maybe a Frog. You know, to them we all look alike.'

'And you're not sure, man or woman?'

'Gringo is all I got.'

I picked at McCarthy a little more, trying to jar his memory to get something on the mysterious gringo. Finally, he said, 'You make my ass tired, pilgrim. I told you all I know. We have a deal. I done my part. Now you do yours. Scram.'

I scrammed. The gringo had to be Jerry, I thought. Or maybe not.

THIRTY-TWO

The late-day quiet of the beer garden in the sunny courtyard off Calle Santa Rita was a welcome contrast to the jarring noise and grim darkness of Club El Pulpo. The lovely face and warm greeting of Beatrijs Hagan was a far cry from the unfriendly McCarthy.

When I arrived, Beatrijs was already seated, beer in hand. 'Right on time,' she said, smiling.

'I was a Boy Scout,' I said. 'Besides teaching me to be trustworthy, loyal, helpful, friendly, courteous, kind, obedient, cheerful, thrifty, brave, clean and reverent, my scoutmaster added his own personal favorite – prompt.'

'And are you all those other things, too, Henry?'

'Off and on. Less regularly than I want to admit.' I wanted to touch her hair, to hold her hand, to wrap my arms around her.

The salt-and-pepper-haired proprietress came over and took my order for a Presidente. When she turned away, I put my hand on Beatrijs's. I did it then, so the proprietress wouldn't see my humiliation if Beatrijs rejected me. But Beatrijs didn't. She curled her fingers around mine. The sun, already fading, seemed to brighten momentarily. My head swam.

'You make me happy, Henry, when there is so much to be sad about.'

I thought she meant the children dying, though she didn't say. So, being a decent investigator and an awkward romancer, I said, 'I have a lead on the bomber.'

Her smile disappeared, though thankfully, she didn't withdraw her hand from mine. 'What is it?' she asked.

'I found the guy who sold the bomber the explosives. The one who did this to the children is a gringo.'

'An American? Why would an American do that?'

'An Anglo. Maybe an American or a Brit or some other European. And I don't know why they would do that. I can't even imagine why.' While I thought the mysterious gringo might be Jerry Pleasants,

I still didn't have enough to be sure. I decided not to mention him to Beatrijs yet.

'Do you think you can find him?'

'It may not be a "him". The man who gave me the information didn't know. I don't know if I can find him or her. I have no particulars other than it's a gringo who has experience with explosives. No name, no physical description, no address or location. And no hint at the bomber's motivation.'

'And the police? Am I right about them not caring?'

'The PND has already decided the Constitutionalists are responsible. I've got a cop friend who gave me a little information, but he can't, or won't, do more. I can go back to him to get verification of facts but I can't count on his help. I'm at a dead end without some kind of a lucky break. Investigation is frustrating sometimes.'

Disappointment made a fleeting trip across Beatrijs's captivating face. It hurt because her disappointment was with me. 'What can we do from here?' she said.

I had not been thinking in terms of 'we' for this investigation. I was used to flying solo. I had done it in the Air Force OSI. I had essentially worked alone as a private investigator in Havana; my partner, Moncho Mercado, had an abiding distaste for work. Now, though, it occurred to me that Beatrijs could help.

'Would the parents of your kids help us?' I asked.

'They are in mourning now. They are shattered with the loss. But the men especially are frustrated with the PND and would be willing to help. What do you want them to do?'

'My next step would normally be to knock on some doors and ask if anyone had seen a gringo in the area of the explosion. It's grinding work, tedious and tiring. Do you think some of the men could ask around? I'm sure they'll do better than a stranger like me and if we get several of them to do it, the canvass will go more quickly.'

'I'm sure they will do it. I'll ask tonight.' She set her shoulders, resolute.

'Good,' I said. Then: 'Beatrijs, you've never cried about the children. Not that I've seen.'

'I've cried. The first night. But I understand that the children are safe now, safer than they ever were in life. I know that they will be best helped by prayer, not tears. And their loved ones will be helped to heal by the passage of time and the meting out of justice to the one who committed this terrible crime. I do what I do to make a difference in people's lives, Henry. I wanted to make a difference in the children's lives by giving them an education. That opportunity is gone but I can still make a difference in their families' lives by giving them justice. The time for tears has passed.'

I felt strengthened by what Beatrijs said. And I was attracted to her more so for her strength. On impulse I leaned across the table and kissed her, lightly, on the lips. She responded tenderly, timidly, reacting in a way that said she enjoyed the kiss and yet conveying reluctance. I couldn't understand why.

We each leaned back and smiled at the other. There was a wanting, a desire, each of us felt and there was a barrier, too. I couldn't place it, couldn't fathom what my heart was telling me, what Beatrijs was telling me.

I kissed her again. She melted into me, my hands in her hair, hers caressing my neck. And then her hands were pushing gently against my chest, separating us.

'Henry, I can't.'

'Why, Beatrijs? I want you. You want me.'

'It's not that simple, Henry.'

'Is it that other guy? What kind of a hold does he have on you? I can tell the way you feel about us. Don't let him stand in the way of our happiness.'

'I'm . . . confused. I made a commitment. I cannot just walk away.'

'You're not married, are you?'

Beatrijs blushed. 'No, Henry. I'm not married.'

'Then no commitment stands between us.'

'I can't say that, Henry.'

'I'm confused, Beatrijs.'

'Trust me. I need some time to think. Right now, tonight, it's best that we . . . stop. I'll talk to the children's parents and have them canvass the neighborhood. Let's meet in a couple days at the children's school. It's on the road north from the Peynado Bridge. You can see where I work and I'm sure I'll have any information by then.'

'Beatrijs . . .' I touched her cheek.

She cast her eyes downward. 'You had better go, Henry.'

I had been told to scram for the second time today. It hurt more than the first but I scrammed.

THIRTY-THREE

'It can't be a gringo, Henry, whether it's Jerry Pleasants or some other one.' Valerie Spicer sat across the white tablecloth from me, looking polished and professional in an emerald green Dior suit and matching pillbox hat. She had come to my house straight-away from work and found, she said, Camila sniffling and sneezing over the supper she was preparing. She sent Camila home – to rest, she said – and tossed out the mostly-prepared meal to prevent us from catching the housekeeper's cold. With nothing to eat, Val informed me that we were going to a place where all the diplomatic corps went. Like seemingly all the places to get a meal in Santo Domingo, it had no name but in keeping with the image necessary to serve the embassy trade, the waiters were an unlikely combination of officious and fawning.

'All I know is that's the word. Not much to go on.'

Raul, our waiter, hovered an uncomfortable arm's length away, listening to every word. I ordered an after-dinner rum to get him to leave for a few moments. 'Do all you diplomats let the stiffs in this place listen to all your conversations?'

'They don't listen, Henry. They're trained not to.'

Yeah, I thought, and I'm Mick Jagger. 'Well, the only info I've turned up is that the bomber is a gringo and that's what I'm looking for until something tells me to do otherwise.'

'There's no reason for a gringo, whether Jerry Pleasants or someone else, to be setting off bombs under school buses in Santo Domingo,' Val asserted. 'In the Dominican Republic, all terrorism is local.'

'No leads point to any locals,' I said.

'Maybe your gringo was being paid by the locals.'

'Which locals are you thinking of, Val?'

'The junta. They want to make the Boschists look bad.'

'Have you been talking to the PND?' Had Cosme Salazar already gotten his Lothario hooks into her?

'No. I've been using my brain. I thought you were attracted to women with brains.'

'The PND says it's the Constitutionalists who did the bombing to make the junta look bad. To cause terror.'

'I don't know if that's correct. Maybe the whole gringo story is a red herring,' Val said. 'Is your asset reliable?'

I didn't think I could use the word reliable in the same sentence with either Porfírio Melo or one-name McCarthy. 'Sometimes,' I said, the doubt creeping into my voice.

'It sounds to me like it wouldn't hurt to do some digging to see what the junta is up to. Use your connections. Don't put all of your eggs into the gringo basket, honey.' She slipped her foot out of her shoe and slid it along my shin under the white tablecloth. Next was a hand on the thigh. 'I'm not hungry after all, Henry. For food anyway.'

All I could think was that if Cosme Salazar was romancing Val, he hadn't been doing a very good job of satisfying her needs. Unless she was insatiable, which she seemed to be, pulling the embassy Ford into a dark alley on the way home and taking me right there on the front seat. Afterward, she dropped me so abruptly at the curb in front of my place that I wondered if she had another man to seduce yet tonight on her busy schedule.

I went into my house and headed back to the kitchen for a beer. I flipped on the light. Jaime Vargas sat at my kitchen table.

'At least you didn't sneak up behind me this time,' I said.

'I learned from the last occasion that it might get me killed.'

'Good. Beer?'

'*Si.*'

'So, to what do I owe the pleasure of your company?'

'I have information for you and I am hoping you have information for me, Señor Gore.'

'Do we do rock, paper, scissors to see who goes first?'

'What is this?' Jaime asked. 'Do we need a rock?'

'Never mind. I guess it's not a Dominican thing. I'll go first. It looks like our Peynado Bridge bomber may be a gringo. And don't ask me how I know. Let's just say my sources don't seem to have a political ax to grind.'

'Do you have a name?' Jaime was champing at the bit.

'No name from my sources. No description either. The source couldn't even say if it's a man or a woman. They don't know if they just bought bomb-making materials or if they placed it and set it off as well. But the gringo thing is a significant lead. And you know and I know that one gringo who has to be a suspect is Jerry Pleasants.'

'Is he the bomber, Señor Gore?'

'I can't be sure. Hell, I'd all but concluded he got blown into such tiny pieces at the La Españolita that the PND couldn't even tell he was there, or he hightailed it out of town and on to the next island so fast he didn't even bother to tell his friends.' The word 'friends' stuck in my craw.

'I have information that he is alive and still here in Santo Domingo.'

'Damn. Where is he?'

'I do not know. My information is not first-hand. It is not even second- or third-hand. I am to meet a man to find out more.'

'I will go with you.'

'You cannot. If you come with me, the man will disappear. You must trust me.'

'I trust you, Jaime. I just don't want this chance to slip away.'

'It will not. I give you my word. And it is vital that we learn the bomber's identity soon. That is part of the reason I came to you. The mood in the street is ugly. Gualey is seething with anger. The people believe it was the junta who is responsible for the bombing. I, together with some of the cooler heads among the supporters of Bosch, counseled against violence. It is not the way Juan Bosch came to power or the way he ran things. But there are those who say killing must be met with killing or we will be oppressed again for decades, as we were with Trujillo. Bosch is not taking a position. He apparently fears to lose the support of either the hardliners or the more moderate. If this bombing was done by Jerry Pleasants or another gringo and we can show it, that will defuse the situation. President Bosch can go back to his strategy of returning democracy to the Dominican Republic through a combi- nation of international political pressure on the junta and peaceful protest here at home. When do you think you can name the bomber to us? And to the PND, who will then be forced to do the right thing and arrest them?'

'Whoa, there, Jaime. I know almost nothing. The information I have may be wrong. I don't think it is but it may be. Getting the right person or persons may take months.'

'We don't have months, Señor Gore. We have days at most.'

'Before what, Jaime?'

'I cannot say, Señor Gore.' Jaime couldn't look me in the eye when he spoke.

'Cannot say as in don't know or know but are forbidden to tell me?'

'Señor, do not place me in this position.'

'OK, I get it. Something's coming.'

'We must find the bomber. Soon. Doing so will not bring back the children's lives but it may save many more than have been lost up to now.'

'Message received, Jaime. I'll do my best.'

'*Hasta pronto, Señor Gore.*'

'*Hasta pronto, Jaime.*' He was out the door and into the night in a flash.

THIRTY-FOUR

'Drinks, Cosme?' My response to Cosme Salazar's '*Policía Nacional Dominicana, Capitán Salazar*' greeting threw him for a second but only a second.

'It depends. Will you be bringing your shapely blonde friend from the American Embassy with you, Henry?'

'Why?'

'I am having difficulty making any headway with her.' I detected a note of injury in Cosme's voice. Had he suffered a blow to his considerable pride at the hands of Val Spicer?

'I thought by now you'd have her personal telephone number and be able to describe the interior of her apartment. *All* the rooms in her apartment.'

'It seems she is a one-man woman and you are the man, Henry. She positively rebuffed me when I called her at the embassy. At the least you would think she would want to have a contact highly placed in the PND Investigation and Identification Unit. That alone should be worth consenting to drinks and dinner but no, Henry. Not a chink in her considerable armor. Perhaps, if we had that drink, á trois, you could let her know that you would bless the two of us . . . privately conferring over matters of mutual interest.'

'If you're looking for a procurer, Cosme, you're looking at the wrong guy,' I said. 'I told you I wouldn't stand in the way but you'll have to make it on the old Salazar charm and not on my endorsement. Now, about that drink. I'll buy.'

'You buying? Almost as much an enticement as an endorsement of my suit to Miss Spicer,' Cosme chuckled. 'May I pick the watering hole?'

'Sure.'

'Playa de Güibia. There is a little rum bar, just a stand and a couple of tables, on the opposite end of the beach from the casino. Give me an hour.'

'To arrange surveillance?'

'To change into civilian clothes.'

I was at the rum bar early. Cosme had not oversold its amenities. It was just a wooden plank bar with some stools, a bench with a dozen bottles of hooch behind the bartender and four tables in the shade of a venerable sea grape tree at the top edge of the sand. I talked the bartender into leaving a half full – see, I am an optimist – bottle of unlabeled white rum at one of the tables. Also, because I am an optimist, I reasoned that this white firewater wouldn't make me go blind because the rum bar looked to have been there through at least three hurricanes and it would not have that kind of longevity if it served inferior – well, poisonous – product. I was nursing my first glass, wincing with every sip, when Cosme arrived.

'Nice suit,' I greeted him. He was wearing a glen plaid mod suit, very James Bond, and a pork pie hat. 'Have a drink.' I pushed the bottle in his direction as he sat.

'Where did you get this swill?' Cosme asked.

'The bartender picked it from the collection of unmarked bottles of vile snake venom displayed behind the bar. He said it was his best.'

Cosme gave me a reproving look and called to the bartender in Spanish. After reaching into a cardboard box beneath the makeshift bar, the bartender scuttled over with a bottle of Brugal Añejo. Cosme sent away the unlabeled bottle and poured the Brugal. 'Now, that's better, no?'

It was. Much better. Years in Santo Domingo and I apparently still looked like a rube tourist to bartenders with whom I wasn't acquainted. 'Yes, Cosme. Thanks for rescuing me from that horse piss.'

Cosme held his glass of amber liquid up in the sunlight. He was facing the sea so he had in his line of sight three of the best things in the Dominican Republic – good rum, the benevolent sun and the bottle-green sea. He savored the moment and then asked the question he knew would end it. 'So, my friend, what wrongs do we right today?'

'I am hurt, Cosme, that you would attribute such altruistic sentiments and such transparent motives to me in the same breath.'

'You are a man of contradictions, Henry. You want to be good but somehow you go about it in bad ways.'

'I'm not into introspection but now that you say it out loud, that may be true.'

'Oh, it is, *amigo*, it is. It takes one with the opposite tendency, wanting to be bad but going about it in ways that seem good, to illuminate those tendencies in others. So, what do you want? You are paying so the floor is yours.'

'I've got reliable information' – I shouldn't have lied about the reliability; good motive, bad method – 'that the person responsible for the Peynado Bridge bombing is a gringo. And I have a hunch, without any real support, that the gringo may be Jerry Pleasants. And Jerry, I've learned, is alive and well and still in Santo Domingo.'

'Interesting.' Cosme did not so much as twitch when he said it.

'Which means it wasn't the Constitutionalists,' I said. 'Find the gringo, bring him or her . . .'

'Jerry Pleasants is a him. Why do you say him or her?'

'My source was not sure which. Bring him or her in and defuse the situation between the junta and Bosch's people. And do justice. And save lives. It might even be viewed favorably by the junta once it is done.'

'Bullito will think otherwise. And, in case you hadn't noticed, he is my boss.'

'You know that sometimes an investigator has to step outside of his boss's instructions to get the job done.'

'Stepping outside of instructions these days gets you fired from the job. Or worse. Why do you think I changed out of uniform? Why do you think I chose this out-of-the-way place to meet? You are career poison for me, Henry. Requests such as the one you make are unhealthy for me.'

'If I am so poisonous, why did you agree to meet me? You had to anticipate . . .'

'Like a gambler who has already lost his shirt anticipates returning to the tables. A sick addiction.'

'No. I saw it before. You want justice for those kids.'

'What if I do?'

'Put a couple men on it, Cosme. Surely you have a man or two you can trust. Send them out to poke around, ask questions. There aren't that many gringos on the loose in Santo Domingo and even fewer with a background in explosives. And this gringo was knowledgeable in bomb-making. Have them pick up Jerry or any other gringo who fits the description.'

'You expect me to do this and you cannot even give me the gender of this person?'

'Not yet. I may develop that information. If so, you will be the first to know.'

'Well, my son-in-law is now in my unit. And a cousin who can be relied upon.'

'I'll bet that you gave both of them their jobs.'

'Of course. This is the Dominican Republic.'

'Fine. Have them poke around. After hours. Off the books, if you feel uncomfortable.'

'My daughter will be unhappy.'

'Can I count on you, Cosme?'

A heavy sigh. 'Yes, Henry. But not a word to anyone, do you understand?'

'I am the soul of discretion, old friend.'

'You are certainly getting your money's worth out of this drink of good rum.'

'Have another, Cosme.'

'*Dios mío*, Henry. Yes, another. Make it a double.'

THIRTY-FIVE

I spent the next two days doing good old-fashioned flat-foot work. My focus was on the gringo haunts of the city. Not the high-end places. I instinctively believed the gringo bomber, whether Jerry or someone else, would not be palling around with embassy staff and their ilk who frequented the nicest hotels, the best bars and the poshest restaurants that Santo Domingo had to offer. I also avoided places with heavy tourist traffic, figuring my man or woman wouldn't look like a tourist and wouldn't want to place themselves in a setting where they would stick out like a sore thumb. That left me visiting the margins of expat society. The bars where Dominicans and gringos mingled together in search of inexpensive rum. Room-by-the-week hotels away from the beach and the touristy colonial area. Bodegas in the fringe neighborhoods along the Rio Isabela and on the east bank of the Rio Ozama. The shops of low-end cobblers, butchers, bakers and candlestick makers who would have some gringo trade and who might have noticed something or someone out of the ordinary. Certainly the kinds of places Jerry had frequented in the past and would probably return to now.

I carried a wad of *pesos oro* and small-denomination greenbacks, greased a hundred palms with them and got a hundred efforts from desk clerks, merchants, bartenders, waiters, maids and cleaning ladies to remember the gringo that I sought. When first I approached them I chose not to offer a description, even as to sex. If no memory was triggered, I described the exceptionally ordinary Jerry.

All my efforts came to naught. I received the same '*no sé*' each time, striking out like an aging minor leaguer in a doubleheader after a drinking binge, over and over, until I didn't expect anything other than to strike out some more, for eternity.

And then, as the sun was lowering in the sky on the second day, a charwoman washing the stoop outside a decrepit apartment block on Calle Moca had something other than '*no sé*' on her lips. When I described Jerry Pleasants, she said she had seen an American who matched the description. He was new to the neighborhood in the last weeks. She had only seen him three times, all at night, when he had passed by her while she was washing the spot where she stood now. He never spoke to her but she did not consider that unusual; no one ever spoke to a charwoman. The man wore a new Panama hat. It had a flat crown rather than the usual rounded one.

This lady didn't miss much. I thought about giving her extra money and asking her to keep an eye out for the man and to contact me as soon as she saw him again. But she was talkative in addition to being a good observer. I felt that I could not count on her to keep from accidentally tipping the man off. So I gave her extra pesos and swore her to silence. It was probably more money that she made in a week. She made a solemn promise to be quiet. I thanked her and walked north on Calle Moca.

A block away I came upon the perfect spot. A partially burned building, its windows and doors broken out, provided a viewpoint for both the charwoman's apartment building and a bodega catty-corner across the street. I went into the building through a back door in an alley. There was no one inside. There were some dirty blankets and empty bottles on the first floor. Evidently the neighborhood drunks used it as a place to crash. Fine by me; no one would think twice if they saw me entering.

I climbed a charred stairway, hoping it would not collapse under my weight, to a second-floor room. There was no sign of any occupancy. The drunks apparently had the good sense not to risk climbing the rickety stairs. A pearlescent half moon lit the street below. Otherwise, the only light in the neighborhood came from the open door of the bodega and a couple of houses down the block. I found a straight-backed chair in the room, wiped the soot off of it with my bare hand and settled in. The light of the moon came in the front window at an angle. I sat in the shadow and moved with it as the moon sunk lower. At first, there were a few people on the street, nearly all of them headed to the bodega, and all emerging, after of a minute or two, with their purchases. The foot traffic trickled to nothing when the bodega closed at eleven o'clock. By two in the morning, the lights in the houses were all out and the moon had set, throwing the street into total darkness. I struggled to stay awake but made it until the first gray edge of dawn appeared in the east, when I went out the way I came in and walked home.

I crashed in my bed, exhausted, and slept until noon, when Camila began ramming around downstairs to signal that lunch was ready. Starved, I ate and went back to bed. At seven, with the sun almost touching the horizon, I returned for my second night of stakeout. The same routine ensued, the quiet neighborhood, the few visitors to the bodega, moonrise, the bodega closing and the lights winking off before midnight. I must've dozed off. I snapped awake just before the moon set. Across the street almost directly in front of the shuttered bodega walked a figure in a Panama hat so new and white that I could see its flat crown in the fading moonlight.

The figure was a man, I saw by his gait and clothing. He was walking fast. I rose, knocking over my chair in the process. It sounded like a thunderclap in the ruined building. I hoped that it couldn't be heard outside. I ran downstairs, out the back way where I had entered, and around the corner to Calle Moca. The man was ahead of me by two blocks already, barely visible in the darkness and putting more distance between us. His rapid pace counseled against him being Jerry Pleasants. Jerry had never moved at more than a languid stroll that I had seen, although that may have been because he was staggering most of the time when he stepped away from the barstool. For a moment I thought about abandoning the pursuit but I'd waited two days for this and decided to follow through.

I broke into a jog to close the distance. I figured I would follow to see when the man entered a building or residence. I quick-stepped on my toes to avoid clicking my heels on the cobblestones. I was within a block when the man turned a corner, now heading east. I started to run, not wanting to lose him, and skidded to a stop at the corner where he had turned. The man was turning at the next corner, heading south again. Another running block for me and another stop at the corner where he had turned. I was now breathing hard. It was difficult to be silent.

When I poked my head around this corner, he was stopped in the middle of the block, leaning against the door frame of a shuttered shop, lighting a cigarette. His head was tilted down to reach the flame to the coffin nail and the Panama hat hid his face. I froze, hoping that the lack of motion and darkness would conceal me. He lifted his head from the match and I saw his face in profile. It was Jerry Pleasants.

I wanted to call out to him. Hey, Jerry, how about a mamajuana down at La Españolita? Hey, Jerry, want to go to the fights next Friday night? Hey, Jerry, have you heard the latest single from The Animals? Hey, Jerry, why did you leave me to be blown into a thousand pieces? Hey, Jerry, why did you blow up a bus full of kids? I almost did. I stopped short as I opened my mouth. If I called to him, he would run or he would stop and give me one of his bullshit stories to misdirect me and then he would disappear once more. I knew it in my bones. I kept silent and still.

Jerry took a drag on the cigarette and started off again, slower. His path was now a turn at every corner, sometimes reversing to the north, sometimes drifting around an entire block to end back where he had started five minutes before. He was onto me or, at least, onto the fact that someone was following him.

I dropped back further, hoping he would see no one behind him and resume his path to wherever he was going. It seemed to work. The twists and turns he took were fewer and his direction was generally south again. He turned a corner that would take him west and, I realized, back to Calle Moca. Just as he made the turn, he broke into a dead sprint. I was wrong about him thinking he had lost me.

Fortunately, the block where he chose to sprint was familiar to me and unique, in that it was bisected at an angle by an old colonial street that was really just a cobbled mule path. I could short cut to the end of the block and his sprint would be for naught.

The diagonal path was darker than the regular grid streets, if that was possible. Halfway through it, I banged into a barrel and fell, got back up and kept going. I felt blood running into my shoe from a cut on my shin. I picked up my pace to an almost-run, and seconds later, popped out onto Calle Moca again. Across the street, a house had lights on inside, providing the first real illumination since I had begun following Jerry.

I pulled up. My shin hurt. Jerry was nowhere to be seen in any direction. I listened. Not a sound. Then a thump, a heavy object hitting something that made a meaty sound, followed by a gasp. In my last wink of consciousness, I realized that the meaty sound was made by my head and the gasp had come from me.

Then I was out.

THIRTY-SIX

'*D* *ios mío*,' Camila exclaimed. 'He is awake.' She grabbed my hand from where she sat beside the bed, holding it against her face, wetting it with tears.

My head was roaring. I moved my neck and the pain seared. I blinked my eyes and the pain stabbed. I tried to sit up and the pain flowed through my skull like hot lava. I decided to stay still. Very, very still.

'Glad to see you've rejoined the living, Henry,' Val said, coming in the door trailed by a nurse. A nurse. I was in the hospital. 'Two concussions in such a short time are not good, my dear. One more and the doc says you'll be reduced to a gibbering idiot. And I don't like my men to be gibbering idiots, although they might be more compliant that way.'

'What happened?' I asked and by doing so I learned that speaking also caused the hot lava to course through my brain.

'A fishmonger found you on the street, head bashed and bleeding. You were too well dressed to be a drunk, so they brought you to the hospital. A nurse found your ID and sent someone to your place. Camila was there and came to the hospital immediately.' Val cast a disapproving eye toward the crying housekeeper. 'She told them she was your wife.'

That seemed funny. I chuckled. My head reacted with bolts of fire bouncing around inside my skull. No more laughing, I told myself.

Camila looked up from my soggy hand. 'I am more of a wife to him than you.'

'You nag more, that's a fact,' Val said to Camila. Then, to me: 'She finally let me know where you were after I stopped at the house twice. She said that you had been out all night two nights in a row. You're not cheating on us, your wife and me, are you, Henry?'

I wanted to be with Beatrijs. But I wasn't on the two nights I had been staked-out, so I felt justified in saying, 'No, I wasn't cheating. I was on stakeout.' I winced when I said it because it hurt. And then the wincing hurt. All that must've made me appear pitiful enough to convince my faux-wife and my wanna-be girlfriend that

I was in no condition to lie. They dropped the line of questioning about cheating on them.

That didn't deter Val from other questions. 'What, or who, were you staking out?'

'Jerry Pleasants.' I'd gotten away with one lie. Best to stop there.

'You found him?'

'Yes.'

'What did he have to say for himself?'

'We really didn't get a chance to speak.'

'Did he do this to you?'

'I don't know. I was tailing him and lost him. Then someone slugged me from behind.'

'The doctor said it was a sap. It made a nice indentation behind your ear in the flat shape of the weapon. It could have killed you, Henry, but whoever used it mostly wanted to send a message.'

'Like?'

'Like "Stay away" or "Stop following me". Or "Stop following my friend, Jerry Pleasants."'

'Jerry didn't seem like he had those kind of friends,' I said. I found out it hurt less if I exhaled as I spoke. I sounded like some smoky-voiced torch singer.

'Maybe it was Jerry himself who slugged you. I know, next you'll say that Jerry didn't seem like that kind of a guy and anyway you're his good friend so he wouldn't do that to you. That may be the case, lover, but maybe it's not. And haven't you satisfied yourself about Pleasants now? You wanted to know if he is alive. He is. Question answered. End of story. He obviously doesn't want to see you. So leave him alone. There are plenty of people who want to see you right here in this room.'

Camila gave a vigorous, teary nod to the last part.

'Not so simple, Val,' I said. 'I located him canvassing for the bomber who killed those schoolgirls on the Peynado Bridge. I think he might be the bomber.'

'Why would he do that? He's an American with no ax to grind here in Dominican politics.'

'You would think. But I've learned that the bomber, or at least the guy who bought the explosives, is a gringo. And Jerry Pleasants is the most gringo of any gringo I know.'

'Who told you it was a gringo?'

'The seller of the explosives.'

'And he had first-hand knowledge?'

'Not exactly,' I admitted.

'Second-hand?'

I was silent.

Val scoffed. 'Third-hand? Fifth? Did his dog know the bomber's dog?'

'A street kid told him.'

'You talk to the kid?'

'The kid's gone. Melted back into the streets.'

'Jesus Christ, Henry, you think Jerry Pleasants is the bomber based on that? With everybody and their brother saying it is the work of the junta to punish the kids' village for being a Bosch stronghold? With the PND carrying out an investigation you know is false to pin it on the Boschists just like the junta wants? Pleasants isn't a red herring, Henry, he's a whole net full of red herrings, a boatload, a cannery's worth of the damn fake fish. Don't waste your time on him. He's the small picture. The big picture here is to look at who the PND is not looking at.'

'Maybe you should be doing the investigating instead of me, Val.' It hurt to say that, physically and in my pride.

'Oh, lover, I don't want you to feel that way. I just want you to feel better,' Val cooed. 'You need to rest. You need to get over this Jerry Pleasants obsession you have. You need to let me take care of you.'

'I will take care of him.' Jealousy raises its ugly head again, eh, Camila?

'You'll make the meals, mop the floors and change the sheets of our bed,' Val said, with a digging emphasis on 'our'. 'Nothing more, Camila.'

I felt like some kind of a pathetic prize as these remarks ping-ponged back and forth between Val and Camila. I did not feel that either of them loved me. They both wanted me, for whatever reason, but want is not love.

'I'll take care of myself. I'll follow who I want to follow and investigate who I want to investigate.' I said it mustering all the forcefulness I could, leaving the breathy torch singer voice behind.

Both women looked at me, shocked. Then they looked at each other. Finally, Camila spoke for both. '*Si*, Señor Henry, you will do as you must. We will be there for you, whatever you do.'

For once, Val had nothing to say, just nodding in agreement.

I had myself discharged from the hospital that evening, against doctors' orders.

THIRTY-SEVEN

'A lo, digame,' Cosme Salazar said at the other end of the telephone line.

'A little casual on the phone etiquette today, aren't we, Captain Salazar?' I asked.

'Ah, Henry, I thought you were someone else calling in. One of my two investigators I mentioned the other day.' Cosme's comments were vague enough to convey a concern that our telephone conversation might have other listeners.

Vagueness called for vagueness. 'How are they doing?' I said.

'They are fine but not accomplishing much.'

'That's too bad.'

'How are you, Henry?' I'm sure Cosme meant 'How is your investigation going?' but I gave a literal response.

'Better since I got out of the hospital. I still have a splitting headache but I'll recover.'

'Hospital, Henry? What happened?'

'I was walking on one of Santo Domingo's picturesque streets at about three o'clock in the morning night before last and fell backward into a beavertail.' I remembered a conversation we'd had years ago about that nickname for a sap and how Cosme had been amused by it, thinking it had sexual connotations. I was sure he would understand but the odd slang would give any eavesdropper fits.

'Did you see the . . . animal?' Cosme played along.

'I did. But it got away.'

'The one we spoke about?'

'Yes.'

'Where?'

'Along Calle Moca.'

'The whole length of it?'

'Just about.'

'Did you report your fall?'

'No.'

'OK. I will have an animal control officer take a look in the area.'

'Just remember, this animal is nocturnal.' I continued, 'And, Cosme, I am going for a short trip today to see a friend. I may get back to you with some more information. If I have more, perhaps I can interest you in a drink to celebrate.'

'At our new favorite place?'

'Yes.'

'OK.' The line clicked dead. I'll never get used to the way Dominicans just end a phone conversation by hanging up.

I rode the bus north out of town that afternoon. It was full of locals returning to the countryside from their excursion to the big city. Most had packages, tied up bundles of cloth to make clothing, a pair of new shoes, a box of tractor parts, new hoes and cane knives. I was the only gringo on the bus, both avoided and looked on with curiosity and suspicion, because why would any gringo leave the cosmopolitan luxury of the Spanish Empire's New World capital for the sweaty, insect-filled jungle where most of my fellow travelers lived? I looked out the window most of the way. My seat mate, a woman who appeared ready to give birth at any moment, squirmed uncomfortably whenever the bus hit a rut in the road, which was often.

We crossed the Presidente Peynado Bridge, restored to full use after the bombing just days ago. It was as if nothing had happened. Wild parrots squabbled over fruit in the trees. On the north side, naked children splashed in the river. The road turned to a washboard dirt track immediately after leaving the bridge deck. My pregnant seat mate's discomfort increased. After half an hour of jouncing progress, the path widened slightly and the jungle gave way to some cleared fields and a village of corrugated metal, concrete block and simple wooden houses. There were no streets separating the three dozen homes; well-trod footpaths wound between the structures. Chickens wandered. Here and there was a pig in a sty. There was no sign identifying this place but I knew it was the place I sought. It was Beatrijs Hagan's village.

The bus ground to a halt in the center of the cluster of buildings. My seat mate rolled out, as did a half dozen others. I was last to leave. There wasn't a breath of wind in the afternoon heat. The air hummed with the sound of insects. It was not long before the mosquitoes found my soft white flesh and began to feast. I knew if I stood still I would be carried away, so I swatted and walked, eventually spotting a large open-air structure with a palm thatch roof. Children from toddlers to teenagers were seated at four rough-hewn tables while a nun at a blackboard gave a lesson.

I stopped outside, still swatting. The nun spotted me and, after giving a reading assignment to the children, walked over to me. As she approached, I saw she was elderly and very pale, surely a gringo of some sort.

'May I help you, sir?' she said. Her accent was the same as Beatrijs's, which I now recognized as Dutch.

'My name is Henry Gore. I'm looking for Beatrijs Hagan. I'm not sure if this is the right place.'

The old nun scanned me top to bottom with hard blue eyes. She seemed to be weighing something in her mind. Finally, she said, 'This way.'

We walked a hundred feet along a meandering path to a shack of corrugated iron no different from the other shacks that made up the village. The sister walked up to the door, told me, 'Wait here,' and stepped inside. I heard muffled voices within and then the old nun emerged and walked past me without a glance. I stood for a moment, unsure of what to do. Then Beatrijs stepped through the door.

She was dressed in a habit identical to the nun, except she wore a simple white veil instead of the elaborate winged coronet worn by her older counterpart. She looked me directly in the eye as she always did, almost as a challenge.

'Hello, Henry,' she said.

'You're a nun,' I blurted.

She allowed herself an almost-smile. 'No, I am not a nun and I will never be one. Nuns are cloistered and devote their life to prayer and worship. Someday, I may be a sister. Sisters are active out in the world, nursing or teaching. But I have not taken vows yet and probably won't for another year. I am a postulant, a candidate to be a sister. I want to teach as a sister of the Holy Order of Saint Augustine.'

I heard what Beatrijs said but I could not begin to fully absorb it. I am not Catholic. I'd been raised as a Protestant in very Protestant Warsaw, Indiana. Catholics were exotic creatures who populated South Bend, fifty miles and a reformation to the north. What little I knew about nuns and sisters I'd gleaned from books and movies. One thing I knew is that they were supposed to wear a wedding ring because they are married to Jesus. And you weren't supposed to kiss them or hold their hand or romance them. And that was what I had been doing.

My mind could not have been working right because all I could think about was Beatrijs's lack of a wedding ring. The words tumbled out. 'Where is your wedding ring?'

'My what?'

'Your wedding ring. That you wear because you're married to God or Jesus or the church or something. Why aren't you wearing it?'

Beatrijs's half smile went full. 'I don't wear a ring. I'm not married, to a man, or the church, or God, yet. The ring is a sign of devotion to God, not marriage.'

'If you'd worn a ring, I wouldn't have . . .'

'Wouldn't have what? Kissed me? Held my hand?'

'Yes.' Now the most stupid thing I could possibly say came out of my mouth. 'Have I committed some kind of offense against God?'

'No, Henry, you have not committed an offense against God. Or against me.' The very direct look from Beatrijs again. 'I rather enjoyed being kissed by you. And holding your hand.'

'Beatrijs,' I began, and the words stuck in my throat. I just shook my head.

'Henry, I see this is difficult for you,' Beatrijs said. 'Confusing. So don't say a word. Let me talk. Let me explain. I am an orphan. I was raised in an orphanage by sisters. It was my entire life until I became an adult. The sisters who raised me were kind, intelligent, devoted to teaching, devoted to God and devoted to making our world a better place. I admired them. I wanted to be like them. When I reached adulthood, I told them I wanted to become a member of the order. A very wise prioress, Sister Maria Annaliese, told me that I wasn't ready, that I had to go out in the world to know my true heart. She gently pushed me out of the convent, the way a mother bird pushes her chick from the nest to learn to fly.

'I went out into the world and taught. I loved the children. I loved my job. I learned to love beer.' She laughed. For the first time since seeing her in her habit, I felt like laughing, too, and did.

'I had a romance,' she continued. 'It was the one thing in life that my time in the convent had not prepared me for. He was a free spirit. He called himself a hippie. I became pregnant. He left me, told me that I'd gotten pregnant to tie him down, to take his freedom and turn him into an establishment drone with a car, three kids, a house in the suburbs and a job that sucked the life from him. I had our baby two months after he walked out. She had a heart defect. She lived a day and then died.'

'Oh, Beatrijs.' Without a thought, I hugged her close. We stayed that way for a while, until she stepped back.

'I continued teaching. Otherwise, I was at loose ends. I went on for a year and then I went back to the convent and asked Sister Maria Annaliese to take me in as a postulant. The order was organizing a mission to the Dominican Republic and I asked to be sent here, to study in preparation for taking my holy vows and to teach.' She stopped there, looking at me with a question in her eyes.

'Beatrijs, I don't know what to say.'

'Say what you feel, Henry.'

'I'm confused.'

'Don't be. This is a part of me.'

'I'm surprised. Not about this place. It's as I expected. Surprised about your . . . postulancy, if that's the right word.'

'I couldn't find a way to tell you.'

'So you invited me to come out here and just popped out in your nun uniform?'

'Habit, Henry. And maybe it was a cowardly way to do it. But when we were together, in Santo Domingo, I didn't want my time with you to end. If I had told you there, it would have ended. You would have walked away, I believe. You would have been justified. I wasn't deceptive but I wasn't forthcoming either. A sin of omission. A sin I was ready to live with if it meant spending a few minutes more with you.'

'But now that I know . . .'

'Now that you know, nothing stands between us.'

'How can you say that? My God, you're trying to become a sister. The vows . . .' I was so rattled I couldn't end a sentence or finish a coherent thought.

'The vows are poverty, chastity and obedience. They are vows that I have not taken. I was questioning whether I should take them before we met. Now, I question even more whether they are right for me.'

'Jesus, Beatrijs,' I blurted, the irony lost on me.

'We are all made by God, Henry. He has a purpose for all of us.

I thought I knew my purpose. Now I am not so sure. I've been talking with Sister Walburga, the sister who brought you to me, about it.'

'About us?' There was a cold feeling in the pit of my stomach.

'Yes. Not at first. At first it was just about my doubts. But recently I told her about us. About everything.'

'Are you in trouble? For . . . us?'

'Don't worry, Henry. There is no trouble. Not unless love is trouble.'

As I've said, I consider myself a man of the world. I'm thirty-five years old. I've served my country in the military. I've traveled and lived abroad. I've been in fights and war, been shot at and beaten. I've killed a man. More than one. I've been with women and I've been in love. But hearing the words Beatrijs spoke, you could not just have knocked me over with a feather, you could have brushed me with the most delicate wisp of down to bring me to my knees.

'I think I may feel that way, too,' I heard myself say, the words 'think' and 'may' sounding so wishy-washy that I instantly regretted using them while saying the most important thing one human being can ever say to another. 'I'm sorry, Beatrijs, I don't mean to sound equivocal.'

Beatrijs put her finger to my lips to stop my bumbling. 'No, Henry, none of that. You feel how you feel. If you said "may", that was the right word, a word I can accept, a word that thrills me with hope. What we have is good. Where we are headed, wherever that may be, is good. We should continue, allow it to happen, whatever it is.' She gave me a full, bright smile and took my hands in hers. 'I am so happy.'

'I am, too,' I said, holding her hands in mine, feeling unwilling to ever release them. 'What do we do now?'

'I will continue to see you, in town. Sister Walburga will permit it but we cannot meet here anymore. The people in the village would not understand. This will give me, and you, time to know our feelings.' She released my hands and stepped back. 'For appearances' sake.'

'Of course,' I said.

'And we do have another purpose for meeting today,' she said.

In the rush of emotion that learning about Beatrijs's postulancy had unleashed in me, I'd almost forgotten the reason I had come. 'Have any of the villagers seen anything that would give us a clue about the bomber?'

'Yes. An old man named Abiezer Peña, who grows maize in a plot near the Peynado Bridge, saw something. One of the village men spoke to him and Abiezer told him he had seen a gringo on the bridge the day before the bombing.'

'This Abiezer Peña, does he live in the village?'

'No, he lives on his land near the bridge. But he has a daughter here in the village and visits often to see his grandchild. I think he is here today.'

'Can we go to him now?'

'Yes.' Beatrijs led the way along a path toward the edge of the village. When we met other villagers, they stepped off the path to allow us to pass, the men doffing their straw hats, the women bowing their heads, some making the sign of the cross. Beatrijs placed a loving hand on the head of any child we met, almost as a blessing. I told myself that this was what dating an almost-sister was like. I felt pretty sheepish by the time we reached our destination, a scrap wood shack with only a heavy blanket as a door. Beatrijs knocked on the frame. A young woman, a baby at her breast, peered out, then quickly set the child in a crate which served as a bassinet and covered herself. A trickle of milk leaked through her blouse.

Beatrijs asked after Abiezer Peña and after an exchange of a few words, said, 'He is around back. Come this way.' We walked around the hovel. The old man, his straw hat tipped low, dozed on a bench set against the back wall.

'*Sor* Beatrijs,' Abiezer said, scrambling to his feet and placing hat over heart when Beatrijs gently shook his shoulder to awaken him. From what I gathered, she explained why I was there and then translated.

'I'm told you have a farm near the Peynado Bridge,' I said.

'Yes, señor.'

'Were you near the bridge on the day the bus with the children in it was blown up?'

'No, señor. I was here with my daughter, Emilia, and my new grandson that day. I was home the day before, though. I understand you, *el policía*, that is, are looking for a man who was around on that day.'

'*Si.*' I didn't disabuse him of the notion that I was a policeman. The surest way to the full truth was to allow the old man to believe he was speaking to a nun and a police officer. He was almost right on both counts.

'I saw a man, as I took my midday rest in the shade at the edge of my maize field.'

'Can you describe him?'

'A gringo. Not young nor old. Like you, señor, or a year or two older. Very white. Of middle height. Of middle weight. Dark hair. I could not see the color of his eyes. A man ordinary in all respects, except that he was a gringo. He was poking around on the edge of the bridge decking near the middle of the span. I thought he might be inspecting the structure of the bridge. He had a roll of wire with him and unrolled it as he walked back to the south side of the bridge. He walked over behind a big tree there, a ceiba, and fiddled around for a while. Then he walked south, back toward Santo Domingo. I lost sight of him when he disappeared around the curve in the road. But after, I heard a car start up and gears grinding, as if the car was put in forward and reverse to turn around in the road. That is all I know, señor.'

'That is very helpful. Did other persons or vehicles pass by while the man was there?'

'No, señor. This road is quiet. Not many pass in the heat of the day.'

'You have been most helpful, Señor Peña. Just one more thing. What was the man wearing?'

'Typical gringo clothes. The tan pants they call khaki. A white shirt. Shoes of the kind many gringos wear on boats. And a hat, of course, to protect from the sun.'

'What kind of hat?'

'A fine one, señor. A new Panama, so clean it was almost white. And it was not of the usual shape. It had a flat crown instead of a round one.'

THIRTY-EIGHT

The bus ride back to Santo Domingo gave me plenty of time to think about what I had learned in the nameless village north of the Rio Isabela. Taken individually, each set of facts was enough to upend my world. Taken together, they caused me to question my judgment, my morals and my sanity. Was it wrong to love Beatrijs? Was it wrong for my love to be a 'maybe' when it was causing Beatrijs to give up her postulancy? And then there was Jerry Pleasants. How had I misjudged him, been taken in by him?

My mind spun, disorganized, jumping from Beatrijs to Jerry, Jerry to Beatrijs, until I had to stop and take a long, calming breath. If I'd had a bottle, I would have supplemented the breath with a drink. Even that would not calm me, I realized. I had to deal with each of the two revelations separately, one after the other, or I would get nowhere.

Beatrijs first, because Beatrijs's situation held some hope of having a pleasant resolution. I could not break up with her, even if logic and convention told me to. Should I ask her to give up becoming a nun or a sister or whatever she was headed toward? No, that would be wrong to ask. It would have to be her decision, free from any influence by me, although just continuing to see her would be an influence in and of itself. I couldn't help that but I wouldn't push her with my words. And, if I continued to see her, how was I to treat her? Like a nun, no hugging, no handholding or kissing? I didn't want the physical bond just established between us to wither and die but with an almost-sister? Would God punish me for that? Not any more than he was going to punish me for the commandments I'd already broken, which were many. And, really, Beatrijs was not a sister – yet. Maybe I was hanging my hopes on a technicality but I needed her touch as much as I needed the sight of her beauty, the sound of her voice and the light scent of flowers that seem radiate from her very being. It was settled, then, I told myself. I would continue with Beatrijs and see where it leads, just as she had so wisely suggested.

Contemplation of the Jerry Pleasants revelation had none of the pleasurable aspects that thinking about Beatrijs did. Jerry had been revealed to me as a betrayer of our almost-friendship and a probable murderer of children. I knew that Jerry had to be brought before the authorities, questioned and subjected to a lineup. Whether this would develop into enough to convict or exonerate him was for the authorities, not me.

So Jerry had to be brought in. I could try it myself but that was a fool's errand. I had no arrest authority and just my bare hands if force came into play. Involving Cosme Salazar could supply the authority needed to arrest, even if he was reluctant to do so. He had to be involved. And if real force came into play, could I count on the PND? Probably not. Most of the rank and file of the PND were in it for the graft and adverse to the risk of taking a bullet from some gringo, if Jerry was armed. I wasn't sure if I could even count on Cosme to step into a real donnybrook if Jerry put up a fight. Cosme was a lover, not a fighter.

I needed fearless muscle to bring Jerry to the authorities. Someone willing to take a risk. The biggest risk taker with skin in this game was Jaime Vargas. It's a sad state of affairs for justice when you are convinced that your favorite barman has more guts than the cops. But that's how I felt about Jaime. He was risking his neck daily against the junta, for democracy and the rule of law. I thought he could be counted on to do any heavy lifting needed here.

I had my plan. Involve Captain Salazar. Involve Jaime Vargas. They could not work together, though apprehending Jerry Pleasants might be their common goal. I would be the link between them. I had to contact them both.

Cosme was already at the best table, the one with only one broken chair, when I arrived.

'Henry, we have to stop meeting like this,' Cosme greeted me. 'While my liver has adjusted to your return into my circle of regular friends, the rum is hindering my romantic performance. And I have a date tonight with a most comely blonde.'

'Miss Spicer?'

'Alas, no, a bottle-dyed substitute for the real article.'

'All right, I'll be brief and I'll cut you off after two drinks.'

'I fear I have already exceeded my limit,' Cosme said. 'Well, my friend, why are we here?'

'There is corroborating evidence that Jerry Pleasants is the Peynado Bridge bomber. He may even be the La Españolita bomber.'

'If you were a woman, Henry, I would say that you have an unhealthy fixation on that man.'

'This is the real deal, Cosme.' I explained what I had learned. Cosme sipped rum and gazed at the blue horizon as he listened. When I finished, he said, 'What is it that you expect me to do, Henry?'

'Stake out Calle Moca and arrest Jerry when he shows. It shouldn't be hard to catch him. Bring him in and sweat him. Put him in a lineup.'

Cosme changed his focus from the intersection of sea and sky to my face. 'I cannot do that, Henry.'

'What? Why? An hour of interrogation and he would crack. You've got more than enough to bring him in.'

'I cannot search for the Peynado Bridge bomber. Or the La Españolita bomber. The Investigation and Identification Unit has been ordered to do the work assigned to it and none other. General Vazquez learned of the search my son-in-law and cousin were doing to find your mystery man. He fired my cousin as a lesson. My son-in-law has been suspended for thirty days. I got off with a stern reprimand by Bullito, which ended with a warning to keep my nose out of this.'

'Cosme, I'm sorry,' I said. 'But this guy is blowing things up in your town, in General Vazquez's town. Don't you want to lock him up?'

Cosme looked at the ground. 'The matter is closed, Henry.' He got up and left, walking like an old man.

I stayed and finished the glass of Brugal in front of me. Then I had another. The PND didn't care. If I wanted help, I couldn't count on the law. I had to look to an outlaw.

I had to talk to Jaime Vargas.

THIRTY-NINE

I went home to lick my wounds. Camila greeted me at the door, worried and effusive at the same time, the little woman waiting for the return of her husband-hero. I will admit to letting her mother me, steering me to a chair, taking off my shoes, fixing another rum to layer on top of the three I had consumed by the time I decided to leave the Playa de Güibia rum stand. Savory scents wafted from the kitchen.

Camila had made *camarofungo*, the shrimp fat and tender, the have mashed plantains garlicky, the *chicharrónes* crispy, salty and porky. I ate a plateful and then a second helping. After Camila denied me another rum, she pointed me upstairs and laid out my pajamas. Apparently she had decided that the war between her and Val Spicer over my sorry carcass would be won in the kitchen, not the bedroom. She tucked me in like a small child.

The food and the rum worked their magic. I drifted off to sleep almost immediately. When I awakened, it was the middle of the night. I lay in bed listening to the few night sounds and thinking of Beatrijs Hagan, what my life had been without her, what our life could be together. It was a sweet dream that didn't even involve sleeping, a waking dream of love and hope and a chance for me to change. Soon the night sounds were replaced by the dawn chirp of the bananaquit and the summons of the fishmonger calling the day's fresh catch. I rose refreshed, the meal, the mothering and the enchanting musings about Beatrijs having done their work.

Camila was not in yet. I went out for coffee and to find my contact for Jaime Vargas. A steaming cup and a quick plate of *buñnelos de viento* at the hole-in-the-wall bakery and I was off to Gualey to find El Pâjaro. He was in his usual place near La Poza del Chino, his tray of gum, hard candy and trinkets before him. There were almost no swimmers or loungers at the pool; the place had a deserted feel. The Birdman came to attention as he heard me walk up, even before I greeted him in my halting Spanish.

'You a gringo, ain't you man?' he replied.

'Yes,' I said. 'I didn't think you spoke English.'

'Seven years in Miami, man, working for the Yankee dollar, like the racist song says.' He rocked back and forth when he spoke. 'You here seeing the fine sights Gualey has to offer, boss? Can I sell you a pack of Chiclets? Maybe a bead necklace for your lady?'

'I'll take the gum,' I said.

'Ten centavos, boss.'

I put a ten-spot in his hand. He felt the size and said, 'I can't make change for American money, boss.'

'I don't want change,' I said.

'What do you want? A tenner will buy a lot of Chiclets.'

'I want to speak to Jaime Vargas.'

'Who? I don't know nobody by that name.'

'Yes, you do. He told me you could get a message to him.'

'Like I said, I don't know nobody by that name. Even if I did know, how do I know you are who you say you are?'

'I'm the man from the land of snow. I'm sure Jaime gave you a way to tell.'

'What? You mean like asking you what have you done for each other lately?'

'He saved my skin by warning me to get out of La Españolita when it was bombed. I saved his skin by pulling him into a store to help him avoid a police beating at the El Conde Gate.'

'OK, you're the man. Where do you want to meet?'

'Catedral Santa Maria la Manor. Where he kidnapped me. Tomorrow at noon.'

'Man, I don't know what kind of kink you two got going on but I'll get word to him. Here, have another pack of gum. On the house.'

It was pouring rain at noon as I stood under the colonnade at the Catedral Santa Maria la Menor, waiting for Jaime Vargas. He materialized out of a side alley like a soggy ghost.

I wasted no time. 'Our man is Jerry Pleasants, Jaime. I've seen him. I have a witness who puts him at the Peynado Bridge fiddling with wires around the structure on the day before the bombing. If I had to bet, I'll bet he is responsible for bombing La Españolita as well.'

'Do you know where he is?' Jaime asked.

'He frequents Calle Moca very late at night. That's all I have.'

'We will find him and execute him.'

'No. We will find him and bring him to the PND, with evidence of his guilt.'

'The PND will do nothing.'

'We will make it so they must. I have a friend there, who I'm sure will help us.'

Jaime hesitated, so I said, 'Aren't the Constitutionalists supporters of the rule of law? Or have they become a group of vigilantes?'

'You are sure this man in the PND will help to see justice is done?'

'Yes,' I said, even though the willingness of Cosme Salazar to do this was the thing I was least sure of in all the world.

Jaime waited a long minute and finally said, 'OK. We can capture him. Do you want to be in on it?'

When I first committed to Jaime, Val and Beatrijs to search for the Peynado Bridge bomber, I had no interest in being present for his actual capture. There was nothing I wanted more now. 'Yes, I want to be there.'

'Is he armed? If so, it could be dangerous.'

'I don't know if he is,' I said. 'But you should be ready for it.'

'We will be. I will bring a compatriot who is good with weapons and we will both be armed. Meet us at the corner of Calle Moca and Avenida Ortega y Gasset at midnight. We will have a weapon for you, Señor Gore.' Jaime melted into the downpour.

I knew the rain would end in minutes, so I waited it out under the colonnade. It had been years since I'd had a weapon in my hands, all the way back to the days with Castro. I could feel the weight of the gun now, feel the danger and the responsibility. The rain had cooled the air but I began to sweat. I thought the days of fear and danger and risk were behind me. I had lived the last few years as a man of peace, a man of ease. Now I was to be back in it. I wasn't sure I was ready, wasn't sure I had in me what I had in Havana in '57 or in the Sierra Maestra in '58. Was I just young and foolish then and older, wiser and careful now? No, I decided. I was no different. I made it through Havana and the mountains not because I was particularly brave but because I was on the side of right, fighting against people who were not only greedy and brutish but evil. And now evil was out there again, a killer of innocent children, a depraved bomber, who struck those who had done nothing to him. A man who needed to face justice. Yes, I was ready.

FORTY

'This is Oscar, Señor Gore,' Jaime Vargas said. 'He will be going with us tonight.' We shook hands. Silently, I'm guessing because Oscar didn't speak English. His appearance made me question why I thought Jaime could supply the muscle needed to capture Jerry Pleasants. Oscar was probably sixteen, whip-thin, with a toothy smile and a deferential manner. Hardly one's idea of a heavy. Then I noticed the Smith and Wesson M&P .38 jammed into his belt.

Jaime was similarly loaded for bear, with a Colt 1911 .45 protruding from his right-hand pants pocket. He produced a Colt Detective Special from his other pocket. 'For you, Señor Gore.' He handed the snub-nose revolver to me butt first and stuffed six .38 shells into my empty hand.

I loaded the gun and we walked the ten blocks from our rendezvous point to the corner of Calle Moca and Calle República de Paraguay, where we huddled in the shadow of a shuttered store. The humidity from the heavy rain earlier in the day lay on my skin like a damp cloth. All the houses and the two or three storefronts in sight were unlit, Santo Domingo not being a party town except along the beachfront.

The sodden darkness seemed foreboding to me, a situation of impaired vision and hearing where anything and anyone could jump from the shadows.

Jaime was clearly nervous, his head on a swivel, walking slightly hunched like he was about to be hit. Oscar was loose and easy, with a sixteen-year-old's on-a-lark self-assurance.

'Do we split up so we can cover more ground?' I asked.

'Yes. We will work both directions on Calle Moca. Take Oscar and go north. I will work my way south,' Jaime said. 'There are no police patrols this time of night. If you capture Señor Pleasants, fire one shot in the air and I will come. If I get him, I will do the same.' How very Wild West, Jaime.

Oscar and I headed north, I on high alert, Oscar shambling along as though he was bored. A few minutes brought us to the burned-out building where I had staked-out and had first seen Jerry. I led Oscar inside and we waited. Oscar softly hummed a Beatles tune, 'A Hard Day's Night'. I wondered if he understood the irony.

We had only been there for a half hour when Jerry Pleasants appeared. He walked up to the bodega across the street and paused to light a cigarette. This time his Panama hat did not hinder my view. It was undoubtedly Jerry.

I gestured to Oscar to be quiet and follow me. We made our way down the rickety stairs as quietly as we could. When we rounded the corner of the house, Jerry saw us. He ducked back behind the store, out of sight. With nothing to lose now, I called out, 'Jerry, it's Henry Gore. Come out. We need to talk.'

The answer was a shot, the muzzle flash bright in the heavy darkness. The bullet went high, tearing into the siding of the building above our heads. I dragged Oscar behind the building. I thought that was the end of it, that Jerry had used the shot to make us do exactly what we did, take cover, and that he would melt into the night while we sought safety.

Jerry and Oscar proved me wrong. Oscar was a teenager who had been given a gun he was itching to use. He barged around the corner of the building before I could stop him, squared his stance and snapped off three shots as fast as he could. I thought that was guaranteed to drive Jerry into the night but I was wrong. A single shot rang out from beside the bodega. Oscar dropped like a rock.

I fumbled the pistol out of my pocket and waited, listening. After two minutes, I poked my head around the wall. Oscar's blood was a black blot on the white sand between the derelict building and the street. I made a two-step dash for the boy, grabbed him under the arms and dragged him to safety. Another shot from across the street whined into the night.

I felt the kid's neck for a pulse. Oscar would never see his seventeenth birthday. His dead hand gripped the Smith and Wesson. I pried it loose and stuck it in my waistband. The way things were going, I might need the three shots it still held. I was breathing hard from the exertion and the stress. Sweat poured off me. I waited, knowing the shooting would bring Jaime. Better to try to take Jerry with two of us.

There was no sound other than my ragged breathing. The quiet was eerie. I thought about calling out to Jerry again and decided it would just draw fire, so I waited.

Soon there was a sound of running footsteps approaching from the south. Jaime was coming. I realized he was running toward the gunfire but he could not know precisely from where it had come, the distance and the darkness cloaking the origin of the shots.

'Jaime, take cover!' I yelled. The running steps halted. There was another shot from across the street. Then two more, one of which struck the wall of the building near me.

I hung back. There was a raw sound from the street, half animal howl and half whimper. Jaime. It went on and on, an agony to hear that was not a tenth of the agony I was sure Jaime was feeling. I waited, fearing to go to his aid, while his torment echoed down the empty street. I told myself not to risk it, that trying to reach him meant death. Finally, the guilt got the better of me. He had warned me of the La Españolita bomb, risking his life to save me. I had to take the risk to try to save him now.

I sprinted to the middle of the street where Jaime lay. I pulled him behind a parked car, putting the car between Jerry and us. There were no shots while I did this, though I imagined myself an easy target during the half a minute it took. I ripped open Jaime's shirt. He was gut-shot. Dead.

It felt as though Jerry was out there, hiding and waiting, watching his old pal deal with the carnage. I was crushed, broken. Two men dead and for what? Then I was angry. This wasn't my fight but it wasn't right, this American just running around Santo Domingo, creating havoc, killing people, sowing the seeds of violence in a place that was already on the edge. I grabbed Jaime's .45, stuffed the snub-nose back into my waistband and ran toward the bodega, expecting to be shot at any moment.

I made it to the front of the little store, slamming into it at full speed, and flattened against the wall. Listening, I heard nothing but the roar of my own pulse in my ears. I bobbed my head around the corner and pulled it back. The maneuver did not draw fire. I did not see any sign of Jerry during my brief glimpse.

I edged along the side of the store to the alley at its rear. No sound. No sign of anything except a shamble of crates and garbage cans. I had a fifty–fifty chance. Pick the wrong direction and I would be chasing down the alley, while Jerry traveled the other way, putting distance between us. Pick the other wrong direction and Jerry was likely hiding somewhere along the path, waiting to turn me into the third corpse of the evening. Not an attractive choice either way.

I picked left and jogged, tentatively, for a block or two and then stopped to listen. There were no nearby sounds but sirens wailed in the distance. Someone in the neighborhood with a telephone must have called in about the raging gun battle in the street. The PND was responding the way the PND often responded to danger, coming in force with lots of noise and the hope that the danger would be dissipated by the cacophony. I'd made my choice and could do nothing now but fully commit to it. I sprinted along the alley, convinced that if Jerry had come this way, he would be running to put distance between him and the converging police. After more blocks, my sprint slowed to a run, then a jog, then a walk. Jerry could have turned off the alley anywhere, at any time. If he had gone the other way, there could be miles between us now.

The sirens wound down as they reached their destination. I thought about going back, hoping that Cosme Salazar would be among those at the scene. I knew that was a remote possibility; he was probably in the bed of his most recent blonde or redhead at this late hour. If I went back to where Jaime and Oscar lay, I would just be some gringo showing up where he shouldn't be, with a cockamamie story and three guns in his pockets, one of which had been fired. There was little doubt that I would be locked up even if I ditched the guns and, these days in Santo Domingo, if you were locked up, the odds were that you wouldn't be out for a long time, guilty or innocent. Besides, I needed the guns. I needed to get Jerry Pleasants, dead or alive, and it was plain that I wouldn't accomplish that without a gun. So I changed direction and walked toward home.

FORTY-ONE

It was two in the morning by the time I reached my door. There were lights on inside, a single lamp upstairs and many bright lights on the lower floor. I hoped it was Camila but it had to be Val. Camila didn't have that kind of chutzpah.

I went straight to the kitchen and poured a double Bruga. My hand shook and the bottle clicked against the rim of the glass. I drained it and felt the burn, which wasn't nearly painful enough. I spilled another into the glass and went upstairs.

Val was on my bed, sprawled on her belly, reading a book. She was naked except for some kind of lacy contraption that was supposed to reveal just enough to be enticing to the male of the species. When she heard me enter the room, she rolled over, the movement doubling the amount revealed.

'Out tomcatting on me, Henry?' she asked. 'You know you won't do any better chasing around town than you can do right here, right now, in your own bed.' For emphasis, she allowed herself a feline stretch that revealed leg until it wasn't leg anymore.

'Turn it off, Val,' I said. 'I'm beat. I've been chasing Jerry Pleasants. Check that. I found Jerry Pleasants. Now two men are dead and Jerry ain't one of them.'

I flopped into an armchair across from the bed and kicked off my shoes. Val sat up and, getting the message that I wasn't in heat like she seemed perpetually to be, wrapped as much of the lacy thing around her as she could.

'Do you want to talk about it?' she asked.

'Not really. It's very simple. Jerry is a monster and he must die. I've got to do away with him.'

'He really killed two men?'

'Yes. Jaime Vargas and one of his friends. And he killed those schoolgirls on the Peynado Bridge. And he killed those seven tourists at La Españolita, probably, and almost me.'

'It sounds like this is work for the police,' she said.

'The police are indifferent, strange as that may seem. They have a narrative that fits well with the views of the junta and catching Jerry would not fit that narrative. I'm on my own.'

'That's too dangerous, Henry. It isn't your fight.'

'Isn't it? I've backed my way into it but I'm all the way there now.'

'Nobody will care, lover. That's why I came over. Jerry and the killing and the bombs won't matter tomorrow.'

'What do you mean?'

'The shit's going to hit the fan, Henry. Tomorrow this place is going up in flames and those schoolgirls and tourists and Jerry Pleasants won't matter. Don't ask. I can't tell you how I know. But the Boschists are going to make their play tomorrow. Folks in the know at the embassy think it might work but it's going to be close. The more likely scenario is that neither the Boschists nor the Loyalists come out on top. It's civil war then. Santo Domingo as we know it ends tonight. I came to tell you. I came to spend one last night with you, while things are somewhat normal. Come here, Henry.'

She pulled me toward her and kissed me, hungry. I felt myself giving in. She pressed herself against me. It was only a few hours until dawn. It was only a few more until war. It was weak of me to give in but I felt weak. She did all the work and enjoyed it.

The sun streamed in through the windows. It was warm already and still muggy, a typical Santo Domingo day in the making. Pans rattled downstairs. I reached across the bed and touched empty sheets. I got up, splashed water in my face and looked in the mirror. I bore a strange resemblance to Hell warmed over. I guess after a night of getting shot at, followed by a tigress making passionate love to me, and chased with only an hour of sleep, I should only expect to look as good as I felt. I tossed on some slacks and went downstairs.

'She's gone.' Camila's tone could have frozen the surface of the sun. 'She got what she wanted and left.'

That's right, I wanted to say. That's exactly what happened. Instead, I gave a tired grunt, not ready to engage with Camila. She had continued on her campaign to win me by use of the stove. She steered me to the table and shoved a massive breakfast in front of me, which I devoured without a word. Camila watched, leaning against the cupboard, and cleared the dishes when I finished, her eyes grim. Now I felt not just tired, but guilty. Then I thought of

Beatrijs. The guilt multiplied exponentially. I headed out of the kitchen for a shower. At least I wouldn't have to look Camila in the eye.

I got as far as the hall when there was a knock on the front door. There was a street kid of eight or nine years old there when I opened the door. He didn't say anything, just held out a folded piece of paper to me. I took it and he dashed down the block and around the corner in the blink of an eye.

I unfolded the paper. In precise script, it said:

AT THE CONFLUENCE OF RIO ISABELA AND RIO OZAMA, ON THE SOUTH SHORE, AT NOON.

JERRY

I checked my watch. It was ten o'clock. Was this legit or some kind of a ruse? Did Jerry want to explain himself? Or turn himself in? Or lure me in to finish what he had started last night?

I knew that, regardless of what the answers were to those questions, I had to go to the meeting. That didn't mean I had to go alone. I went upstairs, threw on a shirt and shoes, and stuffed the snub-nosed Colt into my pocket. In fifteen minutes I was at the post office and paid for a phone.

Cosme Salazar answered on the first ring.

'Who is this?' He was hurried, almost breathless.

'It's Henry, Cosme. I can put Jerry Pleasants behind the gun on two murders last night. And he wants to meet me today at noon.'

There was a commotion on Cosme's end of the line, a jostling, the opening and closing of file cabinets. Cosme didn't say anything.

'Cosme, are you there? I've got Jerry Pleasants coming to a meeting and I need your help in capturing him.'

Still, no word from Cosme. The commotion continued in the background. Finally, he said, 'Henry, you don't know what is going on, do you?'

'What, Cosme?'

'There is a countercoup underway. The PND has been called to the streets. I cannot talk. Listen to the radio.' The line clicked dead.

I walked out of the telephone bank at the Palacio de Correo into the street. People were hurrying now, in all directions. A clump of folks, workmen, businessmen and housewives gathered on the street around a boy with a transistor radio. The radio was turned up all the way; the announcer spoke hurriedly, the words tumbling over one another. I couldn't handle the breakneck Spanish of the speaker and looked around the group for someone I thought might speak English. I settled on a tall man in a business suit. 'What is going on?' I asked him.

The businessman shrugged and said, 'No English.'

A young woman near him spoke up. 'A group of junior army officers asked yesterday to meet with President Cabral today. The president, that spineless puppet of General Wessin y Wessin, feared that there was a plot against him and sent the Chief of Staff to meet with the junior officers instead. The Chief of Staff was arrested. The followers of Juan Bosch, the legally elected president, have now seized the radio station here in Santo Domingo and are calling for action to displace Wessin y Wessin's junta and restore Bosch. The army garrison at the February Twenty-seven Barracks and the Navy's frogman unit have joined the Bosch Constitutionalists. The announcer asks that all civilians who support the constitution and Bosch go to the August Sixteen Barracks and the February Twenty-seven Barracks to receive weapons from their armories. Civilians are also called on to make Molotov cocktails to fight the illegal junta. The announcer says large numbers of the PND are abandoning their posts and throwing away their uniforms to switch sides. We, the people, with the help of the military who follow the constitution, are about to restore Juan Bosch as our democratically elected president!'

I thanked the young woman and started for home. At least this explained why Cosme Salazar was so abrupt with me. He was busy saving his own neck and trying to decide which side to take. The life of a ranking police officer in the coup-ridden Dominican Republic is not an easy one.

It also meant no help for the meeting arranged by Jerry Pleasants. I realized that I couldn't get home and still make the meeting on time if I had to walk. I tried to flag a taxi. Two passed me by, both full of young men brandishing Molotov cocktails, shotguns and cane knives. It was clear that I was walking. I would have to go armed as I was, without the back-up weapon I'd hoped to pick up at home.

I walked north, fast, sweating as the sun moved higher in the cloudless sky. Other than the occasional carload of armed men, the streets were completely empty. I came upon a juice vendor's cart, abandoned, and raided it for some coconut water, leaving ten centavos as payment. At ten of noon, I came to the end of the shell-rock paved portion of Calle Trinitaria. Five minutes more and I had traversed the unpaved remainder of the street and stood on the south bank where the Rio Isabela met the Rio Ozama. There were no people around. The riverbank was a jungle, deeply shaded, filled with parakeets and chittering songbirds. Two hundred feet offshore, a marshy island with no buildings on it interrupted the flow of the two rivers. There was a short stretch of sandy beach on the island. A man stood next to a rowboat grounded on the beach, protected from the sun by a white Panama hat with a flat crown.

Jerry Pleasants lifted a hand and waved when he spotted me.

FORTY-TWO

When I saw Jerry across the water, my mind immediately went to the Colt Detective Special in my trouser pocket. I thought about drawing the gun and firing at Jerry but the distance was almost impossible with the stubby two-inch barrel of the pistol. I could probably unload all six shots and be lucky to hit within ten feet of him. He had picked his spot well.

'Quite a ruckus going on in town today, eh, old pard?' Jerry's voice carried across the smooth water as if he was standing next to me.

'Jerry, what the hell are you doing?'

'Just out for a row, Henry. I stopped for a breather on the beach and here you are. Some coincidence, isn't it?'

'It's no coincidence, Jerry. You asked me to meet you here. And here I am. To find out from you what you are doing and why. And then to kill you.' I shouldn't have said that last part. My blood boiled at his flippant demeanor and I couldn't contain myself.

'Whoa, partner, isn't that a little harsh? After all, we're both Americans and strangers in a strange land. We should be looking out for each other rather than making threats.'

'You mean the way you looked out for me at La Españolita, warning Jaime Vargas and leaving me to twist in the wind?'

'I knew he'd warn you out of the place.'

'You were pretty sure of Jaime. If you didn't actually want me blown to smithereens.'

'I knew I could count on Jaime,' Jerry said. 'I know his type better than he knows himself.'

'Knew himself. Remember, you killed him last night.'

'That was unfortunate but it had to be done. I couldn't take a chance of you and your Boschist friends catching me and queering this morning's events. Bringing in someone claimed to be the Peynado Bridge bomber might have been just enough to derail the junior officers of the August Sixteen Barracks from taking action this morning. I just needed to buy some time and poor Jaime stood in the way.'

'And Oscar, too.'

'Oscar?'

'The kid you killed. He had a name.'

'Again, regrettable but he was a casualty of war.'

'There was no war last night, Jerry.'

'But there is one today.'

'And we should have no role in it.'

'Now there's where you're wrong, pard. We have a role. We are the puppet masters. We pull the strings.'

'Not "we", Jerry. Not me.'

'It could be "we", Henry. There's still time. I still need help here. Uncle Sam still needs help here. Your help.'

'What are you talking about? Are you trying to recruit me for something?'

'I have been. For months, Henry. Don't tell me you're that oblivious. You've worked in intelligence.'

I was that oblivious. Damn. Jerry wasn't my friend or acquaintance or almost-friend. He was trying to become my handler. He thought of me as a potential asset, not a friend.

I guess I was silent too long. Jerry said, 'Jesus, Henry, you didn't get it, did you? You thought we were drinking buddies. Don't get me wrong. I like you. But look at who you are. An American on the ground here in Santo Domingo, tied in to Juan Bosch. You know that is valuable.'

'Then why were you ready to blow me up in La Españolita?'

'Again, sorry, pal, but I thought Jaime would get you out, and he did. It was nothing personal.'

'And if I got caught up in the explosion?'

'The Boschists get the blame from the junta. Uncle Sam maybe changes his mind on who to back.'

'Uncle Sam has backed Bosch since he was elected. That hasn't changed. It's not US policy to support a junta who deposed a democratically-elected government.'

'Not yet it isn't,' Jerry said. 'It will be someday soon.'

'Who do you work for, Jerry? Are you a private contractor?'

'No, my friend, I am a US government employee.'

'CIA? DIA?'

'No. If you insist on knowing which alphabet agency I work for, and you should if you're going to join up, I'm FBI.'

'The FBI has no overseas authority.'

'I'm not here to arrest people,' Jerry said.

'The CIA has the jurisdiction outside the US.'

'CIA has fucked up royally lately, in case you haven't noticed. They misjudged Castro's revolution. They blew it at the Bay of Pigs. Mr Hoover thinks they are in the process of screwing the pooch big time in Vietnam. He's decided our country requires an organization more effective than the CIA handling its overseas intelligence needs. The Federal Bureau of Investigation, to be precise.'

'Does the President know about this? What about the State Department?'

'It's need to know, Henry. And they don't need to know. You do, though. And now you know. You can be in on the ground floor. Mr Hoover needs men with overseas experience, men like you. And there are rewards – service to your country, good pay, Mr Hoover's appreciation, and for you, something special, something I'm betting will be extremely attractive to you after all the time you spent away from the mother country – a ticket home. If you do your duty to your country.'

'You mean to the FBI.'

'One and the same, my boy. If you do your duty to your country here in the Dominican Republic, your past transgressions in Cuba will be forgiven. You will get a fresh passport and an escort through customs and immigration with no uncomfortable questions asked. That label that says commie on your State Department file will be erased. Pretty attractive, *n'est ce pas*?'

'Not attractive enough to let a child murderer go free.'

'Casualties of war, Henry. Casualties of war. There was no other way. Just like the drunk in the gutter I cut the ear from and tossed into the debris of La Españolita to put everyone off my trail.'

'You twisted son of a bitch.'

'Not a son of a bitch. A good soldier, Henry. Ready to do the dirty work that needs to be done so Americans can rest easy in their beds at night, knowing that the commie menace is being held at bay.'

I couldn't stomach any more of Jerry's smug bullshit. There were no more words to be said. I drew out the Detective Special and fired all six shots at him. The range was too great. The bullets kicked up sand and clipped the foliage far from where Jerry stood watching. When I had emptied the gun, he said, 'I guess that's a "no". Your loss, Henry.' He pushed the skiff off the beach, stepped in and pulled on the oars, headed for the north side of the Rio Ozama. I watched the whole time he rowed until he reached the far shore and stepped out of the boat, allowing the sluggish current to carry it away. He took off his Panama hat, waved it at me and disappeared into the jungle.

FORTY-THREE

The next days were filled with all of the uncertainty and chaos of a revolution. Like any effort to overthrow an existing power structure, it was a mess of contradictions and misinformation. In the neighborhoods like mine in the colonial zone, it was almost peaceful. Gasoline suddenly became scarce and so no cars passed along the street. On the first day, mothers kept their children in and the schools were closed. After the second day, the restless children were allowed out to play and impromptu games of *béisbol*, skip-rope and soccer put the empty streets to use. I thought food might be in short supply but the laws of economics overrode any concerns. People in Santo Domingo needed food. Farmers had produce. Fishermen caught fish. Pigs were butchered. The neighborhood stores were open and the people bought. Away from the central area of the coup, there was a somberness in the air, a solemn expectation in people's demeanors. Their lives were about to change, though they had no idea how much or how little. They waited patiently to find out, curious, anxious for information that came in the form of radio broadcasts – the information that the Constitutionalists wanted them to hear – and whispered rumors – the truth that people trusted.

I hunkered down. I'd seen what had happened when Castro's revolution had arrived in Santiago and Havana. It was best to stay close to home, out of crowds and away from the groups of armed men moving through the neighborhoods. If whoever prevailed was going to come after you, they would find you at home or in the streets, regardless. But you were susceptible to the random violence that comes with coups, revolts, revolutions and similar events if you were out in the open. So home is where I stayed. Camila came and worked as a live-in housekeeper. As an unmarried woman, she felt more comfortable in this time of uncertainty in the presence of a man, and I guess I was that man, by default. She slept in a pantry room off the kitchen and seemed, for once, satisfied, not worried that her rival Val Spicer would be coming round and conniving to win my heart.

I assumed Val was confined to the US Embassy, working intensely to help stranded American tourists and more intensely to discern who might come out the winner in this chapter of the contest between the Bosch-Constitutionalists and the Loyalist junta. I did not hear from her and did not expect to. I had no telephone and phone service in such circumstances is dicey anyway. No one was carrying messages, telegrams or letters. I was confident she was safe. She had been in some difficult situations before and had a good head on her shoulders. She was one tough cookie.

Beatrijs was not a tough cookie by any means but I believed she was safe, too, her safety insured by her rural location. All the fighting and the key objectives of the countercoup were in central Santo Domingo. The war would not reach the countryside.

A day after the arrest of the Chief of Staff, President Cabral appointed General Wessin y Wessin as the new chief. Wessin y Wessin visited the barracks that had not mutinied and rallied the Loyalist troops, vowing to suppress the countercoup. The Boschists reacted by storming the Palacio Nacional and arresting Cabral. Later that afternoon, four Loyalist P-51 Mustang aircraft bombed the Palacio Nacional and a number of other Boschist positions in the area. One plane was shot down. On the Rio Ozama, the Loyalist frigate *Mella* also fired on the palace. Ultimately, President Cabral was released by the Boschist commander, who feared Cabral would be lynched by the crowd gathered at the palace. Cabral and the majority of the junta's leadership fled Santo Domingo.

The departure of Cabral and his cohorts was not the end of the Loyalists, although for a while it appeared to be. The Palacio Nacional and other key locations were in the possession of several brigades of Constitutionalist troops and over five thousand armed civilian followers of Juan Bosch. Only three days into the counter-coup, José Ureña was declared the provisional president. Large crowds celebrated the victory in the streets and awaited Juan Bosch's return from exile.

It was time to make my way through the euphoric crowds to find Beatrijs. Most of the large gatherings were in the area of government buildings but even the quiet streets of the colonial zone had revelers out and about. No buses were running, so my trip to the village where Beatrijs lived had to be on foot. I set out at mid-morning with a messenger bag of food and water slung across my shoulder and Jaime Vargas' Colt tucked in the small of my back, covered by a loose shirt.

The weather had moderated, almost as if it, too, was overjoyed at the departure of the junta. A strong east trade wind pushed the humidity from the air. The sun appeared unusually bright and sharp. I started out warily, unsure of what I would find outside my immediate neighborhood. I was soon able to relax. The people I encountered were in a celebratory mood and hardly dangerous. Even the car loads of armed men patrolling the streets were cheerful, offering swigs of rum to passersby and singing songs.

I had no idea where or if I would find Beatrijs. I decided to make a slight detour before heading north out of town. The street gate on the beer garden where Beatrijs and I had met twice was firmly closed when I approached. I rattled the gate and the proprietress with the graying hair appeared from the door inside. I asked in my halting Spanish about Beatrijs, describing her as *la mujer pelirroja*, the red-haired woman. The proprietress opened the gate, motioning for me to enter. Inside, Beatrijs was seated at one of the courtyard tables, a glass of beer in front of her.

She saw me and ran to embrace me. The proprietress smiled for the first time I could remember and left us alone.

'I heard what was happening,' Beatrijs said. 'I wanted to come to Santo Domingo but Sister Walburga wouldn't allow me. She said it was not safe. I waited and worried for two more days and finally, today, Sister said I could go. She made me wear my habit. She said it would provide me with protection. I carried the clothes I'm wearing now. I didn't know where to find you, so I came here. The proprietress let me in and allowed me to change clothes. Then I waited and now you are here.' She kissed me.

I glanced around to see if the owner was watching and saw her face disappear from a window that looked out on the courtyard. What did she think about a sister who asked to come in when the place was closed, changed out of her habit, ordered a beer and then kissed a guy? I had my answer soon enough. The owner appeared with a beer for me and another for Beatrijs, placing them on the table, totally incurious. I guess bar owners in Santo Domingo are like therapists. Our secrets are safe with them.

Beatrijs and I sat and glowed at each other for a while. Then she said, 'I was so worried about you. There were rumors in the village that there were riots and executions.'

'None that I saw or heard about. I was as safe as a babe in mother's arms,' I said. There was no sense in telling Beatrijs about my encounters with Jerry Pleasants. 'And you, you were safe in the village?'

'Yes. Neither the Constitutionalists nor the Loyalists are concerned with our little village,' Beatrijs said. She reached for my hand. 'I have thought more, Henry. I intend to tell Sister Walburga that I am not going to continue as a postulant.'

What do you say when someone studying for a holy order drops out for you? At a loss, I blurted, 'That's wonderful. Come to live in Santo Domingo.' I felt a rush of heat to my ears and neck. Had I just asked an almost-nun to shack up with me? Or had I asked her to marry? I wasn't sure.

Beatrijs took my words to be something less momentous than a proposal to marry or live in sin. 'I want to be near you, Henry, I really do.' She brushed my cheek with her hand. 'But I cannot leave the children and Sister Walburga until a replacement arrives from the Netherlands. I haven't even told Sister yet. And with this revolution, who knows when a replacement will arrive.'

'I hope soon,' I said.

'It will be, Henry.' She glanced up at the sky. 'I left at dawn. I told Sister Walburga that I would return before dark. It took me six hours to walk here. I will need to leave soon.'

'I will go with you,' I said.

'I made a promise to Sister that I would not bring you to the village, remember?'

'I'll turn back on the outskirts.'

'That will put you on the road after dark. It will be too dangerous.'

'I insist. I'll be fine.'

'Come only as far as the Peynado Bridge. I will change into my habit there. No one in the countryside will harm a sister.'

We agreed on that plan. I paid the proprietress, thanked her profusely and fantasized about holding Beatrijs's and my wedding party at the beer garden. In minutes we were on the road.

We passed the afternoon strolling hand-in-hand, chatting and trading stories of our youth. We shared the food I had brought under a spreading ceiba tree in a park. It was so easy and congenial and diverting that I almost forgot Jerry Pleasants, until Beatrijs asked, 'I suppose with all the confusion of the revolution you haven't been able to do anything about finding the man who killed the children?'

'I have learned who he is,' I said. 'He is an American, someone I know.'

Beatrijs grew serious. 'Has he been arrested?'

'No.' Should I tell her that the police were uninterested? That there might not even be any police now, and not for a while? 'I haven't been able to get to the police,' I lied.

'You must turn him in,' Beatrijs said. 'As soon as you can when you get back. He must be brought to justice. For the sake of the children and their families.'

'I will take care of it,' I said. 'I'll do what needs to be done.'

And I meant it.

FORTY-FOUR

Beatrijs and I parted at the Peynado Bridge, as planned. I waited on the southern end of the bridge, watching her cross. She stopped on the other side, waved and disappeared into the brush. In minutes, a sister in a habit emerged and, without a glance in my direction, strode purposefully down the road.

It was late afternoon when I got back to Santo Domingo's core. The crowds were still in the streets, still happily celebrating, chanting, 'Viva Bosch!' I decided it was safe enough to detour to the post office and make a call. When I got there, the clerk who arranged for telephones was not the same one who had been there since the junta's coup. The new man was briskly efficient, though, and in a minute I was in a booth giving the number I wanted. I did not hold a great deal of hope that it would be answered.

'*Policía Nacional Dominicana, Capitán Salazar.*' The voice at the other end of the line was self-assured and businesslike.

'The sky hasn't fallen, Cosme?' I said.

'No, Henry, the blue sky remains above. The Loyalists on the force, most of my unit, disappeared into the *servicio* a few days ago and emerged as civilians minutes later. They haven't been back to headquarters since. There is a pile of their cast-off uniforms in a toilet stall, which is also where their careers are now. Bullito has fled, too, with the rest of the junta leadership. Only myself and my son-in-law remain here in the Investigation and Identification Unit. I expect I will be welcoming old comrades from Juan Bosch's era in the next day or so, and interviewing new recruits. If you are calling for a job, there is a place for you here, no interview necessary.'

'As tempting as the offer is, Cosme, I will have to pass. I have other commitments.'

'Alas, all of the good ones are taken. That is what the last blonde – from a bottle – said to me.' Cosme laughed. 'Why do you call? To meet for a drink at the bar of El Jaragua perhaps? I hear it has re-opened, minus the Loyalist eavesdroppers on the staff.'

'I'll need a rain check on the drink, Cosme. I'm calling on police business. Are you back to that yet?'

'Some, Henry. Are we back to Jerry Pleasants?'

'Yes. You need to bring him in for the Peynado Bridge bombing. And for the killing of Jaime Vargas, and a kid named Oscar. Both Boschists, if that matters. I am your eyewitness on the murders.'

'Where is he? Somewhere I can send my son-in-law to pick him up?'

'I don't know where he is. The last time I saw him, he was on the north bank of the Rio Ozama where it meets the Rio Isabela. He was on the move.'

'I don't have enough people for a manhunt, Henry. I have to stay at the station. The few men I currently have do as well. The countercoup is fragile yet. We need to be here and ready to act quickly if the junta attempts a return.'

'OK, when can you go after him?'

'I really have no idea.'

'It looks like I'm on my own.'

'Unfortunately, yes, Henry, until you deliver him to our doorstep.'

'I don't think that he will come quietly.'

'Be careful, Henry. I want that drink at El Jaragua with you.'

'I'll be fine, Cosme. And I'll buy the first round.' I hung up.

The next day I was up early. Santo Domingo had been quiet all night. The party couldn't go on forever and most folks were back to their regular business. Camila made me breakfast. I was beginning to like the idea of a live-in housekeeper. Maybe she could stay on with Beatrijs and me.

After breakfast, I set out to find Jerry Pleasants. I thought about going back to Porfírio Melo for information but my guess was that he would have his hands as full as Cosme Salazar with the change of regime. There was another person who came to mind, though, who had his ears open and who might have information on Jerry. I headed for Gualey.

The Birdman's business was neither harmed by nor benefited from the countercoup. When I arrived at La Poza del Chino, he was sitting in the same place I had left him days before, his tray of gum, candy and trinkets arrayed in front of him.

'Mr Ten-Dollar Chiclets,' he said, as I approached. 'What can I do for you today?' I had not spoken yet; how could he tell who I was? Smell? Telepathy?

'I'll take another box,' I said, passing him a ten dollar bill.

'I need more customers like you.' He grinned.

'I need something from you.'

'My *mamacita* always said, "You don't get if you don't ask".'

'Jaime Vargas and Oscar . . .' I began.

'They was killed.' No flies on the Birdman.

'I was with them. I know who did it. I'm after him.'

'Who did it was a gringo name of Jerry Pleasants. Do you plan to kill him?'

'I plan to bring him in to the PND.'

'Some of Jaime and Oscar's friends have other, more direct, plans for him.'

'Have they captured him?'

'No. But they will.'

'Do they know where he is?'

'No. If they did, he would be dead right now.' The Birdman rocked back and turned his unseeing eyes up to mine. 'But I know where he is.'

'Why haven't you told the friends?'

'Mr Chiclet, don't get me wrong. I loved Jaime. He was a straight shooter. He did things for folks here in Gualey. But I trade in information. Well, some gum and candy, too, but a man can't live off that. Sooner or later, I'll be able to sell the information I have about that bastard's whereabouts to someone who will go ahead and kill him. So, no, I didn't give the information for free to his friends. But I'll make sure whoever buys it will off him. Now, you buying?'

There was no hesitation. 'I am.'

'Ain't gonna be no ten dollar box of gum.'

'How much?' I had loaded up my wallet with most of my ready cash before leaving home. I considered it about even odds as to whether the cash or the gun I carried would get me Jerry. I didn't care which, as long as it got the job done.

'Five hundred American frog skins, boss.'

I dug out my wallet and thumbed through the bills. 'I've got four hundred and forty dollars. It's all that I've got.'

'You gonna to kill him?'

'I'm gonna bring him in. Testify against him. Someone else will do the execution.'

'That they will. They an unforgiving lot down here. Not like back in the States. OK, I'll take your four hundred and forty dollars and give you the info. Only, because you aren't giving full price, I reserve the right to sell the info again. Deal?'

I thought about it for a second and said, 'Deal. May the best man win.' I put the cash in the Birdman's hand.

'He's in a rented room in a boarding house on Calle Juzgado de Paz near Calle Fifteen Padre Paules.'

'The name?'

'The place ain't got no name.'

Of course. I had the good sense not to ask for an address. 'What else?' I asked.

'This oughta be extra but, for Jaime's memory, the dude ain't there at night. He goes out and prowls around. He ain't there in the day much, either. He's a barfly, a different bar every day. That's all I got, boss. Honest.'

'Thanks.' I turned to leave.

'Hey, boss?' the Birdman called. 'Got a car?'

'No, I'm hoofing it.'

'C'mere,' he said. He put a twenty back in my hand. 'Take a cab. You don't want to miss the bastard.'

FORTY-FIVE

As the cab drove south, the sound of gunfire could be heard across the Rio Ozama. When we started out, the driver, a transplanted Haitian, was glad for my fare. Now he told me in French-accented Spanglish that he would take me to the end of the Duarte Bridge and no further. 'Señor no pay a fare *pour mi ander en coche* into Hell.'

The cabbie dropped me on the east side of the bridge, did a U-turn in the middle of the empty street and hightailed it back west. I don't know why he was so concerned; the gunfire still sounded far off. I didn't mind walking the last few blocks to Calle Juzgado de Paz. Walking allowed for a slow reconnaissance of the area.

Despite the proximity of the Duarte Bridge and the major artery between Santo Domingo and Santo Domingo Este, the neighborhood only a block off the main drag was a sleepy residential oasis. The streets were vacant. Maybe the distant guns had something to do with that. I walked to the corner of the block where Jerry Pleasants' boarding house was supposed to be and leaned against a tree, hoping its black shade would provide some cover for me.

I lingered for an hour and saw no one. The sound of the guns moved closer. I didn't know what was happening but someone was shooting a lot. I told myself that I would give it another hour and if, during that time, the gunfire continued to advance, I would have to leave.

A half hour later, the front door of a two-story house toward the Calle 15 end of the block opened and a man emerged. Short, roly-poly, with a straw hat and a white van dyke beard, he was clearly a gringo. He was lugging a leather suitcase almost as large as he was. By the time he reached my end of the block, he was sweating and winded. Spotting me, he sidled over, dropped the suitcase like it was something offensive and mopped his neck with a handkerchief that smelled like it had been liberally dosed with Aqua Velva.

'Name's Hamannwright. Mike Hamannwright. I sell sewing machines,' he said once he regained his breath.

'Dave Blake,' I said. No sense giving him my real name if he was one of Jerry Pleasants' neighbors, or worse, one of his fellow FBI operatives.

'I should leave the damn sewing machine behind,' Hamannwright said, pointing at the suitcase. 'The thing's a damn boat anchor. But the company would dock me the cost. You getting out?'

'No,' I said. My gut told me Hamannwright really was a sewing machine salesman. Of course, it was the same gut that had told me Jerry Pleasants was just a harmless day-drinker. I decided to take the chance. 'I'm here looking for a buddy of mine. He told me he lives in a rooming house on this block.'

'That would be Señora de Los Santos' place, where I just come from. What's your friend's name?'

'Jerry Pleasants.'

'No one there by that name that I know. He American?'

'Yeah.'

'Only one other American there besides me. Odd fellow. Doesn't talk to anyone. He's out most nights. He's out most days. Don't guess that's your friend. Didn't get his name.'

'Might be. Can you describe him?'

Hamannwright described Jerry to a T. And then added, 'Always wears a Panama hat.'

'Doesn't sound like him,' I said. 'Maybe I'll talk to the landlady, though, just in case.'

'Better move fast, friend. She was packing a bag, just like me. Headed away.'

'Why?'

'Man, you been living under a rock? Wessin y Wessin and a couple battalions of Loyalist troops are headed this way from San Isidro Air Base, about fifteen miles east. A bunch of Constitutionalists in trucks and cars blew by here a couple hours ago to intercept them. Word is that the Loyalists have tanks and the Constitutionalists don't have anything that'll stop them. That's why the gunfire's getting closer. That's why everyone's clearing out or has cleared out. It would be the smart thing for you to do, too, Dave. Maybe you can walk with me and we can share a ride if we can hire one. It looks like there won't be anything until we get to the west side of the bridge, though.'

Hamannwright seemed eager for a companion, maybe to help him lug his suitcase. 'Thanks for the offer,' I said. 'But I think I'll stop in to see your landlady and ask after my friend first.'

The crump of tank cannon fire sounded just then. 'Suit yourself, Dave. I'm getting while the getting's good. I wouldn't linger if I was you. Good luck!'

I waited until Hamannwright turned the corner at the end of the block and started toward Señora de Los Santos' boarding house. When I reached the front door, I saw the silhouette of a woman inside. I knocked but there was no answer. I stepped back from the door and looked into the upstairs windows. No one was there to be seen but when I brought my eyes back down to the ground level, I caught a glimpse of a female figure running between houses toward the bridge. Apparently, Señora de Los Santos was flying the coop with all the other chickens.

I went to the front door and put my ear to it. No sound. I backed away and sidled up to one of the windows, peeking in. No one inside. Back at the front door, I tried the knob. Locked. I sized up the door itself. Luckily, it was as new as the house, not one of those colonial era jobs meant to hold off Sir Francis Drake and his merry men if they came to town. I reared back and kicked with all my might. The frame shattered at the lock. I was in.

I took out the Colt .45 and worked room to room. The lower floor seemed to belong to Señora de Los Santos, plus a common room for the boarders. I climbed the stairs. They creaked. I held my breath with each step.

At the landing was a short hall with two doors on each side. There was nothing to do but work through them one by one. The first two were unlocked and, while furnished, devoid of any sign of occupancy. The third room was locked. I used my foot again and slammed into the room after the door gave, moving the .45 side to side, looking for a target. No one was home but there was an open suitcase in the corner with a couple of shirts I recognized as Jerry's on the top. I backed out of the room and pulled the door closed behind me.

The last room, across from Jerry's, was unlocked. I pushed the door open and immediately smelled the lingering odor of Aqua Velva. Hamannwright's recently vacated room was a perfect place to wait for Jerry. He would expect trouble inside when he saw his room door. He'd be less likely to expect it from across the hall. I pulled a chair up to the door and closed it enough so that it would appear shut but I didn't latch it. Then I listened and waited.

I heard birds singing in the tree outside. A couple times I heard a car speeding along Calle Juzgado de Paz. And I heard gunfire and other sounds of combat, shouted commands and the cries of the wounded growing ever closer. After an hour, I heard the creak of the stairs between the shots. Footsteps, light and wary, made their way down the hall.

I was up and rushed through the door but I was too slow for a pro like Jerry. He was already inside, the door to his room slammed shut. I heard a dresser that had been beside the door pushed to block it just as I hit it with my shoulder. The force moved the door open three or four inches, enough to allow me to fully benefit from the sound of the four shots fired from inside. One of the exiting bullets droned past my ear like an antagonized humming bird. A second cut a bloody path on the surface of my ribs, just under my left arm. The other two thwacked, harmless, against Hamannwright's door across the hall.

I flattened and rolled against the wall to the right of the door. It was quiet in Jerry's room. He had created a problem for himself. He couldn't just pop out the door with the dresser in the way. What had protected him now prevented him from any quick escape.

'Henry, is that you?' Jerry called, no doubt hoping to be answered with a groan to confirm that his shots had hit home.

'It's me, Jerry. And you missed, if you are wondering.' I felt my wound. It burned with pain and was bloody but it was on the surface, a deep scratch.

'Oh, good,' Jerry said. 'For a second, I thought it was those crazy rebel characters who have been after me. They managed to find two of my safe houses already. Almost got me at the last one.'

'I've come to take you in, Jerry. Give it up and come out.'

'Come to take me in? You and what army, buddy? Just you, isn't it? Are you prepared to do it flying solo?'

'I'm prepared enough.'

'What is your thing, Henry? Why are you so persistent? Surely it's not the politics. Tell me you're not as enamored with Juan Bosch as the rest of these *cocolos* are.'

I didn't answer.

'Oh, no, don't tell me. It's not that little nun, is it? The one I saw you with the other day? Lives out in the village north of the Rio Isabela, where most of the kids on the bus came from?'

Jesus, how could he know? I felt real terror now for Beatrijs.

'Oh, that's it, isn't it? Kinky, the nun thing. I didn't think you had it in you, Henry. Nothing to say? OK, I'll do the talking. I'll tell you your future while we're waiting each other out. Waiting for those guns and soldiers and tanks coming from the east to arrive.

'If you're smart, you'll take the offer I made to you back at the Rio Ozama. There's still time. Those guns you hear? Those are the Loyalists marching back into Santo Domingo. They are heavily armed. They have tanks, Henry, and Bosch's rebels aren't going to stop them. The Loyalists will win and when they do, they are going to clean house. And I will be there and you will be there to make sure that they're good allies of America in the war against the commies. You have connections. You can name names to them. Uncle Sam will be appreciative and so will the Loyalists.'

'And I can help save your neck,' I said. 'I can refrain from shooting you or turning you over to the Bosch people hunting you. Right?'

'That would be part of the scenario.' Jerry paused. 'If you find that not to your tastes, if you're not as smart as I hope you are, then there's another resolution. You walk away. Tell me you're leaving and walk out the door. Forget you ever knew me. Forget everything you heard from me or about me. And as a trade-off, I'll forget about the nun. You both go on your way.'

Jerry stopped there, waiting, I supposed, for an answer.

I had one for him. 'You missed the scenario where I take you to the PND headquarters and turn you in for murder.'

'I don't consider that an option, Henry.' Jerry's voice was light and even, as if he was talking to me about the new single that the Dave Clark Five had just released. The heavy dresser inside the door of Jerry's room was shoved aside. Moving the dresser was an invitation from Jerry. I could get up from where I was and rush the door. Or I could wait where I was in the hallway for him to emerge.

'You wouldn't shoot a friend, would you, Henry?' Jerry called. Not waiting for an answer, he burst from the door with a .45 semi-auto in each hand, both the guns blazing, the sound deafening in the narrow hallway, filling the close air with acrid smoke. Jerry had the fire power but I had the advantage. He didn't know where I was in the hall and it took him a split second to locate me. I shot him three times as fast as I could pull the trigger. He collapsed against the wall beside the door, his shirt awash in blood, the guns fallen from his hands. I went over to him.

'I thought we were friends, Henry,' he said, and died.

FORTY-SIX

The sounds of battle seemed to be all around now. I went into Hamannwright's room and peeked around the edge of the window. There was smoke to the east. The clack-clack of tank treads echoed along the main road. I had to get out.

I ran downstairs, out the front door and west on Calle Juzgado de Paz, avoiding the main road. I finally was forced onto the highway in order to cross the Duarte Bridge. At the foot of the bridge, I paused to catch my breath. Glancing back, I saw a ragtag group of Boschists throwing Molotov cocktails at an old AMX-13 light tank, a French leftover from before World War II that had been sold to Trujillo. The tank was impervious to the fire bombs and continued to move toward the bridge.

I made my way across the deserted span, reaching the west end as the retreating elements of the Boschists dug in at the east. I immediately ducked off the main road onto a side street. Not a block away was Hamannwright, still burdened by his suitcase of product. He had flagged a cab that seemed to be the only one on the street anywhere near the Rio Ozama and was haggling with the driver.

'There are tanks coming across the bridge,' I yelled by way of greeting to Hamannwright and the driver.

'He wants twenty *pesos oro*.' Hamannwright said it like an accusation of a crime.

'Pay him,' I said. 'They'll be here in five minutes.'

Hamannwright paid and we sped off along the side streets, ignoring stop signs and the speed limit. The tanks, though, did not cross the Duarte Bridge in the next minutes. I later learned that they had outrun their infantry support and bogged down when they met severe resistance from the Constitutionalists dug in at the end of the bridge.

'I need to find a *teléfono*,' I told the cab driver.

He ignored me, putting more distance between us and the sound of gunfire, until he finally pulled over at a bodega, pointed inside and said, '*Teléfono*.'

I jumped out. Hamannwright said, 'I don't want to linger.'

'That's OK,' I said. 'Go and thanks for the ride.'

'*Hasta la vista*,' Hamannwright said merrily and the cab took off.

The bodega's owner cowered when I opened the door. He probably expected gunmen instead of a guy who needed to make a call. At my request, he pointed to a telephone in the corner. '*Cinco centavos.*'

I paid and picked up the receiver. Miracle of miracles, there was a dial tone. I spun the rotary for Captain Cosme Salazar's number. Second miracle of miracles, he answered.

'I just shot and killed Jerry Pleasants,' I said, foregoing the usual badinage. 'In a rooming house on Calle Juzgado de Paz. It was self-defense.'

'How interesting,' Cosme said.

'I'm not sure you can send anyone over there,' I said, about to explain the combat situation in the neighborhood.

'I have no intention of sending anyone,' Cosme said. 'Given the current state of affairs, the PND is not concerned if one gringo kills another gringo.'

'That bad, Cosme?'

'That bad. I'm now the ranking officer at headquarters, given the desertions, first by the Loyalists and, now that they hear the cannon fire, by the Constitutionalists. The former left to save their own skins. The latter left to meet Wessin y Wessin's tanks at the Duarte Bridge. I just had a report that the Americans are mounting an operation to evacuate all foreign nationals in the country. The USS *Boxer* is steaming here from Puerto Rico. There is a battalion of Marines securing a landing zone near the Hotel Embajador, where all foreigners are being assembled to be airlifted out. I am about to leave to liaise with the Americans.'

'Not going to the Duarte Bridge, Cosme?'

'You know I am a lover, not a fighter.'

'You say all foreign nationals are gathering at Hotel Embajador?'

'Yes. That includes you, Henry.'

'Does it include Dutch nationals?'

'Yes. And all non-essential personnel from all the foreign embassies. Would you like a ride?'

'That would be considerate of you, Cosme.'

'*De nada.* Are you near your house?'

'No. I'm not really sure where I am. I guess about a half mile from the west end of the Duarte Bridge.'

'*Dios mío*, Henry, are you crazy?'

'Maybe. Can we meet at my place in an hour?'

'No, my friend, I don't have that kind of time. Be there in a half hour or you will have to find your own way to the Hotel Embajador. I'm sorry.'

'OK. See you soon.' I hung up.

I went out into the street in front of the bodega. A Dodge bristling with young gunmen careened toward me, going west. I pulled out my remaining money – ten dollars – and waved it as the car approached. I traded my ten bucks and the Colt .45 for a ride west, standing on the Dodge's running board and holding on to the roof. In a quarter hour I was dropped three blocks from my house. I walked in the front door with ten minutes to spare.

Camila was gone. I went to the bathroom, cleaned my wound, and slapped on a bandage and a fresh shirt. I packed a duffel with some clothes, got all my reserve cash from its hiding place under a loose cobblestone in the courtyard and stuffed Oscar's Smith and Wesson, with its three remaining rounds, into my waistband. I had just finished when Cosme roared up in a Ford I didn't recognize.

'Thanks for the ride, Cosme,' I said, jumping into the shotgun seat. 'No police car?'

'Not a good thing to be driving these days. This belongs to General Vazquez's adjutant. He left the keys in it. These days in Santo Domingo, possession is nine-tenths, or maybe the entirety, of the law.' He gunned the car westward. The streets, so full of celebrants days ago, were empty, all windows shuttered, the parks, squares and beaches empty.

That all changed at the entrance to the Hotel Embajador. A tangle of cars, buses and trucks made the road impassable. Cosme steered to the curb and we walked to a checkpoint manned by a squad of US Marines.

A gunnery sergeant was checking IDs. 'Can I see your passports, gentlemen?'

I produced mine. Captain Salazar produced his badge.

'Sorry, Captain, I can't admit you,' the gunny said. 'No Dominican citizens permitted inside the perimeter. Mr Gore, if you go to that table over there where the line is, they'll get you assigned a place in the airlift.'

'Gunny, Captain Salazar is here on official business,' I said. 'And I can vouch for him personally.'

The gunnery sergeant turned to Cosme. 'What official business, sir?'

'I have been assigned as the liaison officer between the *Policía Nacional Dominicana*, and the commanding officer of the US forces.' Cosme tried to make it sound grand and important but it came out a tad desperate.

The gunny he wasn't having it. 'Who assigned you, sir?'

'The acting *comandante* of the PND headquarters.'

Damn, Cosme had assigned himself.

'A name, Captain, please.'

'Myself,' Cosme admitted.

The gunny eyed Cosme like he'd caught the rawest recruit shirking on making his bunk. 'No admission, Captain. Step in, Mr Gore.' Then, looking past us to a couple behind, 'Next.'

'So we part ways here, Henry,' Cosme said and turned away.

'*Hasta luego*, Cosme.'

Once past the checkpoint, I did not join the line to the assignment table. I had no intention of leaving Santo Domingo without Beatrijs. I walked among the milling people, looking for a glimpse of her red-gold hair or the white veil of a postulant.

A makeshift helicopter airfield had been set up on the polo grounds just west of the hotel. A lieutenant with a clipboard stood calling names for the next flight. I wandered in the direction of the officer, planning to ask if he had sent off any nuns. A chopper appeared in the distance, the thrum of its blades threatening to drown out the lieutenant.

A hand on my arm stopped me. I turned and she was there, her blue eyes framed by her veil, not a wisp of her lovely hair visible. Sister Walburga's severe presence beside her kept us from embracing but Beatrijs smiled warmly at me. I felt myself grinning back like a fool.

'Oh, Henry, you're safe,' Beatrijs said. 'I was so worried.'

'Safe as a babe in mother's arms,' I said. Sister Walburga harrumphed but I was ebullient and said to her, 'A good day to you, Sister Walburga.'

The elderly sister nodded, a disapproving pucker on her lips.

'Sister Walburga, may I have a word alone with Beatrijs, please?'

Another displeased twist of her lips. 'She is properly addressed as Sister Beatrijs.'

'Yes, Sister. May we have a moment alone?'

Sister Walburga gave me the evil eye and moved out of earshot, hovering well within viewing distance. Beatrijs took me by both hands. 'I am so glad you are safe and we are together.'

'Was it difficult for you? Getting here, I mean,' I said.

'No. Sister Walburga and I walked the entire way, so we are footsore. We encountered no fighting and no other danger. They have given us food here. My main concern is the village and the children but no forces of either faction had arrived there before we left. The village men have joined together to protect the families. I pray to God that they will be safe. I would stay if I could but we have been ordered to leave. Besides, Sister Walburga is elderly and needs a companion for the journey. You are leaving as well, aren't you, Henry?'

'Now that I've found you I am.'

'Sister Walburga says that the government of the Netherlands has made provision for us to travel from Puerto Rico. The *Boxer*, the aircraft carrier to which we will be flown from here, is to take all foreigners there.'

'That's good. You'll be safe there.'

'What of us, Henry? Will we be separated?'

'Maybe for a time. But we will be together again.'

'Of course, we will,' she said, her eyes brimming with tears. She looked away. 'This place, so beautiful, and yet so sad. So much death. I think of all the children in the bus.'

'I found him, you know,' I said. 'Jerry Pleasants, the bomber.'

'You captured him, Henry? That is wonderful. Now that he is with the police, the families of the children will see justice done.'

'He's not with the police, Beatrijs.'

'Where is he?'

'He's dead. I had to kill him.'

'You killed him?' The eyes that a few moments before had looked on me with love now seemed to see a monster.

'Beatrijs, I was forced to kill him. To defend myself.'

'He had you trapped and there was no escape?'

I thought back to the boarding house hallway. Jerry had offered me an escape but I had stayed because it meant escape for him, too. 'Not exactly,' I said.

'You could have walked away safely? But instead you chose to stay and kill him?'

'It wasn't that way, Beatrijs.' But it was that way, in its most raw, essential truth. She saw it in my eyes.

'He was to be captured. To have a fair trial. To be imprisoned for his crime. To pay for his sins but also to have a chance to see the error of his ways. A chance to repent. A chance to change. A chance to save his eternal soul. No matter how bad he was, how evil, he deserved that chance. You took it from him.'

'Beatrijs, I . . .'

'I thought you were a good man. A kind man. Fair. But to kill a man when there was no need to kill . . .' Her lovely face crumpled in on itself, the tears flowing. She turned and ran to Sister Walburga, who took her in her arms and hurried away.

The incoming helicopter landed, its rotors slowly coming to a halt. Supplies and some Marines were offloaded and then the lieutenant called off the names for the flight out. I heard him call for Sister Walburga and Sister Beatrijs. They came forward, Beatrijs with her head held high, tears dried, her posture erect. She walked past me.

'Beatrijs,' I whispered.

She faced forward, didn't turn, moved directly to the helicopter. A Marine corporal helped her in the open door and she sat on the bench seat, looking straight ahead, her smile gone, her face a mask.

The chopper took off. She never even glanced my way.

FORTY-SEVEN

I watched as the helicopter swung out over the sparkling Caribbean and made a beeline to the aircraft carrier just visible on the horizon. It was a gut punch, what had happened with Beatrijs and after the chopper disappeared from view, I just stood there, looking out to sea, the chaos of the Marines just landed and the foreigners anxious to depart swirling around me, a boulder in a torrent of humanity, stolid and unmoving. I don't know how long I remained there, entranced, forlorn and drained of hope.

'Excuse me, sir, may I help you?' A wiry little Marine, wearing black-framed, Marine-issue eyeglasses stood before me. He carried a clipboard instead of a rifle. He was company clerk material for sure.

His question snapped me back to a state somewhat resembling consciousness. 'No, Marine, thank you.'

'Have you registered for a flight out, sir?'

'No, son.'

'If you have been admitted to the secure area, you should be signed up on the fly-out list.' The Marine had no rank on his fatigues, a mere private but he sensed that I was not right. 'Come this way, sir. I'll get you on the list.' I stood stock-still, so he took my arm and steered me to the table I had bypassed earlier.

He presented me to a corporal seated at the table, who asked my name. I gave it. The corporal consulted a stapled sheaf of papers and said to me, 'Sir, you are on the list to go to Hut A. Private Sims here will show you the way.'

The bespectacled private escorted me to a large tent, folded back the canvas door for me to enter and called in, 'Mr Henry Gore.' He was gone in a flash. I stepped inside.

There were two men inside, in fatigues without insignia, leaning over a metal desk. The men saw me and stepped back, revealing the third person seated at the desk. It was Valerie Spicer.

'Henry, we lost you in all the confusion,' she said, rising from her seat. She had traded her cultural attaché wardrobe for the same type of olive drab fatigues worn by the two men. Her golden hair was pulled back into a tight bun. 'Guys, give me a minute alone with Mr Gore.'

The two men obeyed without hesitation, slipping out the tent door and folding it shut. Val came to where I stood and embraced me. 'You're a hard man to find, lover.'

'Val, what . . .?'

'What is all this? Why am I dressed this way? What is going on? I'm sure it's a lot to absorb, Henry, so I'll give you the Cliffs Notes version. This whole shebang that you see – the Marines, the aircraft, the ships, the entire operation – is called Operation Power Pack. The Marines are here for the purpose of evacuating all foreign nationals, including Americans, from Santo Domingo and the surrounding environs. Ambassador Bennett asked for the evacuation due to the risk of injury or death to foreign persons because of the fighting between the Constitutionalists and the Loyalists. President Johnson agreed and sent in the USS *Boxer* and a Marine battalion to get the civilians out. As you can see, it's going well. We should have most of the foreign civilians out in the next two days.

'I expect, lover, that your most pressing question is, What do I have to do with all that?' Val flashed her Doris Day smile. 'The answer is, nothing.'

'Then what are you doing here?'

'You've suspected – no, known – for quite some time that US Embassy cultural attaché was just my cover. You didn't ask to my face and make me tell you lies and I appreciate that. But now that the shit's hit the fan, there's no need to pretend anymore. I'm with the CIA. Those two boys who were here with me when you came in are CIA as well and right now, Hut A, where you are standing, is the CIA's base of operations in the Dominican Republic. And the CIA is not here to evacuate civilians.'

I listened and tried to make this matter but all I could think of was Beatrijs. Val, though, was on a roll.

'The United States of America, as the result of a policy decision of the Johnson administration, supports Juan Bosch and the Constitutionalists as the democratically-elected government of the Dominican Republic. The CIA is here to support and implement that policy. The CIA is also here to implement LBJ's general policy against permitting the establishment of a communist regime anywhere in the western hemisphere. The Wessin y Wessin junta, who call themselves Loyalists but are really only loyal to their own

power, are many things but they are not communists. So LBJ was
content to allow them here and to allow things to play out between
the two sides without any direct American intervention. Johnson
wanted to see Bosch's people regain power for the sake of democracy in the region, but if the Loyalist junta somehow hung on, that
was OK, too. To paraphrase the old policy concerning Nicaragua's
Somoza, they may be sons of bitches but at least they're not communist sons of bitches. But, while no open intervention is the policy,
LBJ is not above putting a covert finger on the scale for the
Constitutionalists. That is my mission here, to gather intelligence,
provide information to the Constitutionalists and provide what covert
aid we could if things blew up.'

'And your intelligence-gathering function included getting whatever you could from me, since I have been a consultant for Bosch,'
I said. I had been used, just a pawn.

'Not initially, Henry,' Val said, taking my hands in hers, I'm sure
to soften the blow she was going to deliver about how I had been
manipulated. 'Initially, I was fulfilling another function I had been
assigned by my boss at Langley – keeping an eye on the FBI and
its activities here.'

'Jerry Pleasants,' I said.

'If that was his name. Let's call him that for purposes of our
discussion. Have you ever heard of COINTELPRO?'

'No.'

'It is a covert program, started by the FBI to disrupt activities
of the Communist Party of the USA about a decade ago. It was
supposed to stay domestic, in accordance with the division of labor
between the FBI and the CIA. But J. Edgar Hoover thought the
CIA was a bunch of screw-ups. We had misjudged Castro and
botched the Bay of Pigs. He thought his boys in the FBI could do
a better job of keeping the communist menace at bay, not just in
the US but throughout the western hemisphere. Without permission
from anyone in the Johnson administration, he began placing FBI
agents outside the country to tackle the commies. One of those
agents was Jerry Pleasants. I'd just learned who he was and who
his best buddy was a couple days before La Españolita was bombed.
Jerry disappeared but you were there, conveniently bundled up in
the hospital.'

'So it was all false,' I said.

'If you mean the story I told you, yes. If you mean my wanting to help in locating Jerry, no. The bastard had gone completely rogue with that bombing and he had to be stopped. If you mean my feelings for you, no. Those are genuine.' She rose on her toes to kiss me. I didn't reciprocate.

'Hurt, huh?' Val said. 'I can understand that. It's a lot to absorb and I have . . . misled you on some things. But not about how I feel about you, Henry.'

'So you knew Jerry was the bomber,' I said.

'I strongly suspected it. Because Hoover didn't agree with LBJ's policy. He thought Bosch was a weak sister and that if he got back in power, the communists would be knocking on the door in Santo Domingo within a week. He thought the junta was strong and wanted to see Wessin y Wessin remain in power. Langley suspected the bombing was done to provide the junta with an opportunity to blame the Boschists and arrest their leaders.'

'And the bombing of the kids on the bus?'

'I was less sure. I thought even the FBI wouldn't pull something that heinous. I wanted you to find whoever it was who did that. And you did.'

'And I conveniently killed him. End of problem for the CIA in their turf war here with the FBI. You must be very pleased.'

'Don't be that way, Henry,' Val said. 'We're both on the side of the angels here. Bosch means democracy and a better life for these people. The junta is corruption and oppression. And, as far as Jerry Pleasants, whether he went rogue or acted under orders, he needed to be extinguished.'

'Extinguished,' I said. 'What a nice, clean, polite word.'

'You were in the AFOSI. You know it's a dirty business. And you know what you did to Pleasants was justice.'

'Justice is dispensed by courts.'

'Not always. Look, I didn't intend for you to kill Jerry. You didn't intend to kill him. He forced you into it. He was a bad, bad person and the world is a better place now that he's gone.'

'I feel so much better now that you've explained that.'

'Sarcasm does not become you, Henry, and, quite frankly, I don't have time for it today. I'll put my cards on the table. I need your help.'

'Oh, my God, Val. Fool me once . . .' I began.

'Straight up, Henry. Hear me out.'

I should have walked out then. Lifted the flap of the tent,

walked out and kept walking, away from the CIA and the Marines and the helicopters and the milling tourists and businessmen hoping to get out of that hellhole. Walked back into Santo Domingo, found a cheap hotel, signed in as John Smith and hunkered down for the duration. But I couldn't. I was weak, dazed by the gut punches that had been coming at me, day after day, since that bomb blew me out the door of La Españolita, like a boxer who's been knocked down three times, and now, in the fifteenth round, was still on his feet but just barely. So I didn't walk. I heard Val out.

'The Constitutionalists are hanging on by the skin of their teeth,' Val said. 'They've got Wessin y Wessin's tanks stopped at the Duarte Bridge for now but if they aren't able to knock them out, sooner or later the tanks will cross over the bridge into Santo Domingo. They will roll right up to the Palacio Nacional and the radio station and Bosch and democracy will be done for in the Dominican Republic. The small arms and the Molotov cocktails that the Boschists have are not enough to stop those tanks. But I have something that will – two M20 bazookas and a box of rockets for them. They will cut through those tanks like butter. I have them stashed in a tomb in Santa Barbara Cemetery, just off Calle Isabel La Católica.'

'What, they don't let you keep your toys at the embassy?'

'I told you, Henry, sarcasm doesn't become you. And, no, I don't keep them there. There are rules about that.'

'I thought the CIA broke rules.'

'On occasion. This isn't one.'

'Seems simple, then. Give the Constitutionalists the weapons.'

'Not that simple. The tomb has a lock. I have the key. It also has a booby trap, which I need to disarm.'

'Fine. Unlock, disarm and hand over the bazookas.'

'You can't just pick up and fire these things, Henry. The Constitutionalists need to be trained. I'll train them. At the Duarte Bridge.'

'So why do you need my help? I don't have training on bazookas.'

'The tubes weigh fifteen pounds each. A box of rockets weighs fifty pounds. I can carry the tubes or the rockets but not both.'

'What about Tweedledum and Tweedledee who were here when I came in? They looked like strong boys.'

'They are. They also don't have diplomatic immunity like me. If we get caught, they go to prison or maybe get shot as spies. I walk because I am a diplomat.'

'I hate to break this to you, Val, but I don't have diplomatic immunity. Or any kind of immunity.'

'What you have, Henry, besides a strong back, is deniability. You aren't CIA or military. You're actually *persona non grata* as far as the US is concerned. If you get caught, the State Department says, "he may be a citizen, but he isn't even welcome in the US". The powers that be might fuss a little but it's not like you are a government actor.'

'But you are, Val.'

'Hey, I'm just a diplomat trying to get you to the airlift if we get caught.'

'You've figured all the angles, haven't you?'

'All but one, Henry. I haven't figured out what I can do if you say no. I can't carry everything by myself and I am under orders not to let the Tweedle brothers out of the International Security Zone. I can't use the Marines. So you are it. And right now you're asking yourself what's in this for you.'

'That would be crass, wanting to have something for risking my neck.'

'Sarcasm, Henry,' Val said. 'Here's what's in it for you. First, the gratitude of your country. Second, me. We keep going and see where things take us.'

'And if I don't, I lose you, is that it?'

'No. No matter what, you have me.'

I didn't know if I believed Val. And I didn't want her. I thought. Then I thought I didn't know what I wanted.

Val continued, 'Third, I can get you back into the United States. I can get the scarlet letter removed from your file at State. You will no longer be seen as a Castro sympathizer. You will no longer be labeled a communist.'

'I'm not, you know.'

'And you know it doesn't matter whether you are or not. It matters what your file says you are. Are you in?'

There were a thousand reasons not to be. This wasn't my fight. I shouldn't risk my neck. But I was too long and too far from home, from the good old US, from my sister, Jan, and the niece I had never seen, from a life that bore some semblance to normal. I was pretty sure I had lost Beatrijs. I was pretty sure I didn't feel about

Val the way she felt, or said she felt, about me. In the end, I decided that what Val was asking put me at risk of losing my neck, all right, but my neck really wasn't worth that much to me or to anyone else.

'OK, Val, I'm in,' I said.

FORTY-EIGHT

I t was easy enough at first. Val ordered Tweedledum to bring the embassy Ford around from wherever they had it stashed. She had Tweedledee fit me up with a web belt, which held a canteen, a pouch with a couple clips of .45 ammunition and a holster containing a brand new 1911 pistol, all of which bore no identifying marks. By the time I had the belt on, the Ford was at the front of Hut A. Val grabbed a manila envelope from her desk, put it in a rucksack and, as a last thought, reached in her desk drawer and pulled out her own Colt .45.

'No girly guns for me,' she said, laughing. Only Val could have such a sunny attitude going into battle. She took the wheel of the Ford and we drove west, past the polo grounds that were now an airfield, through the perimeter of the International Security Zone, where the Marine sentry saluted us smartly, and out onto a paved road I didn't know.

In a quarter mile, the paved road became a dirt road. We passed farms and forest land, and after fifteen minutes turned north, then east. In another fifteen minutes, Val had us back in Santo Domingo on Avenida Maximo Gomez. The streets were completely deserted. Everyone who wasn't a combatant had hunkered down at home. Everyone who was a combatant was massed for the coming battle at the Duarte Bridge. A few more turns and we were at the entrance to the Santa Barbara Cemetery. There was a sexton's building there but the sexton was nowhere to be seen.

The gates were unlocked. Val drove us to a plain tomb in the old section of the cemetery, with no adornment other than the name 'Cortez' etched into the stone. She took a pry-bar from the Ford's trunk and an ancient skeleton key from her rucksack and had us inside in a minute.

'All right, Henry, let's use that strong back,' she said. 'Pry against the corner of the vault on the left. Just slide it slowly and when you've moved it about an inch, stop. If you don't stop, the booby trap will be triggered.'

'You don't need to tell me that twice,' I said. I applied the bar and moved the vault lid the required inch. Val stepped in with a coat hanger wire – so much for sophisticated CIA equipment – and jiggled it around in the inch gap until something clicked.

'OK, Henry, slide the lid the rest of the way,' she said. The bazooka tubes were inside, nestled in a wooden coffin with a box of rockets at the foot. Val shouldered the two tubes and left the wooden box to me. I picked it up. It was OK to carry to the Ford but I hated to think of marching too far with it.

Outside the tomb, the sound of desultory gunfire could be heard to the north. It was just small arms, designed to keep the heads of the other side down but I didn't relish moving toward it, no matter how light the shooting.

Val drove the back streets in a general northerly direction. We were within a half mile of the Duarte Bridge when we encountered the first Constitutionalist checkpoint.

'*Retroceder!*' the teenager in charge of the five teenagers manning the checkpoint said when we drove up. I could tell he was in charge because he had a Thompson submachine gun and the others only had bats and machetes. Val put on her best motherly countenance and explained in Spanish why we couldn't move back.

'He says the road is impassable from here on,' she told me after a long exchange with the teen.

'Have you told him why we're here?' I asked.

Val shook her head.

'Tell him.' She did. The kid demanded to see. Val got out and popped the trunk. The kid's eyes bugged from his head like he'd seen his high school crush with her top off. More rapid Spanish followed.

'He'll take us to the bridge but we have to walk. He says it really is impassable.'

'Ask him if he can spare a couple of his buddies to carry rockets.'

He could. We broke open the box and divided the rockets inside, each kid carrying two except the leader, and a sack of four for me. The Ford remained at the checkpoint with two kids with machetes to guard it.

Progress was slow. We had to keep ducking between buildings. Anytime we crossed an area exposed to the river, we drew a shot or two from the other side. They were long shots and not likely to hit but that's small consolation when one clips a building ten feet in front of you.

We finally reached the approach to the west end of the bridge where the Boschists were dug in. I thought we were going to get shot when we rounded a building and stumbled on them. Guns turned our way and alarmed voices demanded, '*Hacer alto!*' Our teenaged escort shouted in response and we were taken to a nearby building and presented to a *Capitán* Lara, who was all of twenty years old. The first thing *Capitán* Lara did was look Val over from head to toe with an appraising eye. The second thing he did was to take away our escort's Tommy gun, trading it for an old Mauser rifle that he carried and that his grandfather had probably carried in the First Dominican Civil War back in 1912.

Capitán Lara and our teen escort bantered back-and-forth over the gringos until Val said, 'Do you want these weapons or not?'

'Oh, I want them, pretty lady,' Lara said in surprisingly good English. 'I was just wondering how you happened to have them in your possession.'

'There're from my private collection,' Val said. 'How'd you get your English?'

'Until last week, I was a bellboy at El Jaragua.'

'Those tanks across the bridge aren't going to wait forever. Do you want to learn to use these things?'

'*Si, señora.*'

'*Señorita.*'

A leering smile. '*Si, señorita.*'

'Fine. I need four of your best men. They have to be smart to learn how these work and they have to be brave to hold their fire until a tank gets close enough for the rockets to be effective. And speaking English would help.'

Lara said four names to an aide and the fellow ran off to fetch the students. In three minutes, the students ran in. Val conducted a training that included a dry-firing exercise at the end. It all seemed to go well, except for the fact that the loader on Bazooka Team Two stood behind the weapon during the dry-firing. Val emphasized with a strong smack to the back of his head that if he did that with a live rocket, there would be no second chance for corrective action.

Capitán Lara was almost frantic to get the weapons into position. At the end of the dry-firing exercise, he asked Val, 'Are they ready?'

'As ready as they can be, unless there is time for a couple of hours of instruction on aiming and windage.'

'There isn't time,' Lara said. 'To the bridge.'

The two bazooka teams walked out, trailed by two teens carrying spare rockets. Val brought up the rear. 'Are you coming?' she asked.

'Not if I can avoid it,' I said.

'Suit yourself.'

Val wasn't out the door a second when I realized she actually was going to confront the Loyalist tanks. I scurried to follow.

Outside, the day had grown still and hot. There wasn't a cloud in the faultless blue sky. Every few seconds a shot rang out from one end of the bridge or the other but neither side seemed to be taking any casualties from the firing. The Constitutionalists had constructed a haphazard barricade at the west end of the span – a truck, a few cars, odds and ends of lumber, upturned dining tables, concrete blocks. None of it was substantial enough to stop a tank. Dozens of fighters sheltered along the length of the barrier and off to the side of the approach to the bridge. The bridge deck itself was a no man's land, littered with rubble and spent ammunition. At the eastern end, two L-60 light tanks stood side-by-side. I caught glimpses of four or five more L-60s along the road behind them. There was certainly enough fire power assembled to take out the Constitutionalist barricade and, once that was gone, to storm unopposed to the heart of Santo Domingo. I couldn't fathom why the Loyalist tankers didn't do that but they didn't. I had seen the same thing in Castro's revolution in Cuba, where often Batista's troops were more heavily armed or superior in number but failed to seize the advantage against the rebels. Maybe, when push comes to shove, it's just more difficult to get fired up to fight on the side of corruption and oppression than it is to fight against it.

I found a relatively safe spot behind a truck's rear tire to watch. Val huddled a few feet away with *Capitán* Lara and the bazooka teams. Lara blew a whistle, which echoed for a moment in the humid silence, and then his fighters opened up against the other bank with everything they had. Bazooka Team One dashed out, running along the side of the bridge deck to use the girders as cover. At the halfway point, they stopped. Team One's loader inserted a rocket and tapped the gunner on the back of the head. The gunner took a step to the middle of the bridge, aimed and was shot just as the rocket left the tube. The rocket sailed wide of the lead tank and exploded into the second floor of a building just beyond the bridge.

Team Two rushed forward. Its gunner, having seen his counterpart cut down just moments before, hesitated and fired low, skipping the rocket along the bridge deck until it exploded harmlessly in front of the tanks. Team Two, loader and gunner, dropped their weapon and ammunition and ran back to the barricade amid a hail of fire.

Team One's loader had the courage that Team Two lacked. He ran to the body of his fallen gunner, checked to see if he was alive and, upon learning he was not, grabbed his bazooka and returned with it to the barricade, bullets pinging all around him. He flung himself to the ground beside me.

Both sides were now engaged in a full-on firefight. Then one of the L-60s came clanking at us across the bridge, with another close behind. At the halfway mark, it ground to a stop and fired a round into the barricade, demolishing a car and the two men sheltering behind it.

Val duck-walked across the few feet that separated us and crouched beside me. She spoke in Spanish to the Team Two loader and shouldered the bazooka. The loader fed in a rocket and tapped her on the shoulder. Val stood and faced the tank.

A roar brought my eyes to the sky above the eastern end of the bridge. Two P-51 Mustang aircraft, guns blazing, strafed the bridge from its midpoint to the barricade. Val held her ground, triggering the bazooka just as the machine gun bullets from the planes caught her. The lead tank exploded in a fireball. The second tank reversed back to the east end of the bridge. Every rifle, pistol and machine gun on the Constitutionalist side of the bridge fired at the two planes. They made only one strafing run, flashing off to the east, two silver daggers auguring into the flawless blue sky.

FORTY-NINE

'Things went to hell in a hand-basket pretty quickly, didn't they, Henry?' Val grimaced as she spoke. Kneeling beside her, I applied pressure to the wounds on her legs. She had been struck by four or five of the .50 caliber machine gun bullets from the Mustangs. An artery pumped blood from a massive wound in her left leg. Someone was trying to put a tourniquet on it, using a web belt and failing miserably. Her right leg had been shredded. Her face was ghastly gray, heading to ghastly white. There was no hope.

'Hang on, Val. We'll find a doctor,' I said. No doctor would reach her in time to perform what would be a miracle in the best hospital with the best surgical team in the United States.

'I got the tank, didn't I?'

'You did, Val.'

'I'm done for.'

'Hang on.'

Val gagged as blood ran out of her mouth. I wiped it away. She was trying to talk. 'Sorry. I . . . Sorry, Henry.'

'That's OK, Val. There is nothing to be sorry for. Just fight. Stay alive for me.'

'Sorry, Henry. Look for the papers. In the rucksack. Sorry.' She stopped and gasped, then said, 'Destroy the papers.'

I held her hand. 'I will, Val. Now, hang on.'

'I . . . love you.' She shuddered and was gone.

A crowd of fighters had gathered around us, at first exultant at the destruction of the tank, then somber as Val died. One or two of the younger ones wept. I picked up her body and carried it away from the barricade, taking her rucksack as well.

Capitán Lara appeared beside me with a blanket. We wrapped her in it.

'She was very brave,' Lara said. 'She stopped the tank when no one else would. She is a hero to the people of the Dominican Republic.'

I said nothing to Lara. There was nothing to say. All I could think of was that I had to get Val home. I put her rucksack over my shoulder and picked up her body. I began walking south along the same route we had come less than an hour before. She was light, so light, it was almost as if I was carrying just the blanket.

Lara shouted orders behind us. I paid no attention. Then the teenaged escort from the checkpoint and his two compatriots fell in step beside me. They carried a canvas stretcher. They motioned to place Val on the stretcher. I did. We walked back to the checkpoint. I was numb. I felt I should cry but I did not. I felt I should mourn but I could not. I felt I should be angry at someone – the pilots of the planes, the Loyalists, General Wessin y Wessin, Jerry Pleasants, the CIA – but I was not. I carried in my chest a cold, cold stone.

At the checkpoint, I had the boys place Val's body across the backseat of the Ford and drove off west, toward the US Embassy. The streets were still deserted. I was at the embassy gate in minutes. There was a squad of Marines on guard there, with a fresh-faced lieutenant in charge. As the Ford approached, he saw the diplomatic plates and swung the gate open, saluting as I drove through. I stopped just inside the gate.

'Sir, do you have identification?' the lieutenant said.

'No, lieutenant, I don't. I'm an American but without my passport. My name is Henry Gore. I have the body of one of your staffers, Valerie Spicer, in the backseat. She was killed by the Loyalists at the Duarte Bridge.'

'The cultural attaché, sir?' The lieutenant's face told of his shock at the news.

'That's right,' I said. 'She was doing her duty for her country.'

The young officer was momentarily at a loss. Then he said, 'I'll get Ambassador Bennett, sir.' He quick-stepped into the embassy building.

I turned to look on the shrouded body in the backseat. 'Goodbye, Val. You loved the wrong man. You deserved better for your love and for your loyalty to your country.'

I stepped through the embassy gate into the street. None of the Marines tried to stop me. I walked south to the end of the block and turned east toward the colonial zone. I had Val's rucksack on my shoulder. The sun was setting.

FIFTY

I lay back on the smooth sheets and stared at the ceiling. Sleep had only reached me at dawn. Before, the night had been filled with images – of Val, standing firm in front of the tank and planes; of Beatrijs, facing forward, as the helicopter lifted off; of Jerry Pleasants, leaning over a jukebox; of Jaime Vargas, mixing drinks behind the bar in La Españolita. The gentle trade wind rustled the curtains, promising a cooling kiss to make temperate an otherwise warm day. The sun was well up. I heard a bird singing and the clatter of breakfast being prepared in the kitchen.

Roused by the smell of Camila's good cooking and the strong, black scent of perking coffee, I dressed. Val's rucksack, with its papers, lay on the floor where I'd dropped it the evening before. I left it where it had fallen and went downstairs.

Camila was at the stove, stirring a pot. She had the radio on, listening to a broadcast from the Constitutionalist-held main station in Santo Domingo. The voice on the radio was excited, triumphant.

'Good morning, Henry.' Camila turned and smiled at me. It might have been me but she struck me as calm, less needy, less concerned with landing a husband then she had been in months. 'Coffee?'

I nodded and she poured a cup. 'The news on the radio is good, Henry. The junta has been stopped at the Duarte Bridge. Our fighters even destroyed a tank that was crossing the bridge.'

'Val's dead,' I said. 'She was killed at the Duarte Bridge.'

Camila emitted a sound somewhere between a coo and a sob and hugged me. She stepped back and wiped away tears. 'She was a fine woman,' she said. Despite the rivalry she'd had with Val, it was clear that Camila meant it.

'Yes.' My mind conjured an image of Val in the garden at the French Embassy and then one of her yesterday, in her fatigues at Hut A. Both times she was in her element. Both times she was exuberant, lively, happy.

'She would have made you a fine wife.'

'Yes,' I said. So would Beatrijs, I thought. So would you, Camila, I thought but did not say.

The radio announcer's voice elevated to a fever pitch, claiming our attention. It was filled with optimism and fervor, a call to arms for all men not already armed. Camila translated. 'The Constitutionalists have captured the armory at the Policía Nacional headquarters. They are distributing weapons to any who will join. The announcer is calling for an offensive against the Loyalists at the Duarté Bridge.'

More fighting. More bloodshed. I was sick to death of it. This country seemed caught in an endless cycle of it. I tried to think of something to take my mind off all the death. I remembered my promise to Val. 'I have some work to do upstairs, Camila. You may leave if you want to.'

'I will stay if you don't mind.'

'That's fine.' I went up to my bedroom and opened Val's rucksack. The least I could do was to carry out her dying request.

Inside the rucksack, I found some sheets of paper stapled together. They appeared to be some kind of code key. I put a match to them and dropped them in a metal waste basket in the bathroom. Next was a report to the Director of the CIA. It chronicled Jerry Pleasants' activities in Santo Domingo on behalf of Edgar Hoover's Operation COINTELPRO, including his efforts to recruit me and his probable participation in the bombing of La Españolita for the purpose of fomenting violence between the rival elements in the country. I didn't come off particularly well in the report. To be honest, I came off as a naïve pawn who was completely oblivious to Jerry's manipulation. The report was an original and bore no traces of having been typed on carbon paper. I burned it as I had the code sheets.

The last document in the rucksack was a carbon copy, with no indication of where the original was. It read:

To: Deputy Director, Central Intelligence Agency
From: Valerie Spicer, Paramilitary Operations Officer
Re: Communist Elements in the Dominican Republic

In response to the request from the Chief of Staff, National Clandestine Service, this officer has compiled a list of known and suspected members of the Dominican Communist Party (*Partido Communista Dominicano*), Cuban Communist Party (*Partido Socialista Popular*) and the US Communist Party (CPUSA) currently living in Santo Domingo, DR. All the individuals listed are directly involved with the operations of the Juan Bosch Constitutionalist rebels or have had direct contact with Constitutionalist elements.

There followed a numbered list of forty-three names. I read through the names, recognizing none until I came to my own. There it was, in carbon paper blue and white, me denounced to the United States government as a communist by the woman who had said she loved me with her dying breath. She couldn't bring herself to tell me what she had done, so she told me to destroy the denunciation, counting on me to read it before I did. It may be that she intended it as a warning to me. It may be that she just could not look into my eyes when she told me what she had done to me. Maybe she had believed that what she reported about me was true. Maybe it was an accurate report of what someone had told her. I just didn't know. Now I could never know.

What I did know is that the document in my hand was a copy. I rifled through Val's rucksack. The original was not there. It was out in the wide world somewhere, maybe at the US Embassy. Maybe in a diplomatic pouch on its way to Washington. Maybe it was already in the hands of the Deputy Director of the CIA and from there maybe my name would be put on list after list of known communists, out into the future, the lists excluding me from returning to the United States until I died. I sat dumbfounded, hurt and baffled at what Val had done.

Camila appeared at the bedroom door, excited, entering without knocking and not noticing my state. 'Henry, your President Johnson is about to give a speech about the Dominican Republic. The radio station is going to re-broadcast it here, as it occurs and then translate it into Spanish for the people. I thought you would want to hear. Come, come!' She held out her hand. I rose and took it, automatically, and she practically dragged me downstairs to the kitchen. I sat down at the table, just as the President began:

Good evening, ladies and gentlemen. I have just come from a meeting with the leaders of both parties in the Congress which was held in the Cabinet Room in the White House. I briefed them on the facts of the situation in the Dominican Republic.

The President spoke of conflict, revolution and confusion and then:

But certain things are clear. And they require equally clear action. To understand, I think it is necessary to begin with the events of eight or nine days ago.

The President recounted the events of the last week leading to the countercoup, which he blamed on disgruntled elements of the military. That was only partly true. Ordinary citizens had also risen up against the junta. Then, the first hurtful falsehoods: The rebels themselves were divided. Some wanted to restore former President Juan Bosch. Others opposed his restoration. President Bosch, elected after the fall of Trujillo and his assassination, had been driven from office by an earlier revolution in the Dominican Republic.

Those who opposed Mr Bosch's return formed a military committee in an effort to control the country. The others took to the street and they began to lead a revolt on behalf of President Bosch. Control and effective government dissolved in conflict and confusion.

President Johnson then chronicled diplomatic efforts and failures of which I and most or all of the Dominican people were ignorant. He continued:

On Wednesday afternoon, there was no longer any choice for the man who is your President . . . Shortly after three o'clock I received a cable from our Ambassador. The cable reported that Dominican law enforcement and military officials had informed our embassy that the situation was completely out of control and that the police and the Government could no longer give any guarantee concerning the safety of Americans or of any foreign nationals.

Ambassador Bennett . . . went on in that cable to say that only an immediate landing of American forces could safeguard and protect the lives of thousands of Americans and thousands of other citizens of some 30 other countries. Ambassador Bennett urged your President to order an immediate landing.

In this situation, hesitation and vacillation could mean death for many of our people, as well as many of the citizens of other lands. I thought that we could not and we did not hesitate. Our forces, American forces, were ordered in immediately to protect American lives. They have done that.

Then came the horrid surprise:

Meanwhile, the revolutionary movement took a tragic turn. Communist leaders, many of them trained in Cuba, seeing a chance to increase disorder, to gain a foothold, joined the revolution. They took increasing control. And what began as a popular democratic revolution, committed to democracy and social justice, very shortly moved and was taken over and really seized and placed into the hands of a band of Communist conspirators.

And the consequent action:

Earlier today I ordered two additional battalions – 2,000 extra men – to proceed immediately to the Dominican Republic. I directed the Secretary of Defense and the Chairman of the Joint Chiefs of Staff to issue instructions to land an additional 4,500 men at the earliest possible moment.

My God, Juan Bosch was no communist and the people who revolted in his support weren't either. The President went on:

The American nations cannot, must not, and will not permit the establishment of another Communist government in the Western Hemisphere . . . [R]evolution in any country is a matter for that country to deal with. It becomes a matter calling for hemispheric action only – repeat – only when the object is the establishment of a communistic dictatorship.

Concluding, the President said:

I want to say this personal word: I know that no American serviceman wants to kill anyone. I know that no American President wants to give an order which brings shooting and casualties and death . . . We do not want to bury anyone as I have said so many times before. But we do not intend to be buried.

So that was it. The Americans were coming in force to defeat those who President Johnson had been led to believe wanted to destroy the United States: the supporters of the democratically-elected Juan Bosch.

FIFTY-ONE

Camila had listened to LBJ's speech and watched my face during it but still asked, 'What does it mean?'

'It means the United States has completely reversed its policy of supporting democracy in the Dominican Republic,' I said. 'It means that the country is about to be invaded. It means that the United States, and all its military might, are coming in on the side of Wessin y Wessin and the junta.'

'But how can this happen?'

'I don't know, Camila. We will probably never know,' I said. We think the fate of a nation turns on high principles, on strong leadership, on fairness and truth, when, in fact, it turns on a lie whispered in the right ear, on political expediency, on an ego pushed or pulled in one direction or another, on a quest for individual power or one man's desire for a place in history.

'What will happen next, Henry?'

'To the Dominican Republic? The US will make sure that the Constitutionalists don't win, now that they've been labeled communists. Best case, that doesn't mean that the junta wins and gets to keep power. The Americans may even see that free elections happen again in a few years if they think that all the communists they imagine are here have been stamped out.

'To you and everyone else here, it will mean living under America's thumb for a while. They'll make sure, if Wessin y Wessin and his boys remain, that they don't misbehave too badly. There will be a few trials and a few people will go to prison but it won't reach to you and your family. You will live much as you lived under Trujillo, Bosch and the junta.

'For me, I'm not sure. I can't go back to the States. Any chance of that died with Val on the Duarte Bridge. I can't stay here. Once the junta gets back in full control, they'll conduct a severe housecleaning. Anyone associated with the countercoup will be marginalized, as well as anyone who worked for Bosch's government. That latter group includes me. Best case I will be expelled from the country. Worst case I will see the inside of a prison cell.'

There was sudden pounding on the front door. Camila jumped as if the junta's henchman were already there to snatch me away. I confess that it rattled me, too, until I opened the door and saw Cosme Salazar standing there in civilian clothes, with a slouch hat hiding most of his face.

'Can I come in, Henry?' he said, as he pushed past me without waiting for an answer.

'Make yourself at home, Cosme,' I said. He closed the door and moved immediately to a window to check if he had been followed.

'I see you didn't fly out after all,' Cosme said.

'Decisions made by others caused me to stay.'

'I'm sorry to barge in on you like this. I had no place else to go.'

'The PND headquarters is a little uncomfortable now?'

'It is as of the last hour. My son-in-law just informed me that a company from the US Army Eighty-second Airborne Division is marching from the airfield at the Hotel Embajador with orders to capture the headquarters. I decided not to stay around to see how long it takes them to turn me over to the junta as a Bosch sympathizer.'

'I thought you had mastered playing both sides of the fence.'

'This time is different, my friend. I feel it.'

'What will you do, Cosme?'

'What will you do, Henry? They are sure to come for you, too.'

'I suspect you're right.'

'So what is your plan?'

'Right now? I have an almost full bottle of Ron Barcelo in the kitchen. I was thinking of having a drink.'

'That sounds like one of your plans, Henry.'

'Do you have a better one?'

'Point taken. I will join you.'

When we entered the kitchen, I introduced Camila to Cosme. She nodded and scurried off, claiming work to do elsewhere in the house. Cosme looked after her with an appraising eye.

'I admire you, Henry. Even in times of danger, you always have a beautiful woman at hand.'

'Valerie Spicer is dead, Cosme. Killed at the Duarte Bridge.' I poured Cosme a double and one for myself.

'What a waste. She was a lovely woman. To her.' He raised his glass and emptied it.

'To all the departed,' I said. I drank. To Val. To Beatrijs.

I poured another double for each of us. We sat and stared at our glasses. Cosme picked his up, put it to his lips and, without drinking, set it down again.

'I don't feel like drinking anymore, Henry.'

'Neither do I.'

'So we just wait?'

'No, you do not.' Camila stood in the kitchen doorway. 'You go, now, Captain Salazar.'

'Where?' Cosme asked. 'One can't get off the island by sea, not with all the American warships swarming out there.'

'You go west,' Camila said. 'Overland to Haiti. I have a brother who lives in Loma de Cabrera near the border. He can get you across. He can get you papers.'

'That is very kind of you, Señorita Camila,' Cosme said. 'Given my current situation, it is an offer I cannot refuse.'

'There is a condition,' Camila said. 'You must take Señor Henry with you.'

They both looked to me.

'We leave at sunset,' I said.

Acknowledgments

Once again, my lovely wife Irene served as my first reader on this book. She did a terrific job shouldering that responsibility, in addition to her usual daily work of ego management, application of common sense and being the overall steadying influence in my life. I am doubly thankful to her.

The background information for this book was gleaned from many sources but two merit particular mention. U.S. Army Center of Military History, Armed Forces Expeditionary Campaigns: Dominican Republic was valuable for the long and, at times, disappointing history of the multiple interventions by the U.S. in the Dominican Republic. Ringler, Jack K., Major USMC and Shaw, Henry I., Jr., *U.S. Marine Corps Operations in the Dominican Republic*, April – June, 1965 provided a concise overview of Operation Powerpack and the role of the U.S. military in the Dominican Civil War.

Much gratitude to Rachel Slatter, my editor. We have now done five books together and I still marvel at your insights and the gentle way in which you convey them.

Many thanks to the Severn House team – to Tina Pietron, for putting the novel together and bringing it those last few steps to completion; to Anna Harrisson, for her adept copy editing; to Martin Brown, for getting the word out through marketing and publicity; to Piers Tilbury, for yet another stunning cover design; and to Mary Karayel, for keeping me apprised of, well, seemingly everything.